PURSUING MR. MATTINGLY

Willful Winterbournes
Book Two

Sandra Sookoo

Dragonblade Publishing, Inc. is an imprint of Kathryn Le Veque Novels, Inc.
P.O. Box 23
Moreno Valley, CA 92556
ceo@dragonbladepublishing.com

Produced in the United States of America

First Edition August 2022
Trade Paperback Edition

ARE YOU SIGNED UP FOR DRAGONBLADE'S BLOG?

You'll get the latest news and information on exclusive giveaways, exclusive excerpts, coming releases, sales, free books, cover reveals and more.

Check out our complete list of authors, too!

No spam, no junk. That's a promise!

Sign Up Here

www.dragonbladepublishing.com

Dearest Reader;

Thank you for your support of a small press. At Dragonblade Publishing, we strive to bring you the highest quality Historical Romance from some of the best authors in the business. Without your support, there is no 'us', so we sincerely hope you adore these stories and find some new favorite authors along the way.

Happy Reading!

CEO, Dragonblade Publishing

Additional Dragonblade books by Author Sandra Sookoo

Willful Winterbournes Series
Romancing Miss Quill (Book 1)
Pursuing Mr. Mattingly (Book 2)
Courting Lady Yeardly (Book 3)
Teasing Miss Atherby (Book 4)

The Storme Brother Series
The Soul of a Storme (Book 1)
The Heart of a Storme (Book 2)
The Look of a Storme (Book 3)
A Storme's Christmas Legacy
A Storme's First Noelle
The Sting of a Storme (Book 4)
The Touch of a Storme (Book 5)
The Fury of a Storme (Book 6)
Much Ado About a Storme (in the *A Duke in Winter* anthology)

CHAPTER ONE

July 1, 1819
Berkshire County, England
Ettesmere Park

L ADY SOPHIA WINTERBOURNE-STRATFORD-FORRESTER lifted her face to the summer breeze that was perfumed by the nearby field of wildflowers. This was, by far, her most favorite season of the year, but at the same time, it was one of the saddest, for this week marked the sixth anniversary of both the deaths of her second husband as well as her sister-in-law.

To say nothing of her father's demise.

I suppose one cannot have life without death. That is the way of the world. Light and shadow. Happiness and grief.

"Days like this make me wish to have Cook prepare a picnic lunch so I can take myself off to an undisclosed location and simply while the day away."

A grunt came from her brother Gilbert. He'd finally arrived at the hall a few days prior from the hunting holiday he'd taken, but he'd come alone without his wife, and as of yet, there had been no explanation for her absence.

Which was odd, but then, over the years, she'd come to expect that from the Winterbourne family.

"Without your daughter?"

"She could accompany me if she wishes, but there is comfort to be found in solitude." Though in recent months, that had been the primary concern preying on her mind. After burying two husbands and then receiving a horrifying diagnosis from the family physician, the prospect of spending the remainder of her life alone—however long that might be—left her shaking with fear most nights after she'd shut herself away from the pitying glances of her family.

After she expired, of course, her daughter would be in the hands of her older brother or her mother, and there was nothing wrong with that, but she secretly hoped to marry one last time before death claimed her so that Hannah could have a father.

"How *have* you been keeping yourself, Sophia?" Concern went through Gilbert's tone as they walked through the wildflower meadow, their pace slow to account for the limp he'd acquired during the first of the year in a riding accident. The flash of sunlight on the silver griffin head of his cane kept them company. "I've been home only a few days yet there seems to be an invisible trailing veil of sadness behind you, almost as if you've given up on life."

In the days of their childhood, she had been close to both of her brothers. Arthur was the oldest, while Gilbert was the youngest. All three of them had golden hair, and they were still the best of friends, had been there for each other when spouses died, when children—or the lack thereof—had sent their lives shooting off into different directions, when bumps in the road of life had taken them off track, and now they were each other's supports now that life was again moving into new territory as they grew older.

"I have good days and bad, Gil." She bent to pluck a daisy. The petals were so soft and the bloom so fragrant. Why was there so much beauty all around her that she would never have the chance to experience for much longer? "As much as I miss both of my husbands as well as Papa, I am not anxious to meet them in the next world quite yet."

"But it *is* inevitable," her brother said softly.

"Yes." Sophia broke off much of the flower's stem and then tucked the bloom behind her left ear. Would she ever experience the exquisite perfection of flowers in the next existence?

"Then what the doctor told you six months ago still holds?"

"I'm afraid so." Her chin quivered from an excess of emotion and a sheen of tears went across her vision, but she rapidly blinked and then swallowed. Now was not the time to dissolve into a watering pot. It was a waste of precious energy besides, especially while the sun was shining and the world beckoned. Once she was alone in her bed, she could take refuge in tears of fear or unfairness, but not now. "I saw Doctor Anderson last week. He stands by his original diagnosis. My heart has weakened to the point that any large shock brought on by sudden circumstances or excitement might indeed cause that organ to experience a massive attack and simply stop."

"Is it due to your age?" His fingers tightened on the head of his cane.

"How indelicate of you to mention it." She snorted. "I have just recently turned one and forty. While that is not young by society's standards, I don't feel exactly ancient." There was much gratitude for having gained that advanced age, though.

"Papa had a bad heart."

As if she didn't already know such a truth. "He did." Perhaps that was to be her fate as well. "It's one of the reasons I believe Doctor Anderson didn't do much in the way of an examination. He assumes I have inherited Papa's poor health. The symptoms presented don't appear wrong."

"You have my sympathies." He took her hand and threaded it through his crooked elbow, resting his atop hers. "Did he say how long you have left?"

"He did not. It could be as soon as next week or it might be a few months from now or up to six months at best, but he was quite certain I'm not long for the world." Talking about her future—or lack thereof—had the power to steal her breath, but she drew comfort from her brother's strength and presence. Even now her chest had tightened to the point where it hurt and she probably should cease walking for a bit, but the day was so warm and glorious that she hated to spoil it by resting.

She'd been doing that too much lately, and it was beginning to grate.

Gilbert drew her to a halt. He faced her, resting his hand on her shoulders while holding his cane. "There is no shame if you'd like to give into your feelings. You don't need to remain strong for my sake and facing death sooner rather than later is something we all must come to grips with."

That permission was all too tempting! "For the moment, I *must* retain control, else I fear I'll be lost to the very darkness I'm frightened of."

Nighttime, midnight, the absence of light reminded her of death that was creeping all too close. She was more alone during those times than any other with nothing else to do except think of what might be beyond that darkness… if anything.

Where there was probably nothing.

A trace of fear and pain shadowed his brown eyes before it vanished at his next blink. Did he ponder her existence or problems in his? Though he'd been a staunch supporter of hers, he kept his own affairs quite private. And the absence of his wife was telling, yet he spoke not a word. "Life is precious just now. We shouldn't waste it." He tugged her into his arms, and Sophia gratefully leaned on his strength. "How do you plan to use your remaining time?"

"I haven't given it much thought." Oh, but that was a lie! Truth be told, there was so much she wished she could to, so many places she wanted to visit, so many things she needed to tell so many people. "At the moment, my first priority is spending time with Hannah. After that?" She shrugged. "I should try and find someone who can look after her once I'm gone."

"Surely we can do that." Gilbert held her at arm's length. "Between Arthur and me, your daughter will attain womanhood as if you were with her."

"But it's not the same as having a parent, is it?" Sophia sighed. She continued her stroll, smiling when he came with her. "Hannah is twelve, and it is a difficult age for any child. I don't want her to grow up without a steadying influence in her life. Uncles and her grandmother are wonderful, of course, but all of you have your own paths to tread. I fear Hannah might become lost in that."

"It's understandable." Gilbert remained quiet as they strolled back toward Ettesmere Park. The thud of his cane hitting the ground was comforting. "Speaking of brothers, is it true that Arthur is to be married?"

Her heart gave a little thump of excitement, but she quickly took a few deep breaths to discourage a prolonged period of that feeling. "Yes. He met Julianna quite by accident a few weeks back. She's a self-taught astronomer and lives not far from the village." Sophia smiled at him. "The two are adorable together. Once Arthur relinquished some of his guilt regarding starting a new relationship, let go some of the fear he might lose a second wife, too, it seemed love came sailing in."

Oh, how she envied him that!

"Why the devil would he wish for a second marriage when he'd barely survived the first?" Genuine astonishment wove through Gilbert's voice. "I cannot imagine wishing to go through that gauntlet again."

How interesting. "Arthur is perfectly happy with Julianna. They are in that sickeningly sweet, new-love stage where they are practically in each other's pockets and kissing when they think no one is looking." She remembered those days with each of her husbands. What she wouldn't give to go back in time and experience them just once more.

To hear their voices, know that everything would come out right in the end.

To share a kiss and become lost in those lovely sensations and escape the fear if just for a moment.

"So I've already noticed." Bitterness wove though his voice. "However, I wish him well. He is a man who needs a woman in his life in whatever capacity, and I've never known him to take a mistress."

In this, both of her brothers were quite honorable. To her knowledge, her father had been the same, and they all proved an example of what a true gentleman should be. "Though Arthur had been very much in love with his first wife, eventually loneliness made him seek something different, and Julianna is that. She is nothing like Ellen. I'm thrilled for him. Perhaps I can convince them to marry before I run out of time." A waver entered her voice. "I do so adore weddings and the chance to dress in pretty clothes."

It was rather one of her shortcomings, that vanity. Beautiful gowns and luxurious fabrics were a weakness, and then paired with sparkling jewels and beaded slippers, her heart was happy. She loved the way she felt when wearing pretty things, as if such happiness could last forever.

"Bah." Her brother huffed. He tapped his cane against the ground. "Love is quite fickle. It never lasts and betrays all too easily. Quite frankly, I wonder if it's even worth a man's time."

Sophia shot him a look with a raised eyebrow. "Why are you so bitter?"

"I have just cause."

"Will you tell me?"

"I'd rather not right now." Strain lined his face.

What exactly had occurred in his own marriage? "Why didn't your wife come to Ettesmere Park with you?" In fact, had he even visited with her at all in London? When he returned from India where he'd been making his fortune, he'd spent time at this property, and then as their mother summoned them all to the countryside, he'd taken himself off for a short hunting holiday. How very odd indeed. Was there trouble in the union? They hadn't been married long before he went away. But she refused to ask. "When the two of you married, you were as thick as thieves. The attraction ran so hot, even I was embarrassed for you, and I'm usually one to champion delicious scandal."

"Marriage is more than heat and scandal." A muscle ticced in his cheek. "Suffice it to say, Madelene keeps her own schedule. If she wished to come to Ettesmere Park, she would have. No doubt Mama invited her as she did us. I haven't spoken to her in person since I left for India." At her gasp, he shook his head. "Though I do send a weekly letter."

"Does she answer them?" Her heart tugged for him. Whatever had gone wrong, she hoped he would make it right. Love was too precious for separation.

"It depends on her mood." Gilbert's body tensed beside her. "As for love," he fairly bit off the word, "I wonder if I even believe in such an emotion any longer. After what my wife and I have been through, disaster after disaster, to say nothing of disappointment, I rather think it's a thing of fairy stories only."

That was the most personal admission she'd heard from him. "Is everything well between you and Madelene?" She hadn't seen her sister-in-law for a good six months or so, and that had been while in London. The woman kept to herself and didn't visit often, neither had she invited the Winterbournes over for dinner or anything else. No one knew exactly why but considered she might be finding her path within the family, or she wasn't weathering the loneliness well since Gilbert had gone off to India. When he'd left, they'd been married barely two years, but Madelene wasn't a social butterfly to begin with.

It had been one of the reasons she'd caught Gilbert's eye.

And in Sophia's defense, she'd had her own crisis to come to terms with.

"Ha!" He shook his head. "That all depends on one's viewpoint, doesn't it?" The pain had returned to his eyes, and though she desperately wished to know the story behind it, she refrained from asking. This was his mess, and he would need to extricate his way out. When he'd married Madelene, he'd not given the family much warning, had claimed love at first sight. Perhaps his current contretemps was a result of that.

Her time was too precious to try and sort someone else's life.

"My dearest baby brother." She grabbed his free hand and squeezed his fingers. "I truly hope you'll discover the truth behind your animosity. For both your sakes, because love, when you find it, should be fought for by both parties. There is nothing like it in the world, and you should hold tight to it."

"That very well may be true for some couples, but…" His words trailed off and he shook his head. "Well, I'd rather not talk about my troubles at the moment. It's too nice a day for those sort of storm clouds." He thumped this cane on the ground for emphasis.

"I agree."

"And please, don't tell the rest of the family any of what I've let slip today." Worry shadowed Gilbert's eyes. "I'd like to keep the matter as private as I can until I can figure out what to do about certain… things. Additionally, I don't wish to worry Mama. For her sake, she needs to continue thinking all is right between Madelene and me."

"You have my discretion, of course, but should you ever wish for advice, I am here for you."

"Also," his swallow was audible. "I'd rather not tell you about my troubles right now for fear the shock of it would cause your heart to stop. The story is rather sordid and scandalous."

Oh, the poor thing! "Is it that bad, then?"

"In some ways, I think so, and I'm not certain there is a way to fix the union… or even if I wish to." The admission came out on the heels of a whisper. "Things are too far gone."

"I understand. We all have valleys we must pass through." *Though some of them do not lead to happy endings.* "You shall be in my thoughts." She kept hold of his hand as he nodded. In silence, they made their way back up the lane. Once the outlines of the manor house of Ettesmere Park came into view, she let go of him. "Will you stay here, or will you return to London once Mama's celebrations conclude later this summer? Since her ball not long ago was such a success, she is determined to throw at least one more." This made her happy, for she did so love to dance. At least the sets that weren't as strenuous.

And soon enough, there would be no more dancing.

"I haven't decided yet. But I do know one thing with certainty."

"Oh?"

"I will *not* return to India."

Sophia couldn't help but giggle. "Was it very hot?"

"Quite frankly, it was miserable, but I learned much about tea while I was there, and because of that, I hope to encourage business away from the East India Company, perhaps become a buyer for local tea cafes and shops." When he glanced at her, excitement danced in his eyes. It was the first she'd spied in all too long a time. "I found an affinity for being able to pair food with the appropriate tea from different regions, and I adore sharing that knowledge with others. It is quite fulfilling."

"That makes me happy. You need more of that, I think."

"I can brew up some of my samples for you if you'd like."

"I actually would. It all sounds so fascinating." As they stepped over a small bridge that went over a wide creek, Sophia removed the daisy from behind her ear. She kissed the bloom and then dropped it into the water, where the current took it and sent it meandering downstream. Perhaps the flower would make someone smile, and perhaps it would bring her good fortune.

"I hope you'll find that same happiness soon." He once again linked their arms and set them off. "Please don't waste the time you have remaining on things that don't matter. Live it doing something you love, something you have always wished to do, something that will leave an impression and make us all smile when we think upon it."

Their conversation had come full circle. "As best that I can, I shall try." If she let it, worry over the future and the terror of the unknown would swallow her whole. "I only wish I had the time or the opportunity for one last romance."

Gilbert glanced at her with speculation in his eyes. "Would you marry again, then?"

"Honestly? Yes." Sophia nodded. "If I had the chance and that chance arrived soon, I think I would marry again. Not only for Hannah's sake, but also for mine. When one is facing one's possible last days or months on this mortal coil, one wishes to spend it with a man who adores them." She flashed him a grin. "And I wouldn't mind enjoying the physical acts that come along with being married."

"Good God! Is there nothing you *won't* talk about?" Her brother gawked at her with an expression of awe mixed with apprehension. The hand on the head of his cane tightened.

She laughed, and it felt good to do so. "Open and honest communication is the key in every situation." Then she shrugged. "It is not a crime to enjoy intercourse. Nor is it a sin to bring oneself to that same state of release. However, it's not as enjoyable." Oh, she did so enjoy making her brothers squirm with her plain speaking.

A flush rose above Gilbert's collar. "Yet, you were diagnosed with your heart ailment well after your last husband passed." He frowned. "Are you certain that organ could take the strain of such… activities?"

How unseemly it would be to have a maid discover that she'd passed in the night beside her husband as a result of physical exertions. But she giggled anyway. It was simply marvelous to think about. "I don't suppose it's any more exerting than waltzing, and I only just indulged in that last week at Mama's ball." Tingles of need danced briefly through her core, for it had been a while since she'd lain with a man or brought herself to that state with her fingers. "In many ways, after achieving release, a woman is quite relaxed."

"Sophia, please." The pleading his eyes was almost frantic. "You *must* cease this vein of the conversation. It's not right to discuss such things with your brother."

Oh, but it was such fun to tease! "Fear not. I'm quite finished with this discussion." She patted his arm. "The likelihood of an interesting candidate presenting himself while we're in the countryside is highly unlikely." With a sigh, she turned her gaze to the manor. "I know this is a fact, for at the ball Mama threw just a week past, the eligible men there were either vastly too young or far too old to suit me."

Such was life.

"Don't give up hope. If a third marriage is what you wish for, perhaps fate in all its fickle wisdom will bring a man to your doorstep." Then he pulled a face, much like he had when they were children. "And if not, I suppose you'll expire a wrinkled and desperate shell of yourself."

"How rude, Gilbert." Playfully, she smacked his shoulder. "As of yet, I've managed to keep the worst of the wrinkles from my face." Yet there were silver threads sprinkled throughout her blonde hair. If it weren't for that, no one would ever guess her age.

"I just want you to remember to think realistically." He bussed her cheek. Then, once he pulled away, he touched a gloved finger to the pink enamel rose pinned to one side of her chignon. "Remember what this signifies, but I do hope you are able to find what you need that will make the remainder of your life pleasant."

Her papa had gifted her the hairpin on the eve of her first wedding. He'd told her it represented that hope sprang eternal and to never give up on her dreams. She wore it every day, not only as a remembrance of him, but of his words. They had become a mantra of sorts.

"As do I." To say nothing of the fact that she still needed to tell her daughter of her health crisis. For the time being, she simply hadn't found the words that would soften such a blow, and she would rather wrench out her weakened heart that break Hannah's.

Why is life so cruel at times?

CHAPTER TWO

July 3, 1819
Berkshire County, England

M R. OLIVER MATTINGLY, the American ambassador to England, leaned back against the worn upholstered bench of the traveling coach. It must have been an age since the vehicle had been updated, for a broken spring drilled into his right shoulder blade while another dug into his left thigh. It made for a highly uncomfortable experience, yet his passage was conducted in peace, for he'd been the only passenger going that way. Because of that, he'd promised the driver a few extra dollars—pounds, he supposed he should be thinking of instead while here—to make up for the bother. Further, the driver had then explained the coach belonged to the Marquess of Grantmore—who was hosting his visit—and there would be no further coin needed.

He was on his way to an estate in Somerset, which would require more than a few more days of travel, but for now, the Berkshire countryside he moved through was bucolic enough, and the summer sun wasn't as nearly as intense as it would be from his home in northern Virginia in America during this time of year. For the moment, he was content, and anxious to spend the next two months as the guest of the marquess. He was one of the

English gentlemen Oliver had often spoken with each time he visited London when Parliament was in session.

But this trip had come up in the dead summer, where apparently the affluent in London fled to their country estates for the relatively cleaner air and for leisure activities. As it had sounded like good fun, Oliver had agreed. He looked forward to enjoying the food and traditions of his English friends, as well as the opportunity to study their lifestyles and try to puzzle out the hierarchy of their social structure.

As he glanced out the window, he pushed his wire-rimmed spectacles higher on the bridge of his nose. Terribly near-sighted without the spectacles, he could literally not see past the end of his nose, which had made the early part of his life quite miserable for himself but comical to his peers. Now they were a part of him, a definition perhaps; he thought wearing them made him that much more distinguished, which helped in his ambassadorial duties. It was much better than growing hideous mutton chop sideburns to help him seem older than his then twenty-seven years when he'd began his tenure.

However, wearing spectacles didn't win him any female admirers, even if he'd been blessed with looking younger than his age. Perhaps that was part of his problem and one of the reasons he remained unmatched and hadn't much experience with women. Though he'd indulged in kissing over the years, for whatever reason, those kisses hadn't translated into the actual bedding of those women. In many ways, he felt the act of intercourse was all too sacred to be treated without regard and respect. To his perhaps antiquated way of thinking, when a man took a woman to bed, he needed to have deep feelings for her and wished to spend his future with her.

If being alone was a curse to that testament, so be it. There were other things to fill his time with. Eventually, he would find the right woman.

Because it was one of the things that made him unique, Oliver put a hand into an interior pocket of his jacket and then withdrew a folded handkerchief. As the coach swayed upon the oftentimes rutted road, he carefully peeled back the layers of much-used linen. At the heart of the fabric, a ring rested. The ring itself was done in gold, but the stone was a ruby of deep, clear red and shaped into a heart. Sunlight winked off it and made the gemstone fairly glow. It was the only thing of value he had in his life and had been passed down through a few generations until it came to land in his possession.

He was the last of his line, the last of the Mattinglys, for his relatives didn't seem to have been granted long life or even good fortune, which is why the ring had been given to him when his father had died several years back. To Oliver's way of thinking, that ring meant that love would always triumph, that love would always win. The last woman to wear the bauble had been his mother, but she'd expired ages ago in childbirth when he was a boy of ten.

And now it's mine.

The ring would either go with him to the grave or it would grace the finger of his wife. There was no other option. With a faint grin, he carefully folded the handkerchief about the bauble, and then once more tucked it away into his pocket. Even at the age of thirty-seven, he had faith that he would fall in love. Every man in his family had, and what was more, it had always been a love at first sight that had burned bright and deep.

It was merely a matter of finding that one special woman.

As the coach rumbled past a flock of sheep, he grinned. There were a great many sheep here in England. With a gloved hand, he tapped on the book with its red linen cover that reposed on the bench beside him. *The Lady of the Lake* was what he'd chosen for his reading this day. A narrative poem by Sir Walter Scott, it involved three men vying for the affections of a woman in Scotland. The romance of it played to his heartstrings. But he'd packed many other books in his trunks. One of his favorites rested, even now, in the valise at his feet. *A History of New York*, by American author Washington Irving, who was a master of the short story, was an especial favorite. All of his characters were unforgettable and made the reader think. That spoke to his intelligence.

Reading was how he enjoyed spending his leisure, and perhaps there would be time enough to do that during his holiday. However, he did enjoy a rousing set of pall mall every now and again. He also hoped the marquess would travel about England to show him the sights, for Oliver wasn't due back at his office in London until the first of November.

As soon as he reached for his book, a sickening snap and crunch of wood rent the air. When the coach lurched drunkenly to the left, he, his valise, and the book slid sharply in that same, directly. Everything slammed against the side of the vehicle, and the door popped open from the sudden halt of momentum.

From outside the coach, the driver's curses floated to his ears. The second driver answered the first and then seconds later, he appeared in the open doorway.

"Looks like we've broken an axle, Mr. Mattingly." He whipped off his slouch-style cap and wiped at his sweating forehead with the back of his sleeve. "Won't go any further today, I'm afraid."

Oliver frowned. "What does this mean?"

"Without a replacement part, we're done for. The journey won't continue. Breaks like that are a nasty business, and the damned road's too rutted from recent rains."

"How interesting." He cast about at his feet for his errant hat. "Well, then, I can't very well sit here, can I?"

"I wouldn't advise it." The driver extended a hand and assisted Oliver from the leaning vehicle. After that, he handed him the valise as well as the book, which Oliver tucked into the bag. "Looks like we're out in the middle of nowhere, but there's a manor house about three miles from here to the northwest. Ettesmere Park, and I believe the Earl of Ettesmere is in residence this time of year."

"I suppose it's a good a place as any to regroup." Then he

frowned. "What of my luggage?"

The driver shared a glance with his fellow and shrugged. "Once you reach the park, have them send a cart out this way to retrieve the luggage and us. We could wait a fool's age out here and still never see anyone."

"That sounds reasonable." The change in plans, though, didn't sit well in his belly. The marquess would wonder what had happened to him after a while. With a glance at the badly leaning coach whose wheel had fallen off and lay on the road next to it, he sighed. "I'd best get on with it, then."

Hoping he was pointed in the correct direction, Oliver set out on the new adventure with both trepidation riding his spine and curiosity filling his chest. One often read about such things in novels, journeys that changed the course of one's existence, but rarely did they ever happen in real life. Perhaps this was a good sign that his holiday would prove amazing.

Two hours later, because he kept stopping to admire blooms and plants that weren't native to his home in Virginia, Oliver came upon lane that branched off the man road. Another meadow filled with colorful wildflowers flanked it. In the midst of the sea of color, as if she'd been painted there, was a young girl of perhaps eleven or twelve. Her blonde hair shone in the sun and hung in a braid down her back. The child hadn't worn a hat or gloves, but her dress in a bright blue was quite striking against the field. She held a bouquet of flowers in one hand while she plucked more with another.

"Excuse me, miss." Oliver shaded his eyes with his free hand. "I believe I am lost."

The girl glanced at him with a soft smile. "Then how do you expect I know where you are if you don't?"

He couldn't help his grin. "Fair point. However, I'm on my way to Ettesmere Park," he explained as he came closer to her. "My traveling coach has broken an axle, and my driver said that was the nearest home."

Quite frankly, he was hot and sweaty and wouldn't mind the

opportunity to escape the heat. But though he'd been walking and walking, he still hadn't managed to find a manor house or even a cottage.

"I am from Ettesmere Park," she said promptly as she resumed picking wildflowers, coming closer to the fence where he'd paused. "It belongs to my uncle, but Grandmother lives there currently."

Oh, thank goodness.

"Excellent." The English accent in children was especially fascinating. Oliver rested a gloved hand on the upper rail. All around him, summertime insects buzzed, and birds chirped as they went about their work-a-day business. "Would you be kind enough to point me in the right direction? My throat is parched, and I could do with a cup of tea before attempting my alternate plans."

"When it is hot like this, I rather prefer lemonade to tea."

He didn't have a preference at this point, but his temporary companion was so fresh-faced and willowy—all limbs yet—that he didn't mind lingering for conversation. Children were always the most honest of creatures. "I don't doubt it." Needing the respite from the exertion, Oliver set his valise at his dusty boots. "I had no idea the summers would be this warm in England."

"Are they not wherever you are from?"

"Oh, indeed they are sometimes. And when the weather is like this, thunderstorms roll through." Virginia summers could sometimes prove sweltering and humid. "I expected England to be different."

"I'd like to think all the places in the world aren't that different, really. We are all alive and wish for the same things. We all must eat food in order to stay alive. The need for water, understanding, and love is the same as well." There was a certain amount of wisdom in what she said. "Apologies. Mama says I ramble. Where are you from?"

"The state of Virginia. Uh, it's in America."

"That is quite far from here." She nodded. "That is why you

sound different."

"I suppose it is." For a few seconds, he wondered what his accent sounded like to her, but then dismissed the thought. "Do you enjoy picking flowers?"

"Not particularly. I'd rather leave them in the fields, and I don't like it when bugs tumble out and crawl on me." She again glanced at him, and Oliver grinned at the slight revulsion in her expression. "But my mother enjoys having pretty things around the house, so I do this for as long as the flowers are in season."

"That's a nice way to honor your mother." If she took after her mother at all, then the woman must be beautiful indeed. "Where are my manners? I'm Mr. Oliver Mattingly. I'm the American ambassador to England, here on holiday for a bit." He must be desperate if he'd been reduced to blathering to a child.

"Hullo, Mr. Mattingly." When the girl smiled, she was a veritable angel. "You may call me Hannah. Hannah Winterbourne. My family and I are at Ettesmere Park through at least the end of summer because Grandmother wished it."

"I see." Even though he didn't. "You've spoken of a mother. Can I assume your father is also here?"

"No." The smile faded from her face. In its place came a frown that held so much grief he could nearly feel it pouring from her. "Papa died several years ago. I was only a child then so don't remember it much, but my aunt died around then too. It makes this time of year… difficult."

"You have my condolences." That was too much to have resting on one's shoulders at that age. "My own mother died when I was about your age. My father expired around the time yours did. I have no other family, unfortunately."

Why he'd told her that, he had no idea.

"I don't suppose any of us can escape death, no matter where we live." The pronouncement was much too deep and intellectual for any child to have. She bent down and plucked another bloom. "But here we are. At least I've only lost a few people from my life. Mama has lost her father, a sister-in-law, and two husbands."

"I'm sorry to hear that."

"So am I. Sometimes she's very sad, so I bring her flowers hoping she will smile again." Before he could respond, she spoke. "I miss having a father about and feel I was cheated out of that experience. Though I have two uncles, it's not the same, and sometimes I don't wish to tell my secrets to them."

"That's understandable." Why she apparently felt comfortable telling him things was beyond his ken, but he wouldn't break her trust. "Perhaps your mother will marry again."

"I hope so, too, but Mama can sometimes be stubborn."

"All of us can at some point." He grinned. This was the most refreshing conversation he'd had in quite a while. It certainly was more honest than entertaining heads of state or stuffy peers from around England.

"Are you married, Mr. Mattingly?"

"I've never had the opportunity."

Speculation lined her expression. "No good with the ladies?"

Her penchant for plain speaking left him amused, but he bit the inside of his lip to keep from laughing lest she thought he made jest of her. "I suppose not. The spectacles do me no favors, I'm afraid." He pointed to the silver wire-rimmed lenses. "To say nothing of the fact that though an ambassador sounds like an exotic title, the wages for such are rather modest to those ladies searching for a well-heeled match."

"If it were me, I'd rather have a man of little coin if there was love between us." She shrugged. "Mama says that marrying for love is the purest form of joy one can find."

"She's not wrong."

"Most of the time she is quite wise, but I fear she is holding back a secret from me."

"Oh? How so?" This child that would soon enter womanhood fascinated him with her ability to converse with intelligence as well as understanding.

"Her eyes don't look happy."

"There is a saying that the eyes are a window to the soul, so you could be correct." Though, the fact she'd discerned that at her age was somewhat disconcerting. She needed a much longer time to see the world as a child instead of an adult. "I don't mean to interrupt your flower picking, but could you point me in the right direction to Ettesmere Park? There are two drivers stranded on the road with the broken coach, who need picked up along with my luggage. I told those fellows I would arrange for that as soon as I arrived."

Hannah put the flowers in a willow basket at her feet. She lifted it and then pointed at the lane. "Just follow the path. The manor isn't far."

"Thank you." He hefted his valise once more.

"I shall come with you. It's nearly time for tea anyway." She ducked between the rails of the fence and joined him on the lane. "Do you plan to stay with us since your coach is damaged?"

"Honestly, I have no idea what my plans are now. I don't know how long it takes to repair a traveling coach."

"Do you paint or draw?"

"No. Do you?"

"Only marginally, for Mama has made certain I've taken lessons. I'd rather explore the countryside and classify plants and flowers. I think it might be rather fun to become a botanist."

That was surprising. "From the little I know of you, it's not outside the realm of possibility, and if you apply yourself to studies, I have no doubts you'll accomplish it."

A blush stained her cheeks. "I appreciate that, Mr. Mattingly. And please, keep this secret. I haven't told my family yet."

"Of course." His immediate future might be undecided, but he supposed one manor house in the English countryside was much like the other, especially if the remainder of this girl's family was as interesting as she. "Do you enjoy staying at Ettesmere Park?"

"Most of the time, but if I had my druthers, I prefer London."

"I do too. There is life and bustle there. So much to see and do. People all around. It helps when I'm feeling as if I'm alone in the world." Why the hell had he admitted to that?

"That is exactly how it feels in London. And the lending libraries are vastly superior." Hannah shot with a grin. Respect shadowed her eyes. "For a stranger, there is something about you, Mr. Mattingly, that makes my soul feel like it has found a friend."

"Then I'd be honored to accept said friendship." Lord knew everyone could use more friends. "It's a lovely area."

"Agreed, and the park even more so. I particularly like the maze."

"How intriguing. I don't know that I've ever been in a maze."

Hannah smiled. "Then I'll have that advantage over you, Mr. Mattingly." Then she pointed. "There is Ettesmere Park. I hope you'll enjoy your stay."

He glanced at the charming edifice with the trailing ivy on one side and the three-storied façade. Green manicured lawns rolled away from it in the back. "I have a feeling that I just might." And from the way anticipation buzzed at the base of his spine, he knew it might change his life in ways he could never imagine.

CHAPTER THREE

SOPHIA HAD BARELY settled into her favorite chair in the drawing room before the butler appeared in the doorway. "I don't believe you've ever been so quick with tea, Landers."

"Hardly, my lady. I have only just put in the order, but there is another matter that has arisen."

She glanced at her mother and then her brothers as they took seats of their own. "What has occurred?"

"There is a visitor." Landers glanced at her mother. "Lady Ettesmere, the visitor is Mr. Mattingly, the American ambassador to England."

Arthur exchanged a glance with Gilbert. Then he looked at the butler. "*Why* is he here?"

"Miss Winterbourne came across him on the lane. His traveling coach suffered difficulties. Now he is here." He shrugged. "He is requesting to speak to the earl."

Sophia frowned. "Is my daughter still with him?" That was rather odd behavior for Hannah, but then, the girl was friendly enough.

"She is, my lady. Shall I show them both in?"

"Yes, please." She peered at Arthur. "You'll see the ambassador?" How often did that happen?

"Of course." He gestured. "Show him in and see about that tea. If he's walked here from the main road, he is probably parched."

"At once, Your Lordship."

"Oh, and Landers? Please have a couple of the footman go down the main road and search for the disabled vehicle. Bring the luggage and the drivers back here until we can make other plans."

"I'll see to it immediately, Your Lordship. The main road is in sorry shape after all the rain we've had."

"And it will grow worse, for no doubt more rain will fall," Gilbert said into the silence. "This *is* England, after all."

Sophia snorted. "Well, not everywhere can be like India."

He didn't take the joke. "Thank God."

Seconds after the butler had departed, Hannah came into the room looking as bright as a summertime day, but the man trailing after her arrested Sophia's attention from the moment she laid eyes on him.

As tall as her brothers and a good several inches taller than her petite height, he was lean and fit, dressed as a man at his leisure if somewhat dusty. Ivory trousers hugged his legs, an understated tan waistcoat called attention to his flat abdomen, while a brown jacket showed off a decent chest and shoulders that were neither too broad nor too narrow. Clean shaven but with a jaw that could perhaps lend itself to ruggedness in another location. A mop of messy black curls ran riot over his head, but his gray eyes twinkled with intelligence and curiosity behind wire-rimmed spectacle lenses. One would never know by looking at him that he was an ambassador.

"Good afternoon, Mama," Hannah greeted as she bounded over the floor to buss Sophia's cheek. "I brought you some wildflowers. Landers took them to find a vase."

"I appreciate that, dear. You always take such good care of me." Then she rose to her feet. The rest of her family followed suit. "And who is your friend?"

The girl smiled. "This is Mr. Mattingly. He is an ambassador. I've never met one before." With a gentle nudge, Hannah urged him into the knot of the Winterbourne family. They must have struck up quite the friendship earlier.

"Welcome, Mr. Mattingly." Sophia held out a hand. As the man stared—those dear silver wire-rimmed spectacles gave him a studious, mischievous air!—he scooped up her hand and carried it to his lips, where he placed a fleeting kiss to the back of it before releasing her. "I am Lady Sophia. This is my mother, the Dowager Countess Ettesmere."

"Charmed." He gave her mother's hand the same treatment. It was obviously the right behavior, for her mother blushed slightly and smiled. "I can easily see where both your daughter and granddaughter got their looks."

"Oh, you." Her mother tittered. She took over the introductions. "These are my sons. Arthur, the current Earl of Ettesmere, and Gilbert, Lord Yeardly. At the moment, Arthur's children have been left to their own devices, but should you stay, you'll meet them at dinner."

Hannah snorted. "Cousin John is either in the village chasing some miss or another, or he's napping. He is really quite dull." She rolled her eyes. "Cousin Emily is visiting with Julianna. Neither of them wished to catch toads with me to study."

A flush came over Arthur's neck. "Emily is rather enamored of my intended, you see," he said to Mr. Mattingly, as if that man had a blessed clue about the family dynamics.

Sophia grinned. "There is nothing shameful about any of that. And not everyone wishes to study toads or frogs, Hannah. Biology is rather unique to you in this connection." No doubt the girl would be a scientist when she was grown. She gestured to a low sofa. "Come, Ambassador. Sit and tell us why you're here." As everyone returned to their previous spots and Hannah usurped Sophia's chair, she alighted beside the newcomer on the sofa with a cushion between them.

"Well, I hadn't intended to drop by unannounced, but my traveling coach broke an axle." He included them all in his gaze and put them at their ease. It was probably a skill he'd learned long ago that had led him to landing his current position. Though he appeared as if he were a young man, faint lines framed his mouth and crinkled the corners of his eyes, which proclaimed him much older, perhaps a handful of years her junior. "In fact, my destination is quite far from here. The Marquess of Grantmore has requested I spend the summer at his estate in Somerset."

Ah, how interesting this man knew such a highflyer.

Arthur snorted. "Grantmore is only interested in hunting and fishing, and though his property is a bit larger than this one, it hasn't the charm Ettesmere Park features." Pride wove through her brother's voice. "I rather think you'd have a better time of it here."

"From what I've seen of it already, I like it," the ambassador was quick to agree. "It's quite beautiful." The cadence of his American accent was lovely, and she wished he would speak in longer sentences merely so she could listen to him.

"Thank you."

"Mr. Mattingly is a fascinating person," Hannah said as she beamed at the man. "He and I talked at length before coming up here, so we are friends."

"Then he must have a wonderful character." Sophia transferred her gaze to him. A faint flush rose over his cravat that was tied in a knot she didn't recognize. "What do you wish to accomplish during your holiday, Mr. Mattingly?"

"Whatever there can be accomplished." When he shrugged, the scent of him wafted to her nose. Citrus and sage and hints of man. Threads of awareness went down her spine. It had been all too long since she'd had any sort of reaction for a member of the opposite sex. "While I'm quite familiar with London—and vastly prefer that over the bucolic life—I wish to appreciate the countryside as well. Frankly, I'd like to experience everything. Perhaps open another faucet to myself that will help deepen my understanding when performing my duties."

"A fine answer." Approval rang in Arthur's tone. "I imagine it would also help in trade negotiations once you see farmland for yourself and know what sort of agriculture and cattle England has to offer."

"Quite possibly."

Landers returned with the tea service. "Lady Ettesmere, there is some sort of emergency in the kitchens. Two of the maids are fighting, and one has stolen one of Cook's pots."

Sophia exchanged a glance with Arthur, who shrugged.

"I'll attend to it immediately." Her mother rose from her chair. The men scrambled to their feet. "Ambassador, I hope you feel comfortable enough here and if you wish to stay, I'll have the housekeeper ready a room."

"Thank you, Lady Ettesmere." Then he sat and kept eyeing the tea tray. "If you don't mind, I'm parched and have been hoping for tea."

"Of course." Sophia edged forward. She poured out a cup and handed it to him. When their fingers brushed, heat shot up to her elbow. "Cream or sugar?" Had he felt that reaction too?

"This is fine. Thank you."

"You are quite welcome." Her gaze dropped to his mouth while he blew across the top of his cup. Such sensual lips. What would they feel like pressed against hers? Then she chided herself. She'd only just met him, and she wasn't desperate enough to tug him from the room merely for a kiss.

Was she?

Once she'd prepared cups of tea for her brothers, she did one for Hannah, who declined, so Sophia took it for herself. "How often do you travel, Mr. Mattingly?"

"As much as my position allows." When he grinned, flutters danced through her lower belly. "I've been to France, parts of the Italian region, England, and I've had cause to travel through various portions of America."

Hannah fairly bounced in her chair. "Will you tell me about all those places?"

"If you'd like."

"Perhaps another time, Hannah." Arthur cleared his throat.

"Since my mother already asked you to stay, I'll second that opinion. We have plenty of room, and if you don't mind being caught up in preparations for my wedding that is planned for later this month, we'd love to have you." The flush had returned, and it was adorable. He was still so embarrassed about his engagement to Julianna.

Sophia frowned. "When did you decide upon a date?"

Her brother shrugged. "A few days ago? I left the bulk of the planning to Mama and Julianna. They picked a date and I agreed."

Poor thing. He truly had no idea what he was in for. "It's lovely just the same. I'm looking forward to it."

"Yes, quite," Arthur murmured with a distracted air. He glanced at the ambassador. "Regardless, you are welcome here, Ambassador."

"I thank you for that and will accept most readily." The man drained his teacup. "But about Lord Grantmore?"

"Write to him of your change in destination. Enjoy the summer festivities here. My mother is planning a masquerade ball soon. You can always continue on to Somerset at a later date if you still desire it."

"The best of both worlds." When the ambassador smiled, Sophia's breath stalled. He was simply enchanting. "I shall pen the letter as soon as I'm settled."

"Good. Good." Arthur nodded with a pleased grin as he finished his tea. Then he stood. "Well, I'm off. I have ledgers to look over, and then I promised to take Julianna on a stroll this evening along the stream. It's one of her favorite places on property." A trace of red showed over his cravat.

Obviously, that location held some significance to them both.

"You and your romance." Gilbert huffed with apparent annoyance as Arthur left the room. He looked at Mr. Mattingly and thumped the tip of his cane on the floor as if he were a dour lord of eighty instead of a man in his prime. "At least while you're here, there is no danger of being matched to a troublesome woman who will break your heart and your trust." Heavy bitterness clung to his voice.

"Gil, please!" Sophia glared at him. "Control your tongue in front of Hannah." She didn't need her daughter's budding dreams spoiled by her uncle's troubles.

"I apologize." He returned his teacup to the table with such force she was surprised it didn't break. "People always assume every man is after romance and wants a woman in his life." When he looked at the ambassador, he lifted an eyebrow. "*Are* you in the market?"

Yes, are you? Sophia rested her gaze on him more intently than she should have.

"Not actively, but I suppose I wouldn't say no if love and romance came calling." He tossed a grin around the remaining company as if he were perfectly comfortable setting whatever group he was in at ease. "It would sure beat being alone."

How interesting.

"Then you're destined for misery and heartache." Gilbert stood as he shook his head as he struggled to his feet. "I'll see you again at dinner. Welcome to Ettesmere Park, Ambassador. Don't let Sophia and Hannah put romantic rot into your brain." He flicked his gaze to her. "Don't try to match him. At least let him have his holiday in peace. Love has ruined more than a few good men."

For long moments, Sophia stared at Mr. Mattingly while he looked back with confusion and amusement warring for dominance in his eyes.

"Please excuse my brothers. Arthur will be married soon, so he's been at sixes and sevens with the planning, and quite distracted as of late. Gilbert's marriage is rather a secret, but from the way he talks, I believe the union has hit some difficulties, but he refuses to talk about it." She shrugged. "They are both stubborn in their own ways."

Hannah snickered. "My uncles are always *so* dramatic."

"*Men* are dramatic, darling." Sophia waved a hand. "Why don't you go down to the kitchens and ask Cook for some lemonade. Hopefully, the contretemps are over now, and she'll spoil you with those pastries you like."

"Are you certain?" Hannah glanced between her and Mr. Mattingly. "I wanted to talk to the ambassador a bit more. He is an interesting fellow, and clever too."

Never say the girl was smitten. Trying to tamp her amusement, Sophia smiled. "There will be plenty of time for that. While you're in the kitchens, tell the housekeeper to have a room readied for him. I think we can all agree, Mr. Mattingly will be staying on for a bit."

That brought her daughter out of her chair. "Of course, Mama." Then, with a wave at the ambassador, Hannah skipped from the room with her braid swinging behind her.

"It seems you have made quite the impression on the girl in a short time."

Her guest shrugged. "She's extremely congenial. It's easy to talk to her. And she is quite intelligent in her own right."

"That makes me glad to hear. I always wonder if she's being raised correctly." Sophia grabbed the teapot and silently refilled the ambassador's cup. "You must think the family has escaped from Bedlam. According to my mother, we are all a willful bunch."

When he flashed that grin again, another round of butterflies awoke in her belly. "I'll admit, being on my own for so long has certainly made my world much quieter, but in the silence, I begin to miss life and the noise of it. It's why I adore living in London. There is always something going on. Seeing your large family and interacting with them is interesting for me."

"Then I'm glad. I worried my brothers would make it difficult for you to stay."

"Not at all." He took a drink from his cup as if he hadn't had liquid in days, and when he stole a biscuit from the tea tray, he ate it with apparent relish. "I enjoy the banter, and I look forward to knowing your family better. In my line of work, everything thrives on connections."

"What did you and Hannah talk about before you arrived here?"

"Oh, this and that." He shrugged and popped a tiny seed cake into his mouth. "Mmm! That is tasty." With a wink, he washed down his mouthful with another swig of tea. "She wanted to know if I was married. Then told me you were a widow. Mostly, we talked of death and grief."

Dear God.

She hadn't known Hannah thought about any of that let alone wished to speak about it. And she wasn't aware of the secret Sophia held back from her, the one that would leave her an orphan. Her hands shook so badly that she hid them in her skirts. "I'm afraid she's known more than her share of death in her young life."

And it wasn't over.

"So I gathered, but I told her of my experience with grieving so she wouldn't feel so alone." He ate another seed cake. "It speaks to your rearing of her that she's got such an old soul. Your daughter is quite wise, and her intelligence will only grow. That will serve her well in the future."

Sophia eyed him with suspicion. "Did she ask you to catch frogs and toads with her?"

"No, but that would be an interesting way to pass the time." A look of surprise crossed his face that one could assume was plain at first sight. "She did speak of her love of flowers and her wish to further study them as well as plants."

"She must get that from her father, for just the thought of frogs makes me shiver." She offered him a smile. "However, it's true I'm a widow."

"Hannah said the anniversary of that date is upcoming." One of his dark eyebrows rose in question.

"It is." A tiny niggle of pain went through her chest. "It's something I can't escape from no matter how hard I try." She lowered her gaze to her lap. "Not that I wish to forget either of my husbands. I loved them both dearly."

"As one should." Mr. Mattingly devoured yet another seed cake and finished off his cup of tea but declined a refill. "I wouldn't know from personal experience."

"That's too bad, for being in love is most exquisite." Oh, why had she said that?

"I've always assumed that was so." He rested his cup on the low table and then trained his full attention upon her. Had there ever been a pair of gray eyes as gorgeous as his? So clear and deep and understanding. "I am sorry for your losses and hope, if it's your intent, that you'll find a third husband and that he'll give you many happy years."

Years is something I don't have, though.

"Thank you." The errant idea that this man could possibly fill that role for her danced through her head. Not even a hard shake could dislodge it. From all accounts, he lived a good, decent life. A well-rounded and well-traveled life that would prove a wonderful education for Hannah. Then she shoved all of those thoughts away. She'd only just met this man. "Well, I'm glad that accident or fate has dropped you here, Mr. Mattingly."

"As am I." He wiped his fingers upon a linen napkin and then meticulously folded it. "I think there will be no end of entertainment and activity while I'm at Ettesmere Park, and I'd be honored if your brother still wishes for me to attend his wedding."

"Oh, Arthur never says anything he doesn't mean." Though her smile felt weak, she gave it to him all the same. "It's been an age since Ettesmere Park has played host to a wedding." And it was a good opportunity to have a new dress made. "Perhaps I shall indulge in a bit of dancing."

"Is that exercise you enjoy?"

"I do, but I must be careful. If the set is too boisterous, I must decline as it makes my heart race entirely too fast." It would be the height of embarrassment to expire on a dance floor at her brother's wedding in front of this man of the world. "However, if the mood strikes, I shall indulge during Mama's masquerade ball."

And hope for the best.

"I've done the pretty more than a few times over the course of playing at being an ambassador, so if you need a partner, I'm game." He put his folded napkin on his plate and rested them both on the table. Then he stood. "Well, I really should discover where it is your lovely staff has put me. It's already been a long travel day, and I'm a bit exhausted."

"Oh, I apologize. That didn't occur to me." Sophia sprang to her feet. She must have moved too quickly, for darkness crept up along the edges of her vision and she swayed.

"Steady, now." Mr. Mattingly's arm was about her waist to steady her. "Should I holler for someone, Lady Sophia?"

"No, thank you." For a few seconds, she gave herself the luxury of leaning into him on the pretense of finding her balance. "I'm better now." It had been yet another reminder that her time on this earth was measured. "In any event, welcome to Ettesmere Park." Though she rather enjoyed the brief feeling of being protected in his modified embrace, she pulled away. "If you should like a tour guide for the house or grounds, please ask. I'm always walking the acreage in the morning."

"I appreciate that." Confusion shadowed his eyes, and he perhaps stared overly long at her lips, but she couldn't be certain. "If you would be good enough to show me upstairs to my room? I couldn't presume to traipse about someone else's house, even if curiosity is raging."

"Of course. I'll ring for Landers. Surely they have made up the room." It was so easy to smile around him. "Come with me."

He nodded. "Is there a library here? I only brought three books with me, and I'll wager I'll go through them quickly."

Her heart skipped a beat, and though it was alarming enough, it had nothing to do with her health. *A man who reads books! How lovely.* "Of course, and you're welcome to peruse the shelves. Arthur won't mind."

"Thank you."

With every word he uttered, she was more and more entranced, and she couldn't wait to discover everything else about him.

Hopefully without becoming a silly widgeon.

CHAPTER FOUR

July 5, 1819

I T WAS THE second day of Oliver's unexpected holiday at Ettesmere Park, and already he was beguiled with the estate and its lands. His rambling hike of this morning proved no different.

Though the day had started out with abundant sunshine, clouds had rolled in that promised rain in the afternoon, but he didn't care. Though the air in the country was cleaner than in London, there was something interesting to stumble upon at every turn.

At present, a group of bluebells, as well as pink wild foxgloves, held his attention as he approached a hedgerow on the far perimeter of the property. Would Lady Sophia enjoy a bouquet of them?

In contemplating the thought, he sank down onto a fallen tree as his mind jogged to that lovely lady. Ever since he'd met her two days before, he hadn't been able to evict her from his mind. Not only was she one of the prettiest women he'd ever had the privilege of meeting, but there had been a certain air of vulnerability about her that had intrigued him. There were secrets in her eyes, but would she trust him enough to reveal them?

As of yet, he hadn't had an opportunity to speak with her alone since they'd taken tea together the day of his arrival.

"Hullo! Ambassador Mattingly!"

Oliver yanked up his head at the sound of the hail. As the young man approached, he grinned. "Ah, Lord Eglinton." He was the son of the Earl of Ettesmere, and if he understood it correctly, had been given one of his father's courtesy titles, which could not be passed down to a son should he ever have one. The hierarcky of the English *ton* was complex and oftentimes confusing. "How are you this fine morning?"

"I am well. Thank you for asking." Once the blond lordling drew near, he continued his conversation. "I thought I was the only one who enjoyed walking the acreage in the mornings. I guess I take after my father in that way, except he comes out with the dawn."

"That requires more dedication than I can give at present."

Lord Eglinton chuckled. "Indeed. I rather enjoy sleeping."

"As do I." He turned his attention to the wildflowers again. The riots of purple and pinks pulled a grin from him. "I might do what your young cousin does and bring back a bouquet to the house. Flowers are rather cheerful things."

"Yes, well, Hannah has very specific reasons for doing that."

"Oh?" When he hoped the other man would expand the topic, nothing else was forthcoming. Why was everyone in this family dancing around secrets?

"It's of no importance just now." The lordling frowned, and then seated himself beside Oliver on the fallen tree. "Might I ask you something, Mr. Mattingly?"

"Of course.

"Well, ever since you arrived, I've been curious about what you do for your livelihood."

"What, being an ambassador?" Oliver's eyebrows shot up. "I don't think anyone has ever shown an interest in me before." In that way or any other.

"It's quite fascinating. To travel the world, to make connections with those who share other connections, to talk politics and trade! To dance with ladies from all walks of life. That's immensely more exciting than learning how to be an earl someday."

"Yes, but that is your heritage, your birthright. You should take pride in it." Though, from a young man's perspective, he supposed it might seem like a prison of sorts.

"Perhaps, but if one were interested in doing that sort of thing before the reins of responsibility came due, how would one manage it?" The light of interest shone in his eyes.

Oliver sighed. "Well, in my case, my father had been involved in politics for many years. As you said, from those connections there came a need for a clerk in the ambassador's office. I had no direction for life at the time, so I applied. A few weeks later, I was selected." He once more contemplated the wildflowers. "As the years went by and I learned the duties and became trustworthy, it was only natural that I was eventually selected and approved for the ambassador's position."

"Then it wasn't based on skill or intelligence?"

"I'd like to say there was some of that involved, for I'm not a stupid man." He chuckled when the other man sputtered and flushed. "However, luck played a large part. But once I was appointed to the position, I had to work hard and prove myself."

"Do you think that someone like me would have a chance to do something like that? To prove myself and show my father I am capable of so much more than being a future earl." There was such a note of wistfulness in the younger man's voice that Oliver wished to help.

"I don't see why not, but for that, you can't just stroll into the offices and order people about. You have to put in the time, come to know everyone involved, take an interest in whatever the position demands." He shrugged and glanced at him. "However, if you believe my position is glamorous and a way to meet beautiful women, perhaps you haven't matured enough in life."

Drat. That isn't my place to say.

For long moments, Lord Eglinton stared at him. Finally, he

nodded. "What you say holds merit. I *did* think that, but how did you know?"

Oliver snorted. "Because that's what every man thinks an ambassador does. At first." He grinned. "While I agree there is a fair amount of travel involved and I do attend more social events than I probably should, that is only a small part of it. There are long hours behind a desk writing out contracts or trying to iron out disputes between nations. Diplomacy is a delicate operation. However, none of that has helped me find a wife, and neither does it allow me to go home to the land of my birth often." He pushed his spectacles higher onto the bridge of his nose. "Only you can choose the sacrifices you'll need to make throughout life."

"How do I know what I want from my life though?" He planted his elbows on his knees, leaned forward, and buried his head in his hands. "My father assumes I cannot wait until it's my turn to be the Earl of Ettesmere, but I'm not excited about it. And I didn't go into the military like many of my friends. Neither do I have an affinity for the church. What else is there in life?"

Ah, to be young again and think the world was so vast and without possibility. Oliver bit back the urge to grin. "How old are you, my friend?"

"Three and twenty, and quite frankly, I'm not ready to settle down either."

"No, and you shouldn't do anything merely because it's expected." He truly hoped the earl wouldn't give him a dressing down for offering counsel to his son. And unsolicited at that. "Perhaps over the next few weeks, you should spend time alone with paper and pen and decide what you are interested in and what sets your soul on fire. Then map out a plan on how to pursue one or three of those things. The only way you'll discover who you are meant to be is to search around a bit. If you delay, you will run out of time, and that leads to regret. No one should have those."

"That makes sense." A heavy sigh followed. "Of course, I had hoped you could just tell me what I should do."

"I'm afraid life doesn't work like that." He flashed a grin. "However, we all feel like that upon occasion, and not just when we're young and searching for our place."

"Perhaps." The younger man shoved a hand through his hair and sighed. "Please don't tell my father we had this talk. I don't wish to disappoint him, and he already has enough to worry about with his upcoming wedding."

"You have my confidence." Oliver frowned. Here was an opportunity to find out more about the fascinating family. "I assume you are pleased with his upcoming nuptials?"

"Oh, quite." The other man sat up straighter. His smile was genuine. "She is good for Papa, and they both deserve happiness. Only…"

"Yes?"

"Only, I think it makes Aunt Sophia even sadder each time the subject comes up."

Oliver's heart beat a tad faster at the mention of her name. "She doesn't approve?"

"No, she does. In fact, she was a big champion for the relationship to begin with, but she's been married twice before, and I think she's lonely."

"And perhaps even jealous," Oliver added in a soft voice. When the other man nodded, he sighed. "It's a valid emotion."

"Yes. She's had wretched luck with men living long enough to appreciate her."

"Does she wish to marry again?" That was also overstepping the line, but the more he could discover about her, the better equipped to talk with her he would be.

"I honestly don't know." Lord Eglinton met Oliver's gaze. "But if she does, she'd best do it, for she might expire soon."

"What?" Oliver's stomach dropped, and he reeled as if he'd been given a gut punch. "Why do you think that?"

An expression of slight panic crossed the other man's face. "It's not my place to gossip, Mr. Mattingly. Please excuse me. I need to return to the house." He jumped to his feet. "But thank you for your insight. I'll ponder your words."

"For as long as I'm in residence, I'd be happy to give you further counsel." For long moments after the young man left, Oliver sat on that fallen tree and thought about Lady Sophia.

HE SPENT MUCH of the day outside, only returning to the house to take luncheon, which he shared with the dowager, for the remainder of the company had scattered to their own devices.

"Where is everyone today?" he finally inquired as he took the last spoonful of white soup and then popped the final morsel of a piece of bread into his mouth. "I assumed the Winterbourne family spent much of their time together."

A laugh escaped the elegant lady's throat, and the copious threads of silver in her blonde hair winked in the sunlight. "How refreshingly naïve you are, Mr. Mattingly." But she smiled, and he thought the day a success because of it. "Arthur is closeted away with his intended, finalizing wedding plans, even though it will be a small, private ceremony. Gilbert has taken himself off to the village, no doubt to while away the afternoon in a tavern. There is trouble with him, I'd wager, if I did that sort of thing." She shook her head. "And my grandchildren have decided today was a good time to go swimming in one of the ponds on the property. No doubt the girls will talk of gowns and costumes for the upcoming masquerade, while poor Charles will indulge them with half an ear."

Oliver nodded. "And Lady Sophia? Where is she?" He didn't wish to seem overly eager, but this was a good chance to find her alone.

The dowager leveled a glance on him that brimmed with speculation. "I believe she's puttering in one of the flower beds. She tends to some at the heart of the maze, but there is also a larger bed in the gardens. It's where she goes when she wants to reflect on her life."

"Does she go there often?" What he truly wanted to know was if the slip that her grandson had made earlier that morning was true. But he refrained.

"More and more often, I'm afraid." Sadness reflected on the older woman's face. "There is much to think about just now for her."

Well, damn. "So, then, what Charles told me this morning is true. Lady Sophia is dying." It wasn't a question, and he hated to be so blunt about it, but the urge to know the truth burned bright inside him. "I apologize for the gossip, but this is too important to avoid."

"It is." The dowager's chin trembled. "Never did I ever think I would outlive one of my children, but we are facing that very thing."

"I am truly sorry." He dabbed at his lips with his linen napkin and then rested it on the table. "How long does she have, if you don't mind me prying."

"Who can say? Her doctor cannot divine the future, but perhaps you should talk to her if you wish for more specifics." The dowager shrugged. "I don't think she's even shared with me the true nature of her illness."

"I will. Thank you." When he made ready to stand, she laid a hand on his, staying his flight.

"Despite the hectic schedule we maintain here at Ettesmere Park and despite the looming pall of Sophia's malady, we are glad to have you here, Mr. Mattingly. You are quite a breath of fresh air, and that is exactly what we need right now."

"That's appreciated, Lady Ettesmere." He patted her hand, though that responsibility would grow heavy. "I've been around long enough that studying human nature and interactions fascinates me. When a man sits back and observes without wishing to be the center of attention, that man learns much about people."

And already he'd learned Lady Sophia was imminently unhappy as well as frightened, and her family didn't know how to adequately set her mind at ease.

Perhaps he could help.

"I suppose it takes an American viewpoint to see us differently." The smile she offered was small and tight. "Enjoy the remainder of your day, Ambassador. I'm afraid rain will arrive before too long and then you'll be treated to the typical English weather."

"It won't matter a bit, Lady Ettesmere, for this is my holiday, and I look forward to everything that comes my way." With a nod, he stood, pushed his spectacles back up the bridge of his nose, and then took himself off.

In next to no time, Oliver found Lady Sophia. Indeed, she was ensconced within the strolling gardens set out between the manor house and the maze. Beneath a network of arched trellises, where wild rose bushes and other climbing plants trailed and coiled about the woodwork, she kneeled in the dirt in an effort to pull weeds away from the base of the plants, but her yellow skirts easily made her as cheerful as any of the blooms.

"Would you care for some company, my lady?" he asked in a low voice so he wouldn't startle her.

When she glanced up at him, pleasure leapt into her green eyes, and the smile that curved her lips immediately banished the worry from his mind. "I would enjoy that immensely, Mr. Mattingly." Having not worn a bonnet, she wiped at her forehead with the back of a gloved hand. "In the absence of a chair, I can offer you a patch of grass. Or we can walk through the gardens for a bit."

"No need for all of that. I noted a bench near a grouping of statuary on the way over. Perhaps we can remove to that location and talk."

"Ah, you are referring to the Garden of Zeus." She left her spade near the rosebush, and once she'd gained her feet, she brushed the worst of the dirt from her skirts. "My grandfather created that feature. There are five statues in total. Each depicting a different god or goddess." When she peeled off her soiled gloves, she let them drop to the earth next to the spade. "But there is something about working in the dirt, smelling the richness of it that reminds that me that being alive is nothing to take for granted."

This was the opening he'd waited for ever since arriving. "This might be overly bold of me, and if it is, please tell me, but your nephew and your mother have both hinted about the fact that you are ill."

"I wondered if they could keep the secret once a newcomer was thrown into the mix. Perhaps they merely need to talk about it to someone." At the grouping of statues, she perched on one of the stone benches, and the sun turned her blonde hair into molten gold. Tiny curls at her nape and temples beckoned to him. Were they as soft as they looked? With a sigh, she peered up at him. "As vulgar as it sounds, yes, I expect to perish soon."

There was no point in dancing about the issue. Not when time was apparently of the essence. "Will you tell me about it?"

"Only if you sit beside me. I don't relish craning my neck."

Those dulcet tones as well as the come hither look in her eyes made the decision for him. "Since it's not every day I'm given the opportunity to sit beside a beautiful woman, of course I'll do as you bid." As soon as he settled beside her and the heat of her seeped through his sleeve, budding awareness tripped down his spine.

"Oh, la. You are quite the charmer, Mr. Mattingly." She swatted playfully at his arm.

"It's not charm if it's true." The lilac scent she wore further enhanced the summertime scene unfolding around them. "Now, tell me why you feel you will die, and too soon, I might add. You seem to be in the bloom of health."

Her smile was tinged with sadness. "That is what my personal physician has told me." The lady clenched her hands in her lap and stared at her fingers. "You see, six months ago, I began feeling rather poorly. My chest was tight all the time. I startled easily, was lethargic, or contrary to that, too stimulated. I didn't show interest in the world around me or my family, would be overheated and lightheaded. To say nothing that my heart—the organ itself and not of a metaphorical sort—ached more often than it didn't."

The high spirits he'd had since waking began to plummet the longer she spoke. "What is the prognosis?"

"Other than I'm going to die sooner rather than later?" When her attempt at a joke fell flat, she heaved out a sigh. "However, it's true. The physician told me to live my life without excitement if I could manage it and without being startled. If I did that, then I could expect to extend my existence perhaps by a few months."

Good God. "But what sort of life is that?"

For the first time since he'd met her, the smile she flashed was genuine and her expression filled with amusement. "That is exactly what I asked him. I am one and forty, Mr. Mattingly, and up until six months ago, my life has been filled with everything a woman could ever hope to experience. I wished to feel everything that I could, try new things, conduct myself with abandon because we were given a heart in order to do exactly that." Once more she looked at her hands. "And now that organ is betraying me."

From the way she described herself, the lady sounded lovely. "How long have you been in the countryside?"

"Perhaps a month?" When she shrugged, the bodice of her simple muslin day dress pulled taut over her full breasts. "But while in London, I did nothing more than keep to my townhouse or visit Arthur's. I've been reduced to existing in a half-state for fear that anything that makes my heart race will kill me. It's maddening and a tad pathetic."

"I am deeply sorry to hear that." How could this vibrant woman manage the wait for death? It would have driven him mad. "Is that why there is unfathomable sadness in your eyes every time I look at you?"

"Why, Mr. Mattingly, just how much time *do* you spend watching me?" With teasing clear in her voice, her smile widened, and his world tilted.

"Uh, not overly much, I would like to think." How had his cravat suddenly become too tight? He resisted the urge to tug at the knot. Yet she'd occupied his thoughts from the moment he'd met her.

"Mmm, perhaps." Briefly, she touched his hand. Heat shot up his arm to his elbow. "What you've seen is how I feel. I mourn, and I worry over the fate of my daughter. Once I pass, Hannah will be lost. Both of her parents will have died, and while I trust my brothers with my life, leaving her with them isn't the same as knowing she would have a father looking after her."

"I can understand the concern." When his gaze dropped to her mouth, the budding awareness burgeoned into a wave. What would it feel like if he were to press his lips to hers right now without warning? "How much time do you have left?"

"The doctor told me it could be a week, a month, or perhaps a few months if I'm fortunate and I do nothing of consequence for the remainder." A tiny waver set up in her voice. "Yet in doing so, I am merely waiting for death instead of living. It is quite distasteful."

"A conundrum indeed, but I agree. Waiting for death to find you is no sort of life, and what does that teach Hannah?" He shrugged. "It's never acceptable to call defeat unless every other avenue has been exhausted. You wouldn't want to quell her spirit before it has a chance to grow. She is not suited to a fearful life."

Lady Sophia's eyes widened. "That's exactly what I think too. And I certainly don't wish to miss out on time with her or my family during these last days, especially when I feel perfectly fine some days."

"It does seem counterintuitive." For long moments, Oliver looked at her. "Do you mean to marry again in the time remaining to you? I assume a woman as vital as yourself might have a craving for companionship during her last days."

"If the right circumstances and man present themselves." A knowing light jumped into her eyes. Did she know what he was thinking? "And I *do* rather adore the married state. Especially when there is love involved."

"Are you actively searching for that?"

She shrugged. "Is anyone when it happens to them?"

Despite the gravity of the conversation, his heart squeezed. He might have been enamored with her two days ago, but now it was heading into full-blown infatuation. "I suppose not." Of course, he didn't have the experience to back up that summation. All he knew right now was that she fascinated him, and he wouldn't soon tire of spending a string of days in her company.

"At this point, I know love isn't probably possible, for there is no time, but I do believe I can find a man with whom I get along well with enough that a marriage would be feasible." When she turned toward him, their knees knocked. Intense heat shot up his leg into his groin. "When one's existence is sharply limited, one learns how to boil things down into what is the most important."

"I envy you that. For far too many years, I've sat behind my desk and wondered if there was more out there than drafting a new agreement for trade or trying to appease both sides of an argument between countries over trivial things."

"It's never too late to discover everything you're capable of, especially now that you've been afforded leisure time." When she raised a hand and rested her palm against his cheek, his breath stalled. "And you, Mr. Mattingly, are ripe for a woman to pursue you, I think. You are quite adorable in those spectacles, and forgive me, but I've wanted to do this from the moment I saw you." As he watched her with varying degrees of alarm and anticipation, she moved, surged into him, and pressed her lips to his.

Heat and surprise streaked down his spine and shot through his chest to make him gasp, but just as he went to put an arm around her, she pulled away. "I, uh, well that was…" Every thought he had flew out his head, for that tiny kiss had only set fire to his blood.

Dear God, I need more.

"Oh, I beg your pardon." A pretty blush stained her cheeks as she gained her feet. "Actually, I don't. I wanted to kiss you, and so I did. After all, there is no time for consequences, and you have quite a kissable mouth, Ambassador." She waved a hand as confusion filled her eyes. "I should go. There are things to do…"

"Even knowing the future you face? Are those… things truly as important as living your last days on your own terms or for finding one last adventure?" Oliver wanted nothing except to experience her kiss again and apply himself with passion now that the shock of the gesture had worn off.

"I… I… Let me think about it." Then she fled with her yellow skirts streaming behind her.

Now he was even more intrigued and enamored with her than he'd been before. It might be rather nice to be pursued, if that was her intent. So, what should he do now?

CHAPTER FIVE

July 6, 1819

SOPHIA ALTERNATELY BATTLED grief and hope today. Not only was it the anniversary of her second husband's death, but it was also the same for her sister-in-law's passing. But putting grief aside for one moment, her heart continued to trip and tremble, not because of its weakened state, but from that fleeting kiss she'd taken from Oliver yesterday.

He'd been so dear and genuine when she'd spoken about her ailment and her future, or rather Hannah's, and he'd understood what she'd talked about. In addition, just as she was prone to prefer a man in a military uniform, apparently a man with spectacles sent flutters into her lower belly just the same.

So, she'd kissed him.

Ordinarily, that would have been the end, and she would have been satisfied with that, but there had been such a connection, an attraction, a pull between them in that one moment she'd panicked. For the first time in her life, she'd fled from a man. It was silly, of course, but for all her talk of wishing to marry again, there were certain walls thrown around her heart. Losing two previous husbands had left scars. Did she want to open herself up to potential feeling again? To say nothing of what would become of Oliver once she perished.

For it was a certainty.

Yet…

Such things were complicated, and even more so knowing she hadn't much time.

As she stood at the morning room windows, uncertain as to how she would spend her afternoon, she sipped a cup of tea. Both of her brothers were down below on the lawn, and from the looks of things, they were engrossed in a heated argument if their hand gestures were any indication. At one point, Gilbert pointed the head of his cane at Arthur. She frowned. What in the world could they have to fight about? Unless it was Gilbert's penchant for secret keeping. There was something most certainly wrong in his marriage, but that was between him and his wife.

The rest of the family needed to stay out of it.

Unless Gilbert had done something scandalous when he'd been away in India that had just now circulated to Arthur's hearing. *Oh, dear*, she hoped he hadn't betrayed his marriage vows while separated from his wife.

Whatever it was, she didn't wish to be involved. That wasn't an efficient use of the time remaining to her. And neither was it in Arthur's best interests, when he would marry soon. She sighed and sipped at her tea. Having brothers was trying.

A soft knock on the open door wrenched her from her thoughts. In some gratitude, she glanced that way. "What is it, Charles?"

Her nephew came into the room with an expression full of speculation. "I was told to give this to you by Mr. Mattingly."

"Oh?" Flutters danced through her belly at the sound of the ambassador's name. "Is all well? Is he ill?"

"I wouldn't know, but he appeared quite well. He didn't say what the nature of the missive was, yet he did look quite mysterious. Hannah was with him. They left the manor directly after." Once he'd crossed the room, he held out an envelope.

How very odd. "Thank you." When Charles didn't exit the room, she raised an eyebrow. "Is there something else?"

"I suppose not, except..."

She frowned as she rested her teacup on the windowsill. It wasn't like him to hedge around an issue. Arthur had taught both his children to talk about what bothered them, which was quite funny since he'd had trouble doing the same, and it had nearly cost him Juliana. "What is on your mind?" Though curiosity to know what the note contained burned through her consciousness, if her nephew needed her attention, he would have it.

"Well, I rather thought... That is to say Mr. Mattingly is a congenial sort..." Charles shifted his weight. When he clasped his hands behind his back, he put her in mind of Arthur when he'd been a young man. "The ambassador would make a decent third husband if you were of a mind, Aunt Sophia. I mean, he is here and so are you, and time grows short..." He huffed and then worry clouded his expression. "I am concerned for you."

"Oh, you dear thing." With her chest tight, Sophia stepped forward and briefly hugged him. "I shall think about what you've said, but I cannot make such a decision lightly." *Can I?* With her first two husbands, due to their status in the military and the timing of their leaves, enjoying long engagements wasn't possible. And now, she didn't have that luxury either. But what sort of a woman would it make her if she coerced the first man she'd connected with since becoming a widow again into a hasty union? "My time might be limited but aligning myself with a man who I don't know all that well could prove a disaster. That would be counterintuitive to the quiet life I'm supposed to be living."

Desperate or clever? That was the question.

"I highly doubt Mr. Mattingly has even one deceptive or cruel bone in his body. It's something to ponder." Charles shrugged. "Hannah seems to like him well enough, and you know how difficult it is for her. Honestly, Auntie, she just wants a father."

That was true enough, and their straits had apparently grown dire if her nephew had become attuned to them. "You are far too young to carry the weight of other's troubles upon your shoulders." Though what he said held merit. Like her, Hannah had found it difficult to trust others since so many people had already left her life. Perhaps having Mr. Mattingly here was fate's way of extending a kindness they both sorely needed. "I promise to seriously consider your idea."

"That is all I can ask." He grinned. "Enjoy your day. I'm off to the village. A group of young people are getting up a fishing party, and I aim to be among them."

"Behave yourself while there. Your father doesn't need your scrapes and scandals on top of everything else he is giving attention to."

"Aunt Sophia, you should know me better than that by now." With a wink, Charles left the room. Seconds later, cheerful whistling echoed down the corridor.

Oh, to be young and carefree again!

Then she opened the envelope and withdrew a folded sheet of paper. Bold, confident handwriting lay scrawled in orderly lines. So easily could she see the ambassador at a desk writing missives or contracts in conjunction with his position.

Lady Sophia,

Please join your daughter and me in the wildflower field located just off the lane that leads to Ettesmere Park at half past two this afternoon. You deserve a peaceful outing in the sunshine while we have it. Beyond that, Hannah and I will have a surprise for you that will further help to usher in relaxation.

Yours respectfully,
Mr. Mattingly

How very interesting! What did the man have planned, and why had Hannah gone along with him? As she put the note back into the envelope, she drifted to the window and glanced out. Her brothers had left the area. Perhaps it was time to focus quite selfishly on herself and live the remainder of her life for her own happiness and that of her daughter's. She hadn't the luxury of delay or dancing about the issue of a possible romance.

It would either happen or it wouldn't, and since there *was* a heated attraction already between her and the ambassador, logic dictated she should chase it. *It's time to trust fate.* After all, hadn't she done just that with her first two husbands? Sophia grinned as she left the morning room. Love needn't be involved, not at this abbreviated pass, but there did need to be a bond of trust there if she wished to consider him as a third husband.

Now, what to wear that might entice another kiss from the ambassador? Only then would she know whether to beguile him into a marriage of convenience.

For Hannah's sake.

AT THE APPOINTED time, Sophia strolled down the lane toward the wildflower meadow mentioned in the note. There, beneath the shade of a large oak tree, was Hannah, who sat upon an old quilt that had been spread out over the meadow grass and flowers. Mr. Mattingly approached the area from the direction of the public road. He carried a willow basket in one hand, and when he spied her, he waved with his other.

Silly flutters moved through her belly. This man wasn't of the same bent as her previous husbands. They'd been military men who lived life on a rigorous schedule and followed orderly existences. The ambassador on the other hand apparently went where the wind—and the whim—took him. He did whatever he pleased and seemed to wish only to make the people around him comfortable and at ease.

"Hullo, Mama." Hannah beamed as Sophia reached the quilt. "Isn't it a lovely day?"

For the first time in a long while, her daughter didn't have sadness or worry in her eyes. Was that due to the arrival of Mr. Mattingly or was she truly pushing past the grief she'd been inundated with in her young life?

"Indeed, it is. I cannot remember when the sky was so blue nor bereft of clouds." When Hannah patted the quilt beside her, Sophia gratefully sat and arranged her stamped muslin skirts over her folded legs. The dress was a fast favorite, for it featured lines of green ivy vines alternating with lines of pink and mauve tulips. Soft lace lined the scooped bodice as well as the short sleeves. She'd left the house without bonnet or gloves, but life was exceedingly short to observe the conventions now. Then she glanced at Mr. Mattingly, and her breath caught. Truly, he was a handsome man in a fresh-faced, innocent sort of way. "Good afternoon, Ambassador."

"Hello, Lady Sophia." He set the basket down near Hannah and a mysterious glance passed between them. Then he gave her his full attention. "For now, we'll enjoy a brief rest in the shade. Perhaps once we stroll back toward the manor, you can tell me about some of your favorite places on the property. Hannah has told me all of hers."

The smooth baritone of his voice coupled with the enticing scent of his shaving soap, as well as the impeccable way he dressed that always seemed a tad more casual than an English gentleman, all worked to strengthen that invisible pull between them.

"We could do that, certainly." She eyed the basket that she swore had moved slightly. "Is that a picnic lunch?"

Hannah snorted. "No, Mama. Mr. Mattingly has given us gifts."

"Oh?" A shiver went down her spine. What was he about? "You might as well show me what's in the basket."

The ambassador grinned, and her brief foreboding faded. It was silly to feel as if she might lose herself in a man's smile. "I hope you like them. Last night as I was talking with some of the stable boys, I discovered one of the tenants had a litter of them. I knew right away this was the perfect thing for both you and Hannah. May they bring joy to you as well as comfort." So saying, he unlatched the lock from the top of the basket, moved off the lid, and as soon as he did, two little kitten heads popped up from the interior.

"How lovely!" As much as she appreciated the gift—for the kittens were adorable—thread of anger and sadness twisted down her spine, but she did her level best to not let her daughter see that. Instead, she lifted out one of the orange brindled felines with beautiful golden eyes and immediately put it into her lap. When it began to purr, she smiled. "This is appreciated. Thank you."

Hannah took the other kitten from the basket. This one was all white except for its ears and paws, which were orange striped. "Are they so cute?" She hugged the cat and then dropped a kiss on the top of its head. "Mr. Mattingly asked if I'd like to go have a look, and when I did, I had to have them, for the others were already spoken for." When she turned those big eyes on Sophia and looked soulfully at her, there was no chance to turn down the gift. "May we keep them?"

"I suppose we ought, for it would be rude not to." Absently, she stroked the kitten's head. "But you must be mindful of them. They will be your responsibility."

"I will, Mama." The kitten Hannah held sprang from her lap and darted off the quilt to investigate the grass. "Oh, he's getting away!" Then the girl scrambled to her feet and chased after the errant feline, leaving Sophia alone with the ambassador.

"Mr. Mattingly, I—"

"Oliver," he interrupted with amusement dancing in his gray eyes.

"What?"

"My name is Oliver. It would make me happy if you would make use of it."

"Oh." The name sent delicious tingles down her spine. She nodded. "Very well. Oliver, I must tell you that I'm a bit annoyed with you right now."

"Whyever for?" Genuine confusion lined his face. "They are kittens, not a threat to England."

Obviously, he'd never been around kittens or even cats before. "Perhaps, but why would you do this knowing I won't live to see them grow into adult cats? It seems cruel somehow to give me a gift I'll never have the good of." Her heart ached, and with the pain came a swath of panic. She massaged her fingers over that faulty organ. With the other hand, she entertained the kitten as best she could. "I shall miss out on so much."

"I meant no disrespect, my lady. I merely thought that you and Hannah might welcome a diversion from impending sadness."

"Please, leave the titles and formalities behind. I am merely Sophia." She shook her head and glanced at her daughter where she chased the white kitten. Laughter echoed in the sunlit air, which was at odds with the conflict raging in her head. "I suppose I'm not just angry with you. The kittens are lovely, but Hannah doesn't know yet of my impending demise."

"Ah. Now it all makes sense." He put the lid back on the basket then moved the whole thing off the side.

Before he could give her empty platitudes or advice she hadn't asked for, Sophia plunged ahead. "Continuing in that same vein, I won't survive long enough to see Hannah grow into adulthood." Tears choked her voice and sprang into her eyes as the reality of the situation came all too close. "I won't be able to experience her Come Out or learn what she will accomplish and bring to the world." The more she attempted to keep the tears at bay, the more they pooled in her eyes. When she blinked, a few fell to her cheeks. "I won't be there when she marries or when she has her children. Never will I know the joy of holding grandchildren in my arms." Now she understood why he'd given her the kittens, for cuddling one against her neck, for burying her face into its soft fur *did* bring a modicum of comfort.

Drat the man.

"Nothing I can say will make your situation any better, but I *can* sit with you until you feel more like yourself." He attempted to tease the kitten away from her, but the feline was having none of it. "I thought that perhaps you could tell the kittens of your heartbreak, and it would make your anxiety less, for I doubt you've told your family everything."

"That's a correct assumption." She nodded and swallowed hard around the ball of tears in her throat. "I rather think you are a good listener."

"It's part and parcel of my position." Briefly, he touched her hand, and she wished he weren't wearing gloves so she could feel his skin against hers. "You *must* tell Hannah, though. Don't leave this up to chance so that she's caught unawares if you should expire earlier than you assume. No doubt she'll need to have you clarify a few things."

"Perhaps you are correct." The kitten wandered from her lap to Oliver's. When he took the squirming, energic feline into his hands and the animal began to chew on one of his fingers, she smiled. There was something so very masculine and attractive about a man who showed affection to animals. It made sense because he was so kind to Hannah as well. "Will you wait for me while I tackle this task?"

"Of course." He tugged a handkerchief from an interior of pocket of his jacket and passed it to her. "Good luck. I'll check in on Hannah before dinner just in case she doesn't take the news well."

"You don't need to—"

"Sophia, it is what I do every day of my life." He grinned and the delicate skin at the corners of his eyes crinkled. "I am a peacekeeper, a felicitator of satisfaction and success. Essentially, a matchmaker between countries so they'll maintain a good relationship and enter into trade agreements. I believe that qualifies me to soothe the ruffled feathers of a twelve-year-old girl."

Perhaps, but she suspected he was as wrong in this as he was about kittens being harmless. But with a nod, Sophia rose to her feet. "I shall be back shortly." As she approached Hannah's position, her heart squeezed. The girl was so happy right now and the day so lovely. It felt somehow a sin to mar either. "Hannah, darling, I need to talk with you."

The girl cuddled the kitten in her arms. "You aren't going to take them away, are you?"

"Of course not. You're capable of taking care of them, and I think they'll be just the thing to keep you occupied as time goes on." Her voice broke on the last words. As she closed the distance, Hannah frowned.

"You've been crying." It wasn't a question.

"I have."

"Did Mr. Mattingly upset you? Do the kittens?"

"No. In that quarter, everything is fine." She glanced his way, and he gave her an encouraging nod. "But I must tell you something that has been eating at me for the last six months." She cupped her daughter's cheek while the kitten cavorted about their feet. "I'm sure you've noticed that I have been exceedingly careful these last weeks with my health."

"Yes, but I only thought you tired or still in mourning. It's what Uncle Arthur has said."

There was that, of course. "Perhaps a bit." Would that her troubles were that easy to cure. "When I last saw the doctor, he confirmed what he'd told me months ago. My heart has weakened beyond a point where it can be saved. It could give out on me at any moment." She couldn't keep the waver from her voice. "I might die in days, in weeks, or at best, perhaps months, but the doctor was adamant that I probably won't last until year's end."

"What?" Shock and fear warred for dominance in her daughter's eyes. "You will leave me, just as Papa did?"

"I don't have a choice." As Sophia reached for Hannah's hand, the girl recoiled. "If it were my decision, I would never leave."

"Is there *nothing* that can be done?" Her voice had become a wail of pain.

"I'm afraid not. The doctor suggested I shouldn't experience any shocks or surprises of any kind to prolong what life I have left."

Hannah shook her head. "No!" Tears fell fast and furious to

her cheeks. "After everything, after knowing how much I miss Papa and Grandfather, you will leave me too? Just when I need you the most?"

"If I could change things, I would. Surely you understand." Again, she reached for Hannah's hand, but her daughter widened the space between them. "I don't want to die, darling, so we must make the best of the time we have together." Her heart ached, and she didn't know if it was from her ailment or the fact that she was essentially betraying Hannah, that she wouldn't be around for her future.

"You will leave, and I'll be an orphan, an afterthought within the rest of the Winterbourne family." With red splotches on her face and neck from high emotion, she stooped, scooped up the kitten, and glared at Sophia. "How can you do this to me, Mama? And why did you not tell me as soon as you knew? Didn't I garner at least that respect?" Then she turned about and ran through the meadows as if the hounds of hell were after her.

"I think, perhaps, I wanted that to go much differently than it did." Sophia dabbed at her eyes with Oliver's handkerchief. His scent clung to the linen, and though it gave her a modicum of comfort, she walked back to the quilt where he sat with mixed feelings. "She, uh, is quite angry and more than a little hurt."

"And perhaps in denial. Just as you were when you first found." The ambassador nodded. "I'm afraid that is her right but give her some time. She will come to see you have nothing to do with it, and that it is only fate's hand at play." When she dropped to the quilt beside him, he handed her the kitten. "In the meanwhile, I'm certain such an exchange wasn't good for your heart." He changed position, moved up the blanket until his back rested against the trunk of the tree. "Come sit with me a spell."

Oh, it was tempting, but she had a responsibility as a mother. "I should go after her."

"And what? Have the girl slam a door in your face?" Oliver shook his head. "Let her digest the news first. As I said before, I'll check on her before dinner. By then, her emotions will have been spent, and if not, she might be more apt to talk with me over you." He gestured beside him, and throwing caution to the wind, Sophia sat beside him.

When he snaked an arm about her shoulders and held her, an involuntary sigh escaped her. It was lovely indeed to borrow a man's strength. "Thank you."

"It's my honor." For long moments, they sat there while the summer bloomed on around them. The heat combined with the sun and the pleasant drone of insects lulled her into a peaceful state, even as her heart still ached. Eventually, the kitten settled on her chest and fell asleep, but not once did it stop purring. "Perhaps we should go back so you can lie down and nap."

"No." Daring much, Sophia rested her head against Oliver's strong shoulder, and as he pulled her closer, she couldn't help her grin. The man was too honorable for his own good. "I have long grown tired of resting. It's quite dull, and there's no point to it. I refuse to fritter away the remainder of my life doing nothing. Truly, I shall go mad from it."

"I'm discovering that about you with every meeting. You are a woman of movement and fancy." Amusement rumbled in his voice, and that timbre reverberated deep in her chest.

She snorted. "I am stubborn. I'll admit to that. And I won't expire without a fight." For another long swath of moments, she remained quiet and content to sit at his side with a dozing kitten in her lap. It had been the most peaceful afternoon she'd had in many weeks. "At night, the darkness is overwhelming," she confided in a low voice even though they were the only ones around. "Such pressing nighttime makes me think of death, and as the weeks march by, my fear of it as well as death grows substantially greater."

"Understandable. Eventually, those sorts of thoughts come to torment each of us in our lives." He brushed his fingers up and down her arm. "Always keep a lamp burning to keep the shadows away."

"But what of my thoughts? How do I arrest them?"

"Find someone you trust who will talk to you until you fall asleep. Someone who will hold your hand and sit with you, so you don't feel alone. Someone who will tell you romantic and uplifting stories that will send you sweetly into your dreams." His breath skated across her cheek. "Be it a family member or a friend, have someone close. And though it might not be orthodox, if it's a man you wish beside you, do that. No one has the right to protest in the face of your diagnosis."

What he said made sense. "Are you saying the scandal is worth the reward?"

"I'm saying that you are well past the need to worry about such arbitrary rules." When he pressed a fleeting kiss to the top of her head, her heartbeat accelerated. Oh, what she wouldn't do to feel those lips against hers once more or trailing over various portions of her body! "When facing certain death, everything changes. Or, at least, that is how I imagine it will be. There should be no more worries, no more wondering, no more fear. Use your last days on this mortal coil to bring yourself comfort and pleasure, to bring you joy, if not acceptance. Spend them with the people you love, the ones who make you laugh and smile. Nothing else matters."

"You are quite wise for an American." As he chuckled, she grinned, and spurred on by his words, she took his free hand in his merely to hold it, for the tactile sensation of being protected if only for a moment. It was something she'd missed so much since her last husband died. "And if the man I choose for that comfort or distraction, is you? What then?" It was daring and quite bold, but Sophia didn't care. She adored that closeness between men and women, craved that intimacy, wished to experience it once more before her life snuffed out.

He turned his head and found her gaze with his own. Behind his spectacle lenses, desire burned in those stormy depths. "Then I will do everything in my power to make it happen."

What did that mean? She could hardly conduct an affair right in front of her family, not even if she were dying. It simply wasn't done.

"Good."

"Indeed." He nodded and squeezed her fingers. "But first, smooth out the wrinkles between you and Hannah. I won't have her calling foul if we proceed to the next step."

Which was what, precisely? But thoughts of her daughter's future distracted her. "I promise." She inhaled deeply and then let her breath ease out. "Will you accompany me into the Winterbourne maze tomorrow afternoon? It's something you should see while you're here, and I'll need to inspect the roses besides."

"At present, anywhere that you are is where I'm meant to be."

Oh, they were romantic words to be sure, but could she open her heart enough—weakened as it was—and let him come fully in when there was nothing but grief and ache ahead for him? For her?

CHAPTER SIX

July 7, 1819

O LIVER LIFTED HIS face to the cooling breeze that swept over the landscape. It would rain soon, but as of yet, the storm clouds were far away, and he refused to miss this assignation with Sophia. He had an idea that wasn't fully formed yet, but it kept pestering him, nonetheless. Though it might sound insane once he uttered it aloud, he wouldn't know unless he tried.

Shortly after breakfast, Sophia had written out the directions for navigating to the heart of the maze. Did it take some of the satisfaction out of conquering the puzzle? Of course, but if it got him to her side that much quicker, he took no offense.

He'd barely stepped foot into the gardens that would eventually take him to the maze when Hannah caught him up, and from her windblown appearance and reddened cheeks, she'd pelted after him in order to do just that. "What's wrong? Is it your mother?"

Ever since Sophia had told him about her heart, and especially after yesterday afternoon when they'd spent the afternoon together beneath that oak tree talking of everything and nothing, he'd been highly sensitive to any sort of emotional change within the household. Dear God, surely, she hadn't suffered a collapse so soon.

"No, no, Mama is well. In fact, she should already be in the maze." When Hannah laid a hand on his arm to halt his forward progress, a couple of scratches were clear in the sunlight, no doubt made by the kittens. "Will you stay on here at Ettesmere Park long?"

"I have no other plans." In fact, he'd written to the marquess just yesterday explaining his change in schedule and that he would stay with the Winterbourne family for the duration of his holiday. "And since I'm not due back in London until November, I don't see why I shouldn't remain here." Especially since Sophia was in such a delicate state with her health. Something about her held him captive, and now that he'd met Hannah, his conscience refused to let him leave so soon.

And if his newly formed idea—or ramblings of an insane lunatic—took root, there would be even more reason. It was worth it just to see what would happen.

"I'm glad."

Oliver frowned. "Why is that?"

"It's lovely to have you around, and Mama always smiles when you are near." Honesty shone in her eyes, for she was too young for guile. "She hasn't done that for ever so long."

"Ah." Well, that was encouraging. "I trust you and your mother have come to an understanding regarding the bad news she told you about yesterday?"

"Yes." Sadness flitted over her youthful face. "Though I'm sad Mama is dying, my response wasn't becoming, and I know she cannot help this. I was caught by surprise, so I apologized."

"And I imagine you were frightened." The only thing he could do was listen, for he had experience aplenty with death and grief.

"Yes. I still am. Certainly, I am not ready to lose her, but at least it won't be a shock as Papa's death was." Tears sparkled in her eyes. Once more she'd shown a maturity well beyond her years. "I will miss her, and I don't wish to be alone."

"You'll have your family around when that time comes." The

girl would have any number of people to turn to for comfort once her mother passed. Still, his chest tightened with worry, to say nothing of the mad thumping of his heart when he thought upon that inevitability. There was a vibrancy to Sophia he hadn't managed to see yet due to the amount of strain she labored under. Perhaps if some of that were removed, she could breathe easier again.

At least for a little while, and the broken family existing on time, waiting for the next death would have a modicum of joy. If he could be a conduit for that, all the better.

"Yes, but that's not exactly enough." Did she refer to his private thoughts? Again, she rested a hand on his arm. "That's why I wished to talk with you, Mr. Mattingly, before you joined my mother in the maze."

"What do you mean?"

She looked up at him with such large eyes that she would be an instant favorite in society when she achieved her Come Out year. In that, she very much resembled her mother, and suddenly, his thoughts went skidding into imagining the lady as a girl of Hannah's age. What scrapes had she managed to fall into? "Will you marry Mama?"

"I beg your pardon?" Shock plowed through him so much that he stumbled backward a step. That her thoughts were in alignment with his barely formed idea further astounded him. "Why do you wish for me to do that?"

"Well, you are quite handsome, and you are not yet attached." Hannah counted off the items on her fingers. "You like cats, and my grandmother favors you. I can tell. She doesn't scold you nearly as much as my uncles. Additionally, you would make a splendid father, and *I* need one." She shrugged as if that explained everything. "Besides, once my mother does die, I shall be in want of a parent, and since you travel, that's even better. If I cannot have Mama, I would rather see the world than remain in England where everything will remind me of her and all I have already lost."

"Ah, Hannah." He ached for her forgotten childhood where most of it had been overshadowed by death and worry. "You have a large family; you will be well cared for."

"Yes, but that is not the same, and my uncles are busy with their own lives, and quite frankly, I'm not certain Uncle Gilbert has even the first clue of romance or how to be happy. He is bent on becoming a grouchy man."

Despite himself, Oliver chuckled. "I believe he is a man with a whole set of stories to tell."

"If he doesn't run off to India again. Personally, I think he did it to hide." She rolled her eyes to the heavens as if the actions of grown men were ridiculous. "And though Uncle Arthur is wonderful, he'll marry soon, and then his thoughts will be on his own future. He already dotes on Juliana and sometimes, when he is with her, he forgets about everything else."

Oliver smiled. "That's as it should be for a man in love."

"I suppose, but it is quite nauseating. Charles and Emily are young but will soon discover their own paths. Which is why I would like a father, for my own little family I can call mine. Someone who will pay attention to me, talk to me."

His heart went out to her. This slip of a child not yet grown with dreams in her head and hope in her eyes. "Such things shouldn't even be a concern for you."

"But they are, and neither of us can deny them." She heaved out a sigh. "Mama always tells me that the best things in life occur unexpectedly and without planning; it was what happened when she met my father." Shadows clouded her eyes briefly, gone with her next blink. "She needs happiness in her life right now, I think, so do you, so why shouldn't you ask for her hand? It would be a lovely way to make her last days wonderful."

The child's heart was in the right place, but she simply didn't understand there was more to it than magic. "Your mother and I aren't in love, you understand. Such things could affect a union." It was important she understand that. He wanted no misunderstandings, even if his own feelings were already rushing toward such a state. Perhaps that was a good indicator of his inexperience, or perhaps he merely knew what he wanted.

"But you can still marry her as a friend. I know it's done; my friends have older siblings and such. And that will take care of the legalities, yes?"

Clever girl. She'd be trouble down the line. "*How* do you know these things?"

"Everyone assumes children don't have any idea about what goes on around them. They think that because we don't talk about certain things, we remain ignorant of them."

"And why have you selected me over a different man?"

"Don't ask me such a nodcock question." Nothing but sincerity reflected in her face. "I'm not a dunce. I've seen the looks you exchange with my mother."

That was good information to tuck away, even as heat crept up his neck. But she deserved his respect and his honesty. "It would probably be a marriage of convenience only, so that you might have a parent and stability once she dies." His voice faltered on that last word, but he couldn't think of that now.

"You will make her last days pleasant, though."

"To the best of my ability." That was a truth he wouldn't waver from.

"That is the most important thing." She nodded. "But do you think you might fall in love with her if she lives for a few months more?" There was such a wistful tone in her voice, his heart went out to her. "It's something I know she worries over, that finding a new husband who will care for her until the end."

It was astonishing how much this child carried upon her shoulders. If at all possible, he would alleviate that for her so she could enjoy what remained of her childhood. "Well, considering I'm halfway at sixes and sevens around her, it wouldn't take much."

"How wonderful!" Hannah smiled. "Mama is a special person. She adores flowers and pretty gowns and gems that sparkle, people who make her laugh, and watching sunsets." Her swallow was audible. "I suppose those are all things she will miss the most."

"Then we'll do our best to give her those and then remember them for her as we move forward."

"Oh, and kisses! Mama loves those."

"Ah, I see." That was something indeed he would like to give to Sophia. The heavy responsibility he would potentially gain *if* he convinced her to marry him settled over his shoulders. Did he have the mettle to become an instant father? He met Hannah's eyes, caught the hope and anticipation there, and he sighed.

"If it helps, I already spoke to my father about you taking up where he left off."

The announcement made his lower jaw drop. "I beg your pardon?"

The girl nodded. "I often talk to Papa about things that bother me or worry me. Sometimes, when he answers, I feel it here." She touched a hand to her chest. "When I asked if he would mind me having a new papa, all I felt was peace, so I know he approves."

"I see." The maturity of this young girl and how she had managed to cope with her life amazed him. Perhaps he wouldn't be teaching her much along the way, but it would be her teaching him. "I'm telling you all of this in the strictest of confidences." He lowered his voice to make it seem as conspiratorial as possible. "I had already planned to propose to your mother this afternoon, for I'm serious when I say I'm enchanted by her. Only God knows if she'll accept." When she jumped up and down in place, he held up a hand. "But please, you must keep it a secret until we know what she says."

"I will. I promise!" Impulsively, she threw herself into his arms and gave him a hug. "Thank you, Mr. Mattingly. We shall all get along famously, and then I needn't worry so much that I'll be alone when the inevitable occurs. I am so happy I'll have a father again!"

The excitement both bolstered his confidence and discomfited him. "What's the English saying?" He cocked his head to one side. "Oh, yes, don't rush my fences for me." When he flashed a grin, she giggled. "Is there anything I should know about your mother that will strengthen my case?"

"I don't think so, but she already considers you are adorable."

Heat on his neck intensified. "Is that so?"

"She likes your spectacles and that you read. Intelligent men, according to Mama, are quite attractive." When the girl tried to wink, both of her eyes briefly closed, and he bit the inside of his cheek to keep from laughing. "May I come with you into the maze?"

"I'd rather you didn't. If you mother agrees to my suit, there might be kissing."

God, please let there be kissing!

Hannah shrugged. "I don't mind. Sometimes kissing is romantic. Unless Uncle Arthur is doing it."

I don't want to do this in front of an audience. For it might prove emotional for them both. "There might be *lots* of kissing." And if he was lucky, a bit of exploring might follow.

"Yuck." Finally, the girl pulled a face. "I'll stay behind but come find me immediately if you have good fortune. I wish to pick out a dress for the occasion. Perhaps my grandmother will let us clip some roses for vases." With a wave and a wide smile, Hannah dashed away from him and loped through the gardens toward the manor house.

Oliver grinned. He adored how resilient young people were. They could be in the depths of despair with tears one minute and then soaring through the clouds on joyful wings the next. *Would that we can all rebound from grief and trials like that.* He continued his stroll through the gardens, and when he reached the entrance to the maze, he pulled the scrap of paper from his waistcoat pocket that contained the directions.

Thanks to Sophia's written prompts, he made it through the hedge maze without incident, but he vowed to return at some point and explore the mysteries found therein if one didn't have navigational clues, for there were statues around every turn and in every nook. When he reached the heart of the maze, the scene was so perfect he stopped merely to feast his eyes upon it in the attempt to memorize it.

Three stone benches were gathered about a statue. A collection of rose bushes grew from a circular patch of earth in the middle. White, pink, and red blooms were highlighted by the dark green leaves, while most of the area was shrouded in shade. Sophia tended to the bushes with the same loving care that she had in the garden, but this time she'd laid a folded blanket down to protect her gown as she kneeled.

As he took a few silent steps forward, he swept his gaze over her person, for truly, she was breathtaking. Did she know that? Her blonde hair held back in a loose knot at the back of her head gleamed in the sunlight that broke through the clouds and the hedges. A few tendrils had escaped to caress her nape and temples, but the apricot dress she wore made her look like the roses she lovingly tended.

"Did you wish to stand there and gawk at me, Oliver, or will you enter into a conversation?" The teasing in her voice prompted him into movement once more.

"Can not a man simply appreciate the view or admire a woman?" She was a vision, even more so when she rose to her feet as elegant as royalty and peeled off her gloves, letting them drop to the ground. "I'm glad you decided to meet me here this afternoon. Though I'm certain there might be rain soon that will spoil the outing."

"Your note was intriguing, to be sure." Sophia glanced upward, and the breeze played with those escaped tendrils, beckoning him to touch his lips to her nape, her temple, her lips. "Out of all the things in life I'm facing, rain doesn't bother me. Soon enough, I'll not be able to feel that on my face, so I wish to experience that whenever I can."

"Indeed." Once again, he was reminded of the fragile state of affairs and the reason he'd wished for this meeting. But first, he wanted for a bit more background about her. "Tell me about your husbands. Were you in love with both of them?"

"Oh, I was." Her eyes sparkled. "Wonderfully in love."

That was encouraging.

She smiled as she moved through the heart of the maze and toward a patch of sunlight. Was it for the warmth or because she feared the darkness and shadows? "I adored being wed, knowing there was someone out there who was my equal, my partner, my lover, and my support. Someone I could talk to when the nights were long and the darkness complete." With a sigh, she landed her gaze upon him. "Michael was my first husband. I married him after my second Season in London. Actually, I met him at a society event. He was such a handsome man, especially when he donned his military uniform."

"I can understand that connection. Did you enjoy many happy years together?" Hearing about her life and history would help him gain the courage to ask his question.

"We had three." Sophia rubbed her hands up and down her arms, whether for comfort or warmth in the breeze he couldn't say. "But they were marvelous and full of happy memories. And so much physical affection." When she looked at him, a certain wistfulness had settled over her. "Though a child never resulted from the union, I didn't care, for I had him." A tiny sigh escaped her. "During his stint in the war, he was stationed close enough that I saw him regularly when he took leave, but unfortunately he perished due to a freak accident."

"How so?" Oliver approached her location with trepidation, for he didn't wish to break the spell she wove with her words.

"A wagon filled with cannon balls overturned, trapping him and his horse beneath it. You see, Michael was part of a contingent of mounted men tapped to guard the shipment on its way to one of the fronts." The delicate tendons of her throat worked with a hard swallow. "The weight of it crushed his ribs, which then punctured his lungs. I was told in a letter that his death didn't occur immediately and that it was probably painful."

"How terrible." He couldn't imagine the heartbreak she must have experienced.

"Indeed. I was devastated for months after I lost Michael. Long past that year of mourning, I kept close to home, neither entertaining nor going out into society. I couldn't. How could I exist without him?" She paused near one of the statues. This one depicted the goddess Diana with a bow in hand. "I didn't know how to go on without him."

To love someone that fiercely! Was that what would happen to him if he won her hand knowing she wasn't long for the world? "But eventually you did." The emotions that flitted over her face and the shadows in her eyes made him remember the deaths of his parents and the quagmire associated with that.

Yet now he contemplated willingly throwing himself into that murky place again.

For the hope of loving her.

"Yes, for life moves on despite what we're feeling." Once more, she strolled about the area and this time passed into the shaded portion of the garden. "For years I vowed to remain faithful to Michael's memory, but boredom and loneliness got the better of me. As well as a tiny kernel of hope." Her chuckle didn't relieve the pall of the subject matter. "And I wished to have children."

"Ah, a feat that cannot be accomplished alone." He sought to tease her into a better mood, and when she offered him a smile, his chest swelled with pride.

"No." Sophia laid a palm on another statue. This one was of Eros, the god of love. "So, at the age of six and twenty, I once again entered the Marriage Mart, but I wasn't interested in a man who held a title, which is what my family thought was best for me."

The knowledge brought him comfort, for perhaps that would tempt her to accept his suit. "What happened?"

"I was at a ball where the hostess needed to make up numbers. She'd invited a handful of military officers, and since I happen to be quite weak at the knees by a man in uniform, when I met James, things were pretty much left to fate."

"Love at first sight?" For the first time, Oliver bemoaned the fact that he hadn't gone into the military himself, but he wasn't a fighter, and the thought of killing his fellow man made him nearly sick to his stomach. His goal in life was to bring peace and a better world.

"It was, for both of us, and we'd known each other a mere handful of days before I snuck off with him to enjoy him carnally." A pretty blush colored her cheeks. "It's one of my favorite things and another reason I'm partial to marriage."

"There is no crime in that, Sophia." It was adorable, though, that she still felt embarrassment over it. "Love oftentimes has no logical reason. It's unexplainable and wild, will swing toward the highs and plunge through the lows." At least his feelings for her certainly didn't make sense. They were all that included. What he did know was that he'd tumbled tip over tail, and he didn't wish to stop that slide.

"Oh, I know, but the rules of the *ton* being what they are, it was all so scandalous." Her giggle said she hadn't cared. "My poor father when he found out. It didn't help that I told him I showed no regret for lying with James." She shrugged. "Needless to say, James and I were married rather quickly after that, for I discovered I was increasing."

"With Hannah?" There was something intimate in sharing this conversation with her.

"Not at that time." She shook her head as she traced her fingertips along the sculpture's right leg. Oliver shuddered, for so easily he could imagine that light touch on his person. "In fact, I lost three pregnancies early on before I carried Hannah to full term. Throughout it all, James was a rock of support, and he often took his leave to be with me during those dark times."

The loss this one woman had experienced in her life boggled his mind. "I cannot imagine how you've survived through everything."

A pretty pout took possession of her lips. "One does what one must because there is no other choice." Then she turned about to face him and leaned back against the statue. "I was nine and twenty when I gave birth to my daughter. Oh, that was the most glorious day, Oliver. It felt as if all the suffering and grief I'd already been through was worth that moment of joy. But it brought with it a few complications that meant I could never again carry a child."

Dear God. He wanted to rush over and bundle her into his arms, hold her close and protect her from the world. She'd suffered too much for too long. Instead, he cleared his throat. "Hannah is quite unique." And she was a co-conspirator. If he was lucky enough to step in and be a parent to her, it would be his honor to help her reach her full potential. "She possesses intelligence and compassion. Both of those things will take her far in life. I would like to be there to see what she achieves."

"I think so too." Sophia glanced at the sky, for the sun had vanished behind fat gray rain clouds. "Let's bring this tale to its inevitable conclusion, shall we? Sometimes the rain makes me feel sad." Over the span of a few heartbeats, she remained silent before speaking again. "For the next six years, we were blissfully happy as a little family. Hannah and I traveled all over England to be closer to where James was and make it easier for him to reach us when given leave."

"But, of course, such exquisite perfection couldn't last." In many ways, he didn't wish to hear the rest of the story, but it would help him understand her better.

"No, it didn't. Shortly after Hannah's seventh birthday, a battle raged in Belgium that James was a part of. He didn't come home from that theatre of war. In fact, when I received the official letter of his death, his commanding officer had also included a half-finished letter James had begun." A waver set up in her voice. "It was stained with mud and blood." She pressed her lips together. "Oh, he was so excited to see us again since everyone knew the end of the war was near. He'd said he intended to purchase a present for Hannah as soon as he stepped foot back on English soil." With a sigh, she brushed at the tears on her cheeks. "That was five years ago, and to this day, James lies in an unmarked grave in a Belgium field. Untended and unremembered."

"Not unremembered. I'll wager you think about him every day," Oliver said in a soft voice. "And I know that he is not far from Hannah's thoughts." Hadn't her confidence shown that? "It's fully acceptable to mourn those who have passed long after they're gone. There is no timeline for grief or working through it." As much as he wished to close the distance between them and embrace her, that would distract him from what he wanted to say. "I often think grief is the penalty one must eventually pay to have known such glorious love."

Was that what fate would exact from him sooner than he would like? Would he be able to recover from it?

"Agreed. Some days I'm well enough but then on others, grief sweeps me up and I mourn all over again." She wrapped her arms about her person and shivered. "And now, whenever I look at Hannah and see traces of James in her, I worry all over again knowing that I'll leave her alone without a parent." Tears pooled in her eyes. "It nearly steals my breath, for I don't want to go. I'm not ready."

Her obvious distress tugged at his chest. Perhaps it was time for him to get to the point of this meeting. "No one wishes for you to leave either." As he passed the collection of rose bushes, he plucked two—one lavender and one yellow. "That is largely why I invited you here this afternoon."

Surprise flitted over Sophia's face. "What are you trying to say, Ambassador?"

"Just this." He came close and offered both blooms to her. When she still appeared confused, he took her free hand, led her to one of the benches, and then gently urged her onto it.

God help him, but this was the most important question he would ever ask.

CHAPTER SEVEN

S OPHIA STARED AT Oliver as she took the offered roses. In some breathlessness, she waited for him to speak again, for she hardly dared to hope she knew the direction of his thoughts. He had the air of a man on the verge of a life-changing question.

"I've thought long and hard about this decision since the moment I met you." Genuine honesty reflected in his eyes behind his spectacle lenses. "Lavender roses are used to tell someone that you are enchanted by them, but they also represent desire and love at first sight." When he grinned, the brush of multitudes of butterfly wings tickled her belly. "That is what is happening to me right now. I'm enchanted by you, have fallen in love with you, have become beguiled by your strength and bravery in the face of uncertainty and sadness. There is no explanation for it." He shrugged. "It just… is."

What *exactly* was he trying to say? And why was there such warmth raging in her cheeks? Surely, she was past the age of that sort of reaction. "Oh, Oliver, I'm not sure—"

"Please, allow me the freedom to say what is on my heart, else I'll lose my courage."

"All right." She brought the roses to her nose and inhaled their unique fragrance.

"In addition, the warmth of the yellow rose symbolizes friendship, joy, and gladness. They are also used as a sign of remembrance or affection." The ambassador sank to one knee in front of her and took her free hand in his. Was there ever a more attractive sight than a man on his knee on the threshold of asking such an important question? It had thrilled her twice before, and it was no less evident now. "While I hope that our tentative friendship will bring you all of this, I vow to always remember you by having yellow roses in the house. So that Hannah will have the joy of remembering as well."

Merciful heavens! He is serious. "Perhaps you should arrive at your point, Oliver." Her hand trembled in his. "I'd rather not have to puzzle out your intent, even if I have an inkling."

"I apologize. It's not every day a man does this sort of thing." His grin sent heat spiraling down her spine. "Marry me."

As much as she adored a proposal, this one had the power to both shock and flatter her. To say nothing of the hope it brought with it. "I beg your pardon?" The scent of roses became heavy and cloying to her nose, so she set the blooms he'd picked aside on the bench, but she didn't break eye contact with him.

"Please, marry me." He tightened his hold on her hand. "Spend your last days as my wife. We shall pass the time in companionship, happiness, and joy, and perhaps you will find beauty again in the world before you leave this one for the next."

"But…" For a few seconds, Sophia was speechless. "We don't know each other well." Not that she cared. The mystery made everything that much better.

He winked. "If I may be so bold, neither did you and your last husband, and that worked out wonderfully well."

Well, drat. Of course, he was right. She tried again to dissuade him. "It's quite flattering of you to ask me something as life changing as that, but I am older than you, and if you should wish for children…" Her words trailed off, for once more, the reality of her situation came slamming back into her chest. "I cannot give them to you." It was a maddening problem, but he deserved to make a decision knowing that. Some men wanted to further their line above everything else.

Oh, God. Her heart pounded. Would the stress of this conversation usher in her demise?

"Perhaps we should take one step at a time." Immediately, Oliver sobered. He scrambled to his feet and then when she scooted to the edge of the bench, sat next to her. "Right now, in *this* moment, I am only asking you to marry me. A marriage of convenience if you wish, but it will take the pressure off your shoulders of what will happen to Hannah."

"I don't know…" They had met less than a week prior. Men were quite successful at hiding their true natures, and what if he had nefarious designs on her daughter? "This decision cannot be made quickly."

"Sophia, look at me." Once more, he took possession of her hand and peered into her eyes when she met his gaze. "I will be nothing but solicitous and protective of Hannah. In fact, shortly before I came into the maze, she indicated she would like it if you and I wed so I could become her father."

"What?" A feeling of lightheadedness came over her, and her dratted heart pounded all the harder. She pressed her free hand to her chest. "Hannah is trying to force your hand as well as mine?" It was difficult to breathe, and she took tiny, gasping gulps. "You've asked me to marry you because of that?"

"No." Slowly, he shook his head. "Jumping to the worst possible scenarios won't help. Perhaps your circumstances have made you fearful, and now you're hiding behind that as protection of sorts." Concern shadowed his eyes. "I had two thoughts in asking you such a question. One was to make certain Hannah was taken care of. That seems to be your overriding concern each time that I talk to you."

"It truly is," she managed to whisper.

"And the second was to help you live out the remainder of your life with nothing but happiness, joy, and perhaps some much needed companionship so you won't feel alone during the dark of the nights. Let me be there to tell you stories and ease your mind so that you might sleep without the nightmares."

A flutter moved through her heart that had nothing to do with her ailment. "You remembered." She could hardly force the words from her tight throat.

"Of course. It's important to you so therefore, it's important to me. I told you that you've stolen my heart from the first moment." When he grinned, tingles shuddered down her spine. "Regarding your worry about children, please don't. I am well past the age where such things matter. If I am the last of my line, that is how it will be, but if you marry me, Hannah will be my daughter, so I won't have failed completely."

"But an heir…"

"Is not needed. There are other, more important endeavors a man can embark upon. My legacy in my work is one of them."

Tears prickled the backs of her eyelids. This man would up-end his life merely to make hers less frightening and dim. "Somehow, I can picture the two of you together, and that makes me both happy and sad because, eventually, I won't be there with you."

"Yet you will if you answer my question in the way I hope. You will have all of those good times for as long as we can keep you in peace and comfort. I shall talk to you in the night and soothe your fears, and in the daylight, I will make you laugh, try to fill your days with experiences so that you won't have cause to fret about what's coming next." He threaded their fingers together, and she liked the feel of his skin on hers, for he hadn't worn gloves. "In the event you're wondering, I don't care either that you are older than I. What are a few years—"

"—*several* years," she interrupted with a tiny, tearful laugh.

"Piffle." He waved his free hand. "—several years compared to how you make me feel? I rather doubt there is an age limit on romance, and if there is, well, the people who think that can… What's the English expression?" He briefly frowned then his expression cleared. "Oh, yes. Then the people who think that can go hang."

By accident, a giggle escaped her. He was quite a dear man.

"Is love *all* you feel for me?" Oh, why did she ask that? From his own admission, this relationship wouldn't be about anything other than companionship.

Would it?

"Honestly?" When she nodded, he grinned, and her stomach executed a freefall. "All I've been able to think about since I met you has been kissing you senseless. You already have me topsy turvy about you. Anything else is window dressing."

Merciful heavens. This man just might be good for her after all. But those dratted walls around her weakened heart continued to stand. Too many people could be hurt with this decision, including him. Possibly her family. "I…"

"Answer me this." Emotions clouded his stormy eyes that she hadn't the courage to puzzle out. "Have you felt the attraction between us, that invisible pull that connects us, but you don't know why?"

"Yes, but—"

"And haven't I been able to make you laugh?"

"Of course, but—"

"And haven't I already proven I can comfort you when you are upset, without the benefit of time between us?"

Perhaps he had a point. "You have, and you've apparently made a tremendous impression on Hannah. That is no mean feat. She is quite selective of her friends."

"Good." He nodded, and a tiny grin curved his mouth. Oh, why wouldn't he kiss her instead of talk? "And according to your own admission, haven't you married your previous husbands after very little time in knowing them as well?"

"Yes." Obviously, she couldn't deny that truth. He'd successfully routed her lock, stock, and artillery, and had an answer for her every objection. Just like a man of substance should. Finally, Sophia sighed. "I don't know why you wish to do this. I will imminently expire. There is nothing for you to look forward to."

"That's where you are wrong, especially when one lives his life day by day without thinking too much of the future."

Amusement lit his dear, gray eyes. "Have you always been this stubborn?" he asked in a soft voice seconds before he released her hand in order to cup her cheek, leaned into her, and claimed her lips with his.

"Oh." A sigh shuddered from her. Just like when she'd kissed him a few days ago, an electric sort of energy shot down her spine to bury itself between her thighs. Pure, unadulterated want rushed through her body, and that was something she hadn't been cognizant of for years. When they parted, she could only stare at him for a few seconds. "I believe I told you that all the Winterbournes are willful. It would stand that we're stubborn as well."

Oliver snorted with amusement. "Point taken, and that explains the conundrum of Hannah." He grinned. "Can I assume from the reaction between us that you accept my suit?"

"I have one more question first." Oh, this was the very definition of insanity! *I cannot believe I'm actually contemplating this.* But one look into his face and seeing the slight steam in his spectacle lenses had the decision swinging more toward one direction. "How experienced are you at kissing?"

"Oh, I'm quite experienced in that." His chuckle sent heat sailing through her chest. Answering warmth danced through those stormy eyes merely waiting for a match to be dropped. "However, my skill doesn't usually translate past kissing."

Poor thing, but the fact he hadn't lain with a woman intrigued her more than it probably should. "Why not? You are handsome enough and possess a sense of humor as well as often spend time reading. You have an interesting livelihood and are well-traveled. Any woman would jump at the chance to be with you."

"If only that were so, but sadly, I'm not the type of man who inspires carnal endeavors." He shrugged and looked so wry that she couldn't help but laugh. "I suppose since I'm not physically inclined nor am I titled or rich, I don't garner a second glance."

"Then all of those other women have fluff for brains." How fun would it be to initiate this man into the wonders of intercourse? It would certainly distract her from the worries of her own life. As long as those bouts weren't too strenuous. "You are quite the catch, Ambassador." Feeling wildly abandoned but cautious, Sophia took hold of Oliver's cravat and tugged him closer. Then she framed his face with her hands and proceeded to kiss him back.

For a few seconds, she took the time to explore the shape of his lips. She ran the tip of her tongue along that bottom piece of flesh, and when he groaned, she giggled and moved to deepen the kiss. In next to no time, he'd encouraged her to open for him, and she did so gladly, for it had been far too long since she'd felt the rush and warmth that came along with kissing. As soon as his tongue slid against hers, she was lost to the clouds of desire filling her head. Over and over, she moved on his mouth—seeking, questioning, and finally asking for his surrender.

And the dear man gave it spectacularly.

He let her boss his tongue around and then when she drew a hand down his chest, he moaned and took control of the kiss, doing all the things she'd just done to him. Oh, how glorious it was! She'd missed this sort of intimacy too much, and he was right. It didn't matter how little they'd known of each other, for in this, they were well-matched. So it had been with her previous two husbands.

Why did I doubt that?

Eventually, she wrenched away, a tad breathless, and stared at him with a grin tugging at the corners of her lips. "I would say that you indeed know how to kiss, Oliver."

"Thank you." He was adorable with that flush on his cheeks and neck, and when she glanced downward, the impressive bulge at the front of his trousers fired her imagination as well as her blood. "Can I safely assume this means you will marry me?"

"Yes." When he would have uttered a whoop of victory, she laid a hand on his chest. His hard, warm chest that she would give anything to peek at right now. What would his body feel like against hers? "But I want you to know something before we go forward."

"Oh?" Worry creased his brow.

"If we marry, I want *everything* such a union comes with. I don't want the convenience of it. I don't want you to merely lay beside me in the dark so that I might sleep. There is no time for that. I want you in every way a woman can have a man, but I also want your friendship, your companionship, your support." She stumbled over the last words. "If I am alive long enough for love to form between us, then that is merely the frosting on the proverbial cake. If you are not prepared to give me everything you are, then I must decline."

"Ah, Sophia, there is much fire left in you. You don't do things by half, do you?" Respect reflected in his eyes. "I will give you whatever you wish as long as you'll agree to be my wife, for I only want you. After all, I'm already infatuated."

"That is not the same as love, you silly, adorable man." Despite the fact they were doing this because she was dying, a few pieces of the wall around her heart crumbled. "But oh, that's so romantic." Yet, if she hadn't been given this affliction, would he and she be here at all?

That was a worry for another day or perhaps not at all if fate had her say.

OLIVER'S HEARTBEAT RACED in time to the need throbbing through his member. "Then let me ask again." Once more he took her hand. "Sophia, will you please marry me and let me make the remainder of your life happy and full of companionship—and all the rest you need—to the best of my ability?"

"And heat. Don't forget that." Slowly, she nodded. "Yes." Amusement, excitement, and a trace of longing danced through her green eyes. "Will we suit beyond the attraction between us?"

Honestly, he didn't know. He'd merely offered her this

choice so her future wouldn't feel so grim. "I doubt you have the luxury of worrying about that, and at least in this way, your future will have significant less anxiety in it. And, at least, some fun as well." After everything, would she turn him down?

Sophia drifted closer to him, and the fragrance of roses wafted to his nose. "Will you have the proper papers drawn up to ensure Hannah is well cared for?"

"Of course. I promise to summon a solicitor to Ettesmere Park as soon as I can."

"Arthur can assist in that I would imagine." She squeezed his fingers. "Then, yes, I will marry you and am grateful you are giving up so much to do this… for me."

The tears in her eyes tightened his chest and brought every protective instinct he had to the forefront. "I'm not sure there is much to sacrifice, but you are more than worth it." He delved a finger into the pocket of his waistcoat and withdrew the family heirloom ring. "And that means this is for you." His hand shook as he slipped the ruby bauble onto her finger. It fit slightly loose, but it looked somehow right on her.

"You already had a ring?" Surprise flitted over her face. "I don't know whether to be flattered or alarmed."

"It's not like that at all." Oliver brought her hand to his lips and kissed the ring then pressed his lips to the back. "This ring is the only thing of value I own. It's been passed down through my family for years, intended for each first son's bride. Since my mother's death, it's been in my possession, and for a long while, I feared I would never have the opportunity to give it to anyone."

"Yet you've given it to me." Awe rang in her voice.

"Why shouldn't I?" It was the most natural thing in the world. "To me, it signifies that love will always triumph, regardless of the obstacles it faces. Now, on your finger, hope remains alive for us both. Never forget that, Sophia."

"Oh. How sweet." She bounced her gaze between the heart-shaped ruby and then his face. Tears made the green in her eyes luminous. "I'm so honored, even though I probably won't wear it for long."

"You will take it to the grave with you. For you will have been my wife." He clenched his teeth against the pain that invaded his own heart. "We shall enjoy the time we'll have together and not worry about anything else." Wanting better access to her, he rose to his feet then offered her a hand. When she slipped her fingers into his, he pulled her into a standing position. "Truly, Sophia, my aim is to make you as comfortable as possible. To help you see the beauty in each day and to dispel the worst of your fears, so they don't steal the time you have left."

"I appreciate that so much." The breath as she whispered the words skated along his jaw. She fiddled with his cravat, and each brush of her fingertips sent him closer to insanity. "In fact, I doubt many other men would do so much for a woman he didn't know or won't have a future with. That is much of why I've kept myself from society. Pity infuriates me."

His chest constricted for her plight. "Then it's fortunate I happened along when I did, thanks to that broken axle." Slowly, tenderly, Oliver took her into his arms and kissed her. Each time he touched her lips, tasted the faint trace of tea from her mouth, he craved more, and when the first spattering of raindrops hit his cheeks, they did nothing to cool his ardor. When she looped her arms about his shoulders and pressed herself closer—every part of her touching every part of him—need shuddered through him, but before he could perhaps deepen the embrace and start an exploration of her charms, a tiny squeal from somewhere behind him broke through the cloud of passion in his head.

Immediately, Sophia sprang away from him with a hand to her cheek, while he glanced over his shoulder to spy Hannah standing there with wide eyes and a grin spreading across her face. "Hello, Hannah." The dear girl needed to learn about privacy and the respect therein.

"Does that mean you are engaged to my mother, Mr. Mattingly?" she asked with her hands clasped in front of her.

"It does indeed." He cocked an eyebrow. "Are you certain

this is what you wanted?"

"Yes." The girl bounded into the heart of the maze and made her way to Sophia's side. Then she took up her mother's hand to peer at the ring. "This is wonderful and so romantic! Well done, Mr. Mattingly."

Sophia glanced at him with a slight grin. "I agree." Then she gave him a rueful smile. "I told you she's a handful."

"How wonderful!" Hannah hugged her mother and then, being the impulsive creature she was, she did the same to him. His heart was full to the point of bursting, for already he was grateful to have them both in his life. "Thank you for easing some of my mother's worries… and my own."

"It is my great honor. I hope to make you both proud." He set her aside in order to address his fiancée. "When would you wish to wed?"

Sophia appeared both dazed and excited, and it was adorable. "I would imagine as soon as we can. As you've said, time is of the essence, and you'll need to procure a license."

"I don't have any idea of how to accomplish that."

"Oh, dear. I'm afraid you'll need Arthur's help, for you'll have to ask for a special interview with the Archbishop of Canterbury because you are a foreigner." Her expression reflected a rather dismal outlook. "What if he doesn't grant permission?" Apparently, it was a real possibility, for she swiftly sat upon the bench as if her knees could no longer support her weight.

Was this the catalyst for ushering in her early demise? Worry constricted his chest. "Let's not borrow trouble."

Her face had paled. "What if we cannot marry?"

"Calm yourself, sweeting." His heart squeezed from the distress in her voice while Hannah patted her hand. "If it's possible, I will chase it. I can be quite clever when needed, and I won't give up until I've exhausted every possibility." They didn't come this far to only arrive at this moment and stop. "We should tell your family before dinner this evening, and then if the earl is agreeable, we'll go to London and demand an audience with the archbishop." If he had to use every bit of her brother's influence or that of any other peer he could press into this service, he would. "I'm sure there are men of high authority in London that I can persuade to my cause. I know many people in England." He caught her gaze. "We won't fail. I promise."

Please God, let him not be a liar, for he wanted this little, broken family more than he'd ever wanted anything.

CHAPTER EIGHT

S OPHIA PAUSED OUTSIDE the drawing room. Her family was assembled inside the room already: her mother, both brothers, her niece and nephew, Hannah, as well as Oliver. The bell calling them to dinner would be rung in about thirty minutes, which left her just enough time for her to reveal her engagement and intention to marry.

This is going to cause a sensation.

Would that prove too much excitement for her heart? The last six months she'd spent as a shell of her former self, too afraid to do anything, to enjoy anything for fear she would expire prematurely. And now, here she was, with a pretty ruby ring on her finger on the verge of telling her family that she would marry for the third and last time, merely to settle her daughter's future and to make sure her own last days weren't spent in loneliness or boredom.

Were those two things good enough reasons?

Only time would tell, and unfortunately, time was what she didn't have in abundance. As she leaned her back against the wall, low-pitched laughter drifted to her location. Easily, she discerned Oliver's timbre. It tugged a small smile from her. Truly, the man was a gem and as honorable as they came. For him to do this, to give up so much for her sake? She was still in awe of that, but the worry she carried wouldn't subside. How could she look forward to the upcoming wedding? How would they even be allowed a license?

There were so many unknowns.

Finally, Sophia stirred. She couldn't very well stand about skulking in the corridor for the remainder of the evening. After taking a deep breath, she let it ease out between her lips, squared her shoulders, and then entered the drawing room. Both of her brothers held snifters of brandy while occupying two matching chairs. Julianna sat in one opposite Arthur's. Her fat beagle—Regent—reclined at her feet as if he were indeed his namesake. Oliver stood by the fireplace with a hand resting on the mantel. Her mother occupied a sofa with Hannah beside her. One of the kittens lay curled in a ball in a corner of the sofa. The other one was nowhere to be found. Charles and Emily sat on the opposite sofa across a low table from them. Every one of them was so dear to her! How could she leave them with nothing but memories and grief?

"Good evening, family." She glanced at Julianna. "And soon-to-be family."

Regent lifted his head and gave a soft bark of welcome.

Her brothers and nephew scrambled to their feet. The grin on Oliver's face had the power to steal her breath, for in his expression was such pleasure, such pride, that she couldn't imagine her mere presence in a room could affect anyone thusly. If fortune was with her, she would belong to him in days and he to her.

I hope, for I… I need him.

"Good evening, Sophia." Arthur lifted his glass in salute as he regained his seat. "You look like summer itself. It's good to see a bit of color in your cheeks again."

"Thank you." The mint green gown she'd chosen was lined with pink tulle at the bodice. A spattering of tiny pink glass beads and seed pearls decorated the hem and cuffs of the short sleeves. It was a garment that brought her comfort and confidence, both of which she would need tonight, and she felt pretty while wearing it. Her heart ached as she thought of all the lovely gowns in her clothespress she wouldn't have the occasion or opportunity to don if she expired like the doctor warned. With an effort, she shoved those musings from her mind. Now was not the time. "I've decided to dress as if there is no tomorrow—and because it pleases me."

Her mother smiled. "Life is very precious and should be celebrated as a gift each day."

"Yes." Sophia nodded at Gilbert, who rolled his eyes and readjusted his hold on the head of his cane. Then she winked at Charles, who snickered. Once everyone seated themselves, she drifted to a chair near Oliver's location. "I am glad you are all here, for there is something I would say to you."

Truly, there was no sense in dancing about the issue or causing a delay.

Immediately, all attention turned to her. Hannah fairly bounced out of her seat, so great was her excitement. Even Regent glanced in her direction, though she suspected the fat hound assumed there would be food involved.

Concern shadowed Arthur's face. "Are you well? Has your health taken a turn for the worse?"

"Not yet." She refused to think about that at the moment. Instead, she peeked at Hannah, who grinned like a cheeky monkey. "As all of you know, six months ago, my life changed in ways I had never anticipated, in ways that I've been trying to make sense of ever since." Then she looked at Oliver and flutters moved through her belly.

He gave her a nod of encouragement. The affection and support in those stormy eyes of his imparted a modicum of peace.

I have been quite fortunate.

A tiny sigh escaped her. She forced a hard swallow into her suddenly dry throat. "When one faces a certain early death, everything comes into sharp relief." With a small smile, she glanced about at her family. These people had been there for her every step of the way. "I suppose, in a way, death is what gives meaning to life, for we know that we will all eventually succumb, but we don't know when."

Gilbert harrumphed. "Must we be maudlin tonight? What is it you are trying to say?"

"For shame, Gilbert," their mother hissed in a whisper. "Have some compassion. You will miss your sister when she's gone."

One would like to think.

"I apologize." Her brother drained his glass, and his hand shook slightly. "Pray, continue, Sister."

Sophia nodded. Suddenly, everything was just so very… tiring and ordinary. She wished to withdraw into herself, seek wisdom, and solace there, but that wouldn't solve her problems. And she'd spent all too many days and nights like that already.

No more. Now, just as Oliver had said in the maze, it was time to live, to extract every ounce of joy and happiness from the days she had left.

"Earlier today, I had an interesting conversation with Mr. Mattingly." Again, her gaze strayed to him. He straightened to his full height, tugged on the hem of his dinner jacket, and she admired that proud bearing, the handsome profile he made. For a younger man, he was quite fine, and she still couldn't believe she'd said yes to him. "In any event, the ambassador presented me with a sound step for my future." As all the members of her family stared, Sophia smiled. "I have agreed to marry him."

Profound and utter silence met her announcement.

Then, it was as if everyone became animated at once. Her brothers sprang to their feet with protests on their lips. Hannah bounced out of her chair with a smile and sparkling eyes. Charles and Emily exchanged looks of shock, while her mother leveled a speculative gaze on her. Regent stood and barked, whether in agreement or dissuasion or just plain excitement, she hadn't a clue.

"What do you mean you intend to marry the ambassador?" It was Arthur who found his voice before the rest. "The man only just arrived here a handful of days ago, and now you think yourself in love?"

"I never said we were in love." The muscles in Sophia's stomach pulled. "I merely said we would marry."

Hannah jumped up and down in place. "I saw them kissing yesterday in the maze!"

Oh, dear. "Dearest, that doesn't mean—"

"You kissed him?" This was from her niece, Emily, who regarded her with wide eyes. "Was it terribly romantic?"

Sophia couldn't help a tiny grin. "It was, actually."

"You should see her ring," Hannah said with a grin. "It's shaped like a heart!"

"How I envy you and Julianna. Kissing is such a delicious way to pass the time," Emily murmured with a blush on her cheeks. "Would that I—"

"Not now, Emily," Arthur interrupted. "And you are quite too young for all that." He shook his head, disbelief in his eyes as he focused again on her. "I cannot believe you'd do something like this, Sophia. What the devil has prompted this decision? The marrying, not the kissing thing." He set his brandy glass on a nearby rose-inlaid table. "It seems the height of irresponsible."

That struck her as slight funny. "Doing this is exactly the definition of being responsible. When one is facing death, irresponsible is no longer at play." She planted her hands on her hips, and when he didn't appear convinced, she rushed onward. "How do you explain your own engagement? You knew Julianna for only a few weeks before you offered for her. And now you'll wed her soon. Why is my situation any different?"

A red flush crept over her brother's collar. "Because we are in love." He glanced at his fiancée, who blushed but grinned. "It makes *all* the difference."

"I agree. However, I am not afforded that sort of time. Love isn't as instant as attraction or convenience." Her voice wobbled; her chin quivered. "I supported you when you wished to court Julianna. Now I expect the same consideration from you."

For the first time, Julianna spoke. A trace of tears pooled in her eyes as she encouraged the beagle to lay again at her feet. "Your sister is right, Arthur. She championed our match. We owe her our support. What does it matter how long they've known each other if the ambassador makes her happy?"

"Thank you." Sophia looked at Oliver, who wore his concern like a garment. Her heart trembled, for that sort of hero was what she needed most in this moment. "Right now, it is enough there is some sort of heat between us. That is more than some couples share." Belatedly, she remembered her daughter was still in the room, and her cheeks warmed. "Hannah, dearest, will you please leave the room for a moment? This discussion shouldn't occur in front of you."

"I won't." Her daughter shook her head, and of course, her stubborn streak decided to make a showing. "Your marriage directly concerns me and my future, so if Uncle Arthur wishes for a debate, I shall give him one." She took the white kitten into her arms and petted it while glaring at her uncle.

Groans issued about the room, for everyone knew just how much a spitfire Hannah could be when riled. Sophia pressed her lips together to prevent laughing as she glanced at her brother and then her mother, who shrugged. Poor Oliver. He would have his hands full in the raising of her. *And I will miss it all.*

"The girl has a point," her mother said with a nod. "Though the announcement did come as a surprise, I'm glad you're taking steps to see to her care."

"Thank you." Having her mother's tentative support didn't alleviate the anxiety sitting heavily on her chest. "I know you're concerned, Arthur, but please know I have thought much about it, even before the ambassador asked me. I had the thought of pursuing him before he did me." She shrugged. "Marrying Oliver is the best decision I can make, for it settles Hannah's future and makes the time remaining to me a bit less frightening. And I did wish to marry once more. Surely you can understand that."

Perhaps those things were all that mattered.

"I'm only worried for your well-being."

"As am I," she admitted in a soft voice. "And I don't mind telling you, what little remains of my future is terrifying. I believe Oliver can make it less so. Having a man to talk to and hold me when I'm at my lowest is what I need the most right now."

"Ah, Sophia. I cannot imagine what you are feeling, and I sometimes forget." Arthur's expression softened. He locked eyes with Julianna, and then sighed. "Why do you feel the ambassador is the best match? When Mother threw that ball not long ago, surely there were other men that you connected with? Titled men, who could care for you until the end?"

Why did titled men assume women wanted, well, titled men? "I'm certain there were, yet none of them connected with me, and most of them looked at me with pity in their eyes when they discovered my circumstances. I refuse to allow that. However, when Oliver arrived at Ettesmere Park, there was a certain… spark about him, an immediate… something that is rather unexplainable." But it had been the same thing she'd experienced when meeting her previous husbands. Instincts never lied. "He views life in an interesting way, and that speaks to my soul." When she turned her attention to him and he grinned, flutters went through her lower belly. How much did she want to spirit him off to an unused room and do wicked things to him? "I believe he understands what I'm feeling and what I need just now."

Some of that included baring various parts of their bodies and exploring with their mouths…

"Oh, Mama, that's beautiful," her daughter gushed, completely interrupting her naughty thoughts, and when Oliver smiled at the girl, a blush stained her youthful cheeks.

"Poppycock. Perhaps the stuff of fairy stories." Arthur scoffed. "Surely that's irresponsible—"

"No." Sophia held up a hand and shook her head. In this, she would remain immovable. "It's more irresponsible to do nothing and leave Hannah's future up to fate. She is my first responsibility. And Oliver has her welfare uppermost in his mind. That speaks volumes." Her chest tightened. She pressed a hand to her heart. Surely this wouldn't be the shock that ushered in the end before she could do anything fun with the ambassador. "Yes, I know she has all of you, but you have your own lives and will soon be busy with them. And perhaps we all need the hope that fairy stories impart. God knows I could use a dose of that magic."

"You would make an excellent princess, Mama," Hannah said as she dropped a kiss on the kitten's head. "You are already beautiful."

Dear, dear Hannah.

"Agreed, on all counts." Oliver came swiftly to her side and slipped an arm about her waist. "Come and sit. This conversation is proving taxing and quite vexing," her murmured in a low voice that soothed her frazzled nerves.

Grateful for his presence, she nodded. "Thank you." Sophia let him lead her to a chair, and when she sat, he stood slightly behind her with a hand resting on her shoulder. That gentle contact, that reminder of his unwavering presence, that simple sign of possession, ushered in more calm than deep breaths ever could. Then she stared down her brothers as a wave of exhaustion swept through her. "If you take issue with him, voice those concerns, for I will refuse to hear them once this conversation concludes."

Never had she been forceful with her family, but if there was ever a time to guide the direction of her own life, it was now.

"Perhaps I should say something before that happens." Oliver's voice was clear and steady. So easily could she imagine him orating in a room full of heads of state and peers high on the instep. "From the first moment I saw Lady Sophia, I knew our paths would not only cross but impact each other." He met the gazes of her family members as he pushed his spectacles higher up on the bridge of his nose. "While I can appreciate the concern from this unexpected announcement, please know I asked for her hand because, quite simply, she needs me."

For the first time, Gilbert spoke. "But she has us. You she's only known inside a week." He thumped the floor with the tip of his cane.

"This is all true, of course." For a few seconds, Oliver paused. When the kitten escaped Hannah's hold and meandered over to him, he smiled while it twined about his legs. "However, when I put that ring upon your sister's finger, I knew a deep contentment I'd never experienced before. It gives me great pleasure to know I'm caring for Sophia in her hour of need and that I can step in and be the surrogate father Hannah requires." His Adam's apple bobbed. "I now have a family, Your Lordship, and there is nothing I wouldn't do for them. Don't discount that." He glanced at her. "And perhaps I need her in my life, too."

Apparently, her brothers weren't appeased by the impassioned speech. Arthur slowly shook his head. "Regardless of how he makes you feel or how he feels about you, the man is a stranger."

"But—"

Gilbert snorted as he rested his brandy glass on a nearby table. "Better than knowing someone for years only to discover they have betrayed you and have fallen out of love."

Oh, dear Lord!

"Enough!" Sophia's hands shook so she curled them into her skirting. "Enough, boys." A wave of exhaustion slammed into her. "I will remind you that neither of you are my keepers and that I'm old enough to know my own mind. Actually, I have since I was Emily's age." It had always been like that. Willful, yes. Stubborn, of course. Inherently able to understand how to move her life forward in a way that would make her happy.

Absolutely.

When she was certain she once more had the attention of everyone in the room, Sophia sighed, lifted a hand, and touched Oliver's that still rested on her shoulder, borrowed that warmth and strength. "From all that I've seen, Oliver is clever, kind, and resourceful. He's been responsible and respectful toward me as well as Hannah, and he is not without an income." Though she smiled up at him, the urge to cast up her accounts grew strong. "The ambassador is educated and well-traveled. Under his wing, Hannah's future will be incredibly bright."

Confusion skated across Arthur's face. "But Sophia—"

"No." She took a deep breath and let it ease out. The ache in her chest intensified, and it terrified her. *Please don't let me die tonight.* "Let me finish. Additionally, as I said before, there is a connection—an attraction—between us, and this marriage will only be for a short time." Her voice broke, and as hot tears sprang to her eyes, she rapidly blinked them back. "Please, you are my family and I love you all, but I am asking you to let me enjoy the days I have remaining to me in the manner to which I see fit." When she pressed her lips together, she pored over her next words. "I want you to let Hannah spend time with him as well. And why shouldn't I be as happy, feel wanted—even desired—as I can be until the end? If I find that with Oliver, where is the harm?"

Regent uttered a low woof of approval.

"And we will be married, so that is less scandal upon the family name," she added in a soft voice.

At least Arthur had the decency to appear embarrassed. He glanced everywhere but at her before meeting her gaze. "I suppose if it were me facing the same circumstances that you are, I would feel the same."

She nodded and relief shuddered down her spine.

"I, for one, think it's a lovely idea." Her mother stood. "Shame on you boys for arguing with her. Sophia doesn't need that right now, and such added worry will only hasten her demise." After she skirted around the table, she tugged Sophia to her feet. "I'm glad you won't be alone in your last days. No doubt facing each night with no one to talk to is making the situation worse."

"Yes." Her chin quivered. Finally, someone understood. "The dark is terrifying at times. More so now than when I was a child." She had always been fearful of the night, for it clouded the familiar and rendered it strange.

"Your father used to tell me the same thing occasionally. There is something comforting about knowing there is someone next to you in the shadows that will hold you and beat back your fears." When her mother embraced her, a soft cry issued from Sophia's throat, and she hugged her back. "I would say you could make use of the countess suite, for no one is using it, but Arthur will be married soon, and I shall need to relocate."

"Don't worry about any of that right now." She pushed out of her mother's embrace. "The manor is large enough that we'll rub along well enough, and if we don't, we can always return to London."

For long moments, her mother peered into her eyes. Then she nodded. "I trust you know what you're doing."

"I do." Didn't she? Yet those walls remained firmly around her heart even if they were starting to crumble.

"Very well." Then her mother looked at Oliver. "When will you wed my daughter, Ambassador?"

"That is something we need the earl's assistance with." He glanced at Arthur, who looked back with narrowed eyes. "But I must warn you, with or without your help, I still intend to wed Sophia. My position on that won't change, and neither will the obstacles prevent me from achieving the goal. If we need to relocate to America in order to do it, we will."

How brave he was in the face of her family's opposition! Sophia glided to Oliver's side. Daring much, she took his hand in hers and threaded their fingers together. Both Hannah and Emily smiled while Gilbert returned to his seat and Charles assumed an expression of deep boredom. "Since Oliver is an American, he will no doubt require a special audience with the Archbishop of Canterbury regarding this usual circumstance to wed."

Understanding creased Arthur's face. "Well, damn. It didn't occur to me that there might be an issue in that quarter."

"Indeed." Oliver nodded. "Because of this, I cannot apply for a special license outright. It's my hope as well as Sophia's that you might accompany me to London and lend your influence for a meeting."

"As well as offer a donation to the church to… encourage the man's decision if he proves difficult," Sophia hastened to add. When her brother appeared skeptical, she rushed on. "You are an earl of some power. He should listen to you."

"I could write to Lord Grantwood to hasten our cause, but that will take additional time," Oliver said into the silence that had gathered in the room.

Arthur snorted. "So will removing to America," he inserted in a droll tone.

She squeezed her fiancé's fingers. "If it would help, I can write a letter explaining why I wish to marry Oliver so quickly. Surely knowing I'm facing imminent death might usher in a positive decision. Also, he is an ambassador. I'm certain his reputation needs no introduction."

When Arthur kept his own counsel, the muscles in her stomach protested. She released Oliver's hand and then closed the distance between her and her eldest brother. "I know you're concerned. I know you have doubts. I do too." As she laid a hand against his cheek, she caught sorrow and worry in his eyes. Oh, her death would hurt all the people she loved the most. It was too much to contemplate. She forced a swallow around the ball of tears in her throat. "I appreciate the urge to protect me, but Arthur, I need your help just now more than anything else. You can either be a part of this or you can prove an obstacle, but I *must* move forward. There is nowhere else to go and little time in which to accomplish it."

"Have you ever known me to deny you anything?" He crumpled, let his vulnerability show for a tiny moment. "Of course, I'll lend my assistance to you and the ambassador." Over her shoulder, he nodded to Oliver. "We shall leave for London immediately following dinner if you are of a mind."

"I am."

Sophia nearly sagged with relief. She lifted up on her toes and bussed her brother's cheek. "Thank you."

"It's the least I can do." He held her gaze for long moments. "You'll keep Julianna company while I'm gone?"

"Of course. We shall discuss gowns and such. After all, two weddings this month plus Mama's masquerade require much work and planning."

"Good." He glanced at Gilbert. "Will you come with us?"

"I would rather stay, if you don't mind." A flush rose up his neck. "I'll only be in the way, and besides, it will allow me extra time to spend with Sophia before… Well, you know."

"I do, and I had the same thought more than once." Arthur nodded and then looked at his son. "How about you, Charles? Are you up for a small adventure?"

"Absolutely!" He sprang to his feet. "For years this family has done nothing exciting, yet ever since you met Julianna, it's been non-stop excitement. I wouldn't miss it."

Sophia smiled. "Let me dash off a quick letter while the rest of you enjoy dinner. If I finish, I'll join you." As soon as she said that, the butler rang a bell signaling dinner was served. She giggled. "I'd best hurry. Cook doesn't like to hold back the meal." As she left the room, she winked at Hannah.

Please, please, please let this be correct decision for everyone involved.

CHAPTER NINE

July 10, 1819

THE PEACEFUL SHADOWS of the twilight had descended by the time Oliver arrived back at Ettesmere Park. He'd learned much during the three-day trip about the earl and the Winterbourne family and how special Sophia was to them. They'd entertained him with stories from the past and the scrapes the Winterbournes had fallen into. What he'd discovered about himself had been equally startling, for he'd been forced to grow a backbone of steel and try his hand at being aggressive, when none of that had been his lot. It was needed; he had been reduced to opening himself up for ridicule and blatant contempt when he'd been granted a private audience with the Archbishop of Canterbury.

In the end, the impassioned speech he gave, coupled with Sophia's hastily penned letter, the support of more than a few notables throughout London he'd worked with while in his position as ambassador, and the earl's assurances of a few donations to various causes close to the archbishop's heart finally won him the much-sought-after special license.

Now, he was exhausted but beyond pleased.

I am free to marry Sophia and make a life together while we can.

Gooseflesh popped over his skin. As soon as he could arrange it with the local vicar, he would wed. Never in his life did he think this day would come. As soon as the traveling coach rolled to a stop, the young lordling vaulted out with the excuse of needing something to eat post haste. When Oliver moved to follow, the earl stayed him with a gloved hand on his arm.

"A moment of your time, Ambassador."

"Of course." Cold foreboding twisted up his spine. Would the earl prevent the union from taking place after everything he'd been through? He met the other man's eyes. "Is something troubling you?"

"Not any longer, not after spending this time with you, seeing how you handled yourself as you spoke about marrying my sister and your motivation therein." The earl offered a tight smile. "You truly care for Sophia. I can see it in your eyes, hear it in the way you speak about her."

"I do." Oliver nodded in the event the earl didn't understand. "From the moment I laid eyes on her, she's been my reason for drawing breath."

"Even knowing next to nothing about her."

"Must one discover everything ahead of a marriage, Your Lordship? Is that not what a couple does over the course of a union?" He grinned, for he couldn't wait to unwrap the package that Sophia presented. "Surely you have felt that way yourself with your intended."

"I have." Lord Ettesmere's jaw worked as if he were choosing his words carefully. "But my marriage will be different, for there is no expiration date upon it."

"This is true, but conversely, couldn't we argue that every-one's time on this earth is limited? None of us know when we will expire." Oliver sobered. His heart squeezed from the knowledge that he wouldn't have years with Sophia. "If any of us can make someone else's life better, can lighten the burden of another, even for one day, shouldn't we try? Shouldn't we all live as if today is our last?"

"Of course." For a moment, the earl struggled with his emotions. He glanced through the open door at the butler who was directing the footmen to go after the luggage. When he met Oliver's gaze again, the muscles in his throat worked. "I cannot tell you how impressed I am that you're doing this for my sister. You have my respect and my support, but please, promise me you will do everything in your power to make her happy."

"That is my intention. You have my word that Sophia will know nothing except contentment and joy until she breathes her last." Please God help him to uphold that vow. It would be difficult enough, for there was nothing he could do to remove the inevitable thoughts that probably plagued her every waking moment. "And when that time comes, I shall be at her side until I must give her up," he finished in a quiet voice.

"Good." Lord Ettesmere offered a hand, and when Oliver shook it, he nodded. "Welcome to the family. You'll soon find it takes a strong person to join our ranks." He snorted. "Which is odd in and of itself, for this second season of all our lives is full of more emotional upheaval than the first time each of us wed."

"Life, though, requires us to commit to a certain level of emotion in order to remind us that we're alive. Good or bad, we've signed on for every portion of it." And though his union would end with heartache—how could it not—he was determined to enjoy the hell out of every day he was given with Sophia. "Frankly, why would we want it any other way?"

Quite frankly, she was his reason for living at the moment, and he intended to enjoy every moment of having his little family to himself.

"You are quite wise for an ambassador." The earl left the coach since the driver kept slapping his gloves against his thigh as he waited for them to disembark. "It gives me some relief to know Hannah will be in excellent hands when..." His voice broke and his words trailed off.

Oliver nodded as he too left the coach. "Thank you. I'll do my best by her as well, and I think she has quite the talent for politics."

"Well, she certainly can argue."

"Indeed."

The earl gestured with his chin. There, sitting cross-legged on the top step to the manor, was the girl herself. And instead of the dress he expected, she was clad in a loose-fitting man's shirt and a pair of tan breeches. "I wonder if she's waiting for me or you."

"Let's find out." She was like a breath of fresh air though.

Lord Ettesmere snicked. "I don't envy you the raising of her. She'll be a hoyden if we're all not careful, and I suspect you won't remain in London the year around."

"No, I won't, but what is life without a challenge? And from everything you've told me about her mother, perhaps it's in her blood to be bold and curious." Oliver took his valise from the driver with a nod, then he and the earl approached the manor. "It will serve her well as she advances toward womanhood. She will make London take notice, and that's a fact."

Immediately, Hannah squirmed off the wall. She bounded over to them and threw herself into the earl's arms. "Welcome home, Uncle Arthur."

"Thank you. I trust you weren't trouble for your mother while I was away?"

"Of course I wasn't, but I cannot say the same about Uncle Gilbert," she said with a wide grin. "And the more he grouses, the more fun it is to tease him."

"Be kind to him. He grapples with more than any of us realize." But there was a grin on the earl's face. "Come inside. You can tell me all about it while I cajole Cook into feeding us."

"In a moment. First, I wish to speak with Mr. Mattingly."

"Ah." The earl threw an amused glance at Oliver. "It seems it was you she wished for all along." After bussing the girl's cheek, the other man vanished into the house.

Oliver cocked an eyebrow. "What is amiss? Everything is well with your mother?"

"Yes, yes. Mama has spent her days choosing a gown for the ceremony. It's so pretty! You will adore her in it, I think. Oh, and we also planned our masquerade costumes." She took his hand and led him up the steps, and he marveled that she had such faith in him. At the top, they moved to the side and out of the direct line of traffic for the footmen hauling luggage. "I'm glad you came back."

"Why wouldn't I?" He frowned. "I promised your mother I would marry her, and I completed my task in London to do just that." He patted his jacket where the all-important signed paper rested. "All we need now is to ask the local vicar to come by."

"Good." She grinned and bounced her gaze between his valise and his face. "Did you, um, bring me a gift?"

Truly, this young lady who had known so much grief in her life was nothing more than a child still, and he delighted in that. Would that she had many more such years ahead of her, for the world would present its challenges soon enough. "How did you know I would?"

"You are that sort of man, Mr. Mattingly." She held out a hand, palm upward with an air of expectancy. "Well?"

He chuckled. "We shall need to talk later about the risks of becoming spoiled as well as deporting yourself all over the countryside dressed as a boy." Then he delved a hand into his valise and withdrew a mother of pearl hair comb. "Perhaps this might grace your lovely tresses at the ceremony."

"It's beautiful!" She snatched it from his fingers, cradling it in her palm as if it were the most valuable work of art. "I've never owned anything so fine because Mama says I lose things when I'm on adventures."

"Somehow, I suspect you'll keep this safe." He closed his valise with a snap. "Now come inside. As your uncle said, we're in need of food. I trust you've taken care of the kittens?"

"I have."

"Good. Now you can explain to me why you are dressed like this and tell me why you thought that was a good idea."

She huffed but followed him inside as he nodded to the butler. "Will you tell me it's not proper or that I shouldn't do it?"

"That depends on how creative your forthcoming answers are." When he glanced at her, he grinned. Was he up for the challenge of being an immediate father? Indeed, he was. "I'm of a mind that there are various degrees of proper. The problem isn't merely black and white."

"You and I will get along famously, Mr. Mattingly."

Sophia might give him a dressing down, but for the moment, solidifying his bond with Hannah was more important. He didn't just want her mother in his bed; he wanted every responsibility that came along with being wed.

July 11, 1819

OLIVER CLASPED HIS hands behind his back to hide their shaking. His nerves felt strung too tight while sweat plastered his fine lawn shirt to his back beneath his best jacket and waistcoat, both in black. Of course, that discomfort could be due to the heat outside, for the midday sun beamed into the drawing room at Ettesmere Park, and there was very little breeze.

Yet, as most of the Winterbourne family stared at him while waiting for the vicar to arrive, he concentrated on his breathing. It wasn't every day that a man married, and the event was incredible in its own right, but perhaps his nerves stemmed from what he'd be expected to do later tonight. Would his inexperience make Sophia think she'd made a horrible mistake? Or worse yet, would she deride him for it?

Oh, God.

The earl came into the room with a grin. Behind him was an older gentleman and a younger man. One carried a well-worn copy of the *Book of Common Prayer* while the other held a leather folio. "Good afternoon, everyone." He glanced at Oliver. "I must tell you, Mr. Mattingly, I just glimpsed my sister in the upstairs corridor, and she is quite lovely."

"That is good to know." But it simply made him all the more nervous. "Yet I thought that of her all along."

Lord Ettesmere chuckled. "This is Vicar Mitchell, and his clerk, Mr. Mead."

"Hello, and welcome." Oliver shook hands with both men. "Thank you for coming on such short notice."

The man with a ring of white hair around his balding pate grinned. "This sort of thing happens more than you'd think, Mr. Mattingly. Though I must say, your reasons for wedding are thought provoking and heart breaking as much as they are inspiring. You are a true example for us all."

"Yes." He nodded. "But in the doing of it, I hope to make a few lives better."

Vicar Mitchell grinned. "You are a good sort, Mr. Mattingly." He glanced at his clerk. "If you set up the register on a table at the back we can move forward."

With a nod the younger man broke away. He set his folio on the table where a large vase of varied colored roses rested. Oliver had convinced the dowager to let him cut a bouquet for the wedding. Thankfully, she'd gladly agreed. Perhaps it would make Sophia smile.

"Well, I'll leave you to it." Lord Ettesmere clasped Oliver's shoulder. He looked at the vicar. "And I'll be seeing you not long from now." Then he crossed the floor and took a seat next to his fiancée. The ever-present rotund beagle lay at her feet. There were two roses tucked into his collar in honor of the festivities.

Still his nerves continued to plague him, but when the double doors to the drawing room opened and Hannah strolled in, he couldn't but help a grin. She was adorable in a pale blue gown with a cluster of pansies tucked over her left ear. She held a single yellow rose in her right hand. Her blonde hair had been left down, tied back with a matching satin ribbon. With an exuberant wave to Oliver, she settled upon a chair next to the dowager countess.

Then Sophia paused at the doorway, and he completely forgot how to breathe. "Well, hell's bells," he whispered, much to the amusement of Vicar Mitchell.

Her gown of raspberry pink silk had been the perfect choice and showed her curves, making her a veritable goddess. The skirts flowed about her ankles as she slowly approached the top of the room where he stood. A band of gold encircled her waist, which only served to bring his attention to the swell of her breasts over the low bodice. Pretty color stained her pale cheeks, and her golden hair had been arranged into an intricate updo with swoops and braids. Curling tendrils hung at her temples and nape. A strand of delicate pearls encircled her neck with an oval-shaped pink gemstone in the center that winked with her every movement. Her green eyes sparkled, and those soft pink lips curved into a smile that both conveyed delight and wicked promise.

A shiver moved down his spine. Never had he been more certain of a decision before in his life. As a few snickers moved through the room, he glanced about only to find the orange kitten trailing after Sophia's skirts, batting at them with each step she took. He chuckled. "What is life without laughter to help soothe the way?" he asked of the room at large. When she reached his side, he grinned like an idiot. "Good morning, Lady Sophia."

"Good morning yourself, Mr. Mattingly. You are quite handsome today. I adore the sash."

"Thank you." He'd chosen an ivory satin sash for the occasion, to better display his medals and ribbons proclaiming various accolades and honors bestowed upon him during his stint as an ambassador. Since he had no title, he felt this might set him apart from those that did, and that Sophia might be proud of him. "I'm rather proud of all I've accomplished."

"And so you should be. I certainly am and cannot wait to hear the stories." The faint scent of roses floated his way as she nodded at the vicar. "Hullo, Vicar Mitchell. Thank you for coming."

"It's lovely to see you so happy, my lady, all things considered," the older man said. "Shall we begin?"

"Yes, please," she replied with a speaking glance at Oliver. "Delay is not something I wish to indulge in."

The vicar cleared his throat. "Our nuptial couple is ready to start." He opened his *Book of Common Prayer* and turned to the correct page, then he encompassed them both in his gaze and then said, "Dearly beloved, we are gathered together here in the sight of God, and in the face of this congregation, to join together this Man and this Woman in holy Matrimony; which is an honorable estate, instituted of God in the time of man's innocency, signifying unto us the mystical union that is betwixt Christ and his Church…"

Oliver's mind wandered slightly as the words the vicar spoke became caught up in the cloud of worry in his brain. Their lives were about to change. In a mere handful of moments, he would walk from this room with a wife as a married man. Was he up to the challenge? Did she think him good enough? Did it matter she was marrying below her station or that their time together was short?

When Sophia gently touched his hand, the swirling thoughts ceased to chase around his mind, and he concentrated again on what the vicar said. Apparently, just in time, for the older man was addressing him directly.

"Wilt thou have this Woman to thy wedded Wife, to live together after God's ordinance in the holy estate of Matrimony? Wilt thou love her, comfort her, honor, and keep her in sickness and in health; and, forsaking all others, keep thee only unto her, so long as ye both shall live?"

So long as ye both shall live.

A tremble of fear went down Oliver's back. The time he would be given with Sophia was truly limited. Panic bubbled up in his chest. He always thought that when he married, it would be for longer than perhaps a few months to a year without the worry that any sort of large shock or excitement might strike his bride dead. His breathing became labored. How could he prove any sort of good husband in such a short time? Yes, he was infatuated with Sophia and selfishly he wished for more time, yet… He glanced at her, saw the gleam of happiness in her eyes, and all his concerns vanished like mist before the sun.

In a clear voice, he answered, "I will. In fact, from the first moment I saw the lady, I knew my future lay with her."

"I rather assumed you would, Mr. Mattingly," the vicar said to a few titters from their audience. Then he turned his attention to Sophia. "Wilt thou have this Man to thy wedded Husband, to live together after God's ordinance in the holy estate of Matrimony? Wilt thou obey him, and serve him, love, honor, and keep him in sickness and in health; and, forsaking all others, keep thee only unto him, so long as ye both shall live?"

For a horrible few seconds, she didn't answer the question.

"Mama, you are supposed to say yes," Hannah interrupted in the world's worst stage whisper, which made the clerk snicker at the back of the room.

Sophia's smile was as beautiful and beaming as a sunrise. She nodded. "I will." Her answer came out breathless and, in a whisper, said, "This is perhaps the most poignant of my marriages." Tears gathered in her eyes. What thoughts were plaguing her? Did she, too, wish for more time, or was she even now regretting that she'd arrived at this pass?

Damn it all, there were too many unknowns, and on this day of all days!

Oliver was instructed to take her right hand in his right one. Her fingers trembled, and her breath came in short pants. Was the stress of the ceremony too much? Surely, she wouldn't expire right here. As his protective instincts rose, he leaned close, put his lips to her ear, and whispered, "I give you my word and my promise this isn't a mistake, and I will make certain, to the best of my ability, that the remainder of your life will be spent in abundant happiness and pleasure."

"I appreciate that, but not even you and your bright attitude can control fate, Ambassador," she whispered back.

"Perhaps not, but I can put up the devil's own opposition as I fight to give you every good thing while I can." When he smiled, the blush in her cheeks deepened. Never had he felt more passionate about a goal in all his life.

"Should I go on, Mr. Mattingly?" the vicar asked with amusement in his tones. "Or do you wish to continue to convince your bride she hasn't chosen a husband poorly?"

Heat rose up the back of his neck. "Yes, please. I apologize for the interruption. It's not every day I am presented with such unique challenges."

"Indeed." But the vicar smiled as he focused fully on him. "Mr. Mattingly, repeat after me…" As he intoned the words that would forever bind him to Sophia, Oliver drew his bride a tiny bit closer and held tight to her fingers.

"I, Oliver Jonas Mattingly, take thee, Lady Sophia Winterbourne-Stratford-Forrester, to my wedded Wife, to have and to hold from this day forward, for better for worse, for richer for poorer, in sickness and in health…" His voice broke on that word, and to his mortification, moisture rose in his eyes. *God, please give me the strength to love her thoroughly in this limited time so she doesn't feel alone before she leaves me to be with You.* When Sophia squeezed his fingers, he cleared his throat. "…to love and to cherish, 'til death us do part, according to God's holy ordinance; and thereto, I plight thee my troth."

"Oh, Oliver." A tear fell to her cheek, and he wanted nothing more but to kiss it away. "You dear, dear man."

They were directed to release hands, and Sophia was told to then hold his right hand with her right one. The vicar addressed her with distinct emotion graveling his voice. "Lady Sophia, repeat after me." As he said the words, the whole of Oliver's being strained to hear them in her tones.

"I, Lady Sophia Winterbourne-Stratford-Forrester, take thee, Oliver Jonas Mattingly, to my wedded Husband." The delicate tendons in her throat worked with a hard swallow. "To have and to hold from this day forward, for better for worse, for richer for poorer, in sickness and in health, to love, cherish, and to obey, 'til death us do part…" Her words stumbled over themselves and another few tears fell to her cheeks. Oliver's heart went out to her, for no doubt the reality of her limited days had come home to her, but when he squeezed her fingers, she met his and nodded, and smiled through her tears. "…according to God's holy ordinance." She lowered her voice to a whisper. "And thereto I give thee my troth." Her gaze rose to his. "You appeared when I needed you, Oliver, and for that, you will forever be my hero."

Please let me live up to her imaginings.

A few sniffles issued from the dowager as well as the earl's daughter, but Oliver ignored the high emotion swirling through the room.

They were instructed to again release their hands. Oliver gave a thin band of gold to the other man, who then laid it upon his open *Book of Common Prayer* along with a small leather pouch of coins that would pay for the vicar's services. After Vicar Mitchell thanked him and said a short blessing over the ring, it was returned to him. Oliver then slipped it onto the fourth finger of her left hand, nestling the band beneath the ruby engagement ring he'd already given her. According to the earl, it wasn't done, but he'd witnessed a few weddings while in America that had taken up the practice, and he liked it. Besides, it had given him great pleasure to purchase that plain band—his first gift to her.

Vicar Mitchell nodded. "Repeat after me, Mr. Mattingly."

"With this Ring I thee wed, with my Body I thee worship, and with all my worldly Goods I thee endow." His voice wavered slightly, for that had been his intention from the first. "In the Name of the Father, and of the Son, and of the Holy Ghost. Amen."

"Let us all pray for this couple before the ceremony concludes."

As Oliver kneeled in front of the vicar, he gently pulled Sophia down beside him. While the words of a prayer went on, he neglected to concentrate on them, so great was the urge to look at his new bride. Her face had paled, and tears sparkled on her cheeks, but she gave him a smile, and he reveled in that.

Thank you for making this sacrifice, she mouthed to him.

It is not a sacrifice. I am neither saving you nor myself, he mouthed back. Then, he put his lips to the shell of her ear and whispered in a barely audible voice, "I found myself enchanted with you and wished to make your last days as beautiful as you've made mine by merely existing."

The tiny sound she made tugged at his heart. "Oh!"

Finally, the vicar's prayer ended. When he stood and brought her up with him, Vicar Mitchell announced, "I now pronounce thee husband and wife. May God bless you and your days together."

Polite applause broke out from the guests in the room. Hannah bounced out of her chair with a loud, "Huzzah!" The kitten, spooked by the sudden commotion, darted off to hide beneath a sofa.

Regent, however, lifted his head and bayed like only a beagle could.

Laughter broke out through the room.

Oliver grinned. He scarcely felt his feet on the floor as he took Sophia's hand, brought it to his lips, and then kissed her middle knuckle. "Congratulations, my lady. I am so proud to call you my wife."

"You do look ready to burst from it." But she returned his grin. "It's such a lovely day."

The vicar smiled at them both. "If you'll just step over to where my clerk is waiting, there is a paper you need to sign."

"Of course." Oliver pulled her hand through the crook of his arm. "Truly, you have made me the happiest of men today." There wasn't anything he wouldn't do for her.

"Aw, Oliver, you deserve so much more than I can give you." She brushed at the moisture on her cheeks. "I am so grateful to you." Though tears still swam in her eyes, she pointed with her free hand to a small, pink enamel hair pin in her tresses. "My father gave this to me on the eve of my first wedding. It means that hope springs eternal, to never lose my dreams. That is what you represent as well."

His chest tightened. A wad of emotions stuck in his throat. "We'll go together into the future. You are not alone, sweeting."

Before they reached the clerk's location, Hannah ran over and hugged her mother. "I'm so happy you married Mr. Mattingly!" She glanced at him as her stomach rumbled. "Might we go into luncheon now? I'm famished."

Oliver chuckled while Sophia nodded. "Go ahead. It appears the family is heading out to the lawn as we speak."

After they'd signed the register and thanked the vicar for his services as well as invited him and his clerk to the meal, he took Sophia into his arms. "I'm afraid I don't know quite what to do now. I've never had a wife, you see." Though having her close sent acute awareness prickling through his body.

"I'm certain you can figure out what comes next." Sophia held his head between her palms and touched her lips to his. "After all, you *are* a clever man."

With a soft groan, he settled her more comfortably in his arms, and just when he would have spent the next few minutes kissing her senseless, Hannah bolted into the room. "Are you coming, Mr. Mattingly? I want to sit next to you."

He laughed and pressed his forehead to Sophia's. "Well, I suppose I shall *come* in quite a different way later." It was a bittersweet moment, for he couldn't forget theirs was not a marriage of a long lifetime. When his wife snorted and a blush stained her cheeks, he pulled away to glance at his new daughter. "I shall be delighted to indulge you, Hannah."

Every step he made now would prove a new adventure, though he hoped they would all manage to weather the impending heartbreak with courage.

CHAPTER TEN

*W*HERE THE DEVIL *is Oliver?*

Dinner had been over and done with two hours ago, and though he'd gone off with her brothers and nephew, she had assumed he might be anxious to join her. In the meantime, she'd cheerfully made certain Hannah had been tucked into bed—given a few books to read if she wasn't tired—and had handed down strict orders not to wander the halls tonight.

The last thing Sophia needed was for her daughter to creep into her room while she was involved in wicked things with her new husband.

Yet for that to happen, said husband needed to make an appearance.

Common sense told her that she should wait to share such intimacies with him, for she barely knew him, but with the time allotted to her dwindling, she'd meant every word she'd said to him when they'd become engaged. She wanted a husband in every sense of the word, a chance to enjoy being in a man's arms once more. And if she were honest with herself, she enjoyed intercourse all too much to let this opportunity slip by.

Already, the purpling shadows of twilight had given way to the navy darkness of the night. She rubbed her hands up and down her arms. The silk of the thin, Chinese-style dressing gown in shades of green slipped over her skin as she paced to the window. Below was the sloping back lawn of Ettesmere Park. Off to the left, the darkened gardens waited and beyond, the hedge maze.

When the sound of the latch to the adjoining door of her dressing room echoed in the silence, Sophia caught her breath and slowly turned as her heartbeat raced. *He's here!* "Oliver."

"I apologize for the delay," he said as he came into the room. "Your brothers kept offering up toasts followed by stories." Her new husband shook his head as a smirk tugged at the corners of his mouth. "I have learned all too much about the two of them and their marriages." His chuckle reverberated in her chest and set off an avalanche of tingles down her spine. "To say nothing of Arthur's undisguised interest in his bride-to-be."

A giggle escaped her. "Well, he *is* quite enamored of Julianna. It's rather adorable." Would she eventually come to love Oliver in that same way? If she were allowed enough time?

"Anyone can see that, but it's Lord Yeardly—Gilbert, rather— I'm worried about." With a glance about the room, he removed his satin sash, and with care folded it before resting it into a drawer of the nightstand. Then he shrugged out of his dinner jacket and draped the garment over the back of a chair. "He is terribly bitter regarding his union, and I'm beginning to wonder when he last saw his wife. His stories were not complementary as a whole."

"That is my worry too." Gilbert could clean up his own mess. She had other things to occupy her attention. When he removed his cuffs and collar, she stifled a sigh. There was something so erotic about watching a man undress. "I'm glad you are bonding with my family, though. That will help when I... At the end when... Well, when things happen," she finished lamely with a lump in her throat.

"We needn't talk about that now." After tugging off his cravat, Oliver threw it atop his jacket and then joined her at the window. "Especially since the purpose of us marrying is to take your mind off that eventuality. Nothing but happy days, remember."

"I know, but it lurks in the background waiting to pounce."

The heat of him seeped into her. "It's a nice view here. My room is—was, I suppose I should say—on the other side of the house and overlooks the drive."

"Yes." Sophia peeked out the window. "When I was a young girl around Hannah's age, I often took refuge from the storms of life in that maze. My father was tickled I treated it as my own personal play area. Then, when Mama usurped the heart for her gardening purposes, I let her have it, for I'd already been married the first time."

"Is it still the bastion of solitude it used to be?"

"Oh, yes. Upon arriving at Ettesmere Park and knowing I could—can—expire at any time, I've spent an inordinate amount of time there." A sigh escaped her. "Often, I bring an old quilt with me when I'm not caring for the roses. At times I'll read a book or attempt to sketch, but mostly I let my mind wander. Revisit things, dare to hope for others."

Never had she told anyone that before.

"That is understandable."

For whatever reason, she felt that he did indeed grasp what she struggled with. Perhaps she'd been strong for far too long by herself, for when he slipped his arms around her, she uttered a shuddering sigh and leaned into him with her palms resting on his chest. His scent wafted to her nose as a distraction, and for a few seconds, she closed her eyes and merely let herself enjoy the moment. They were here and on the verge of something wonderful. "I still can hardly believe I'm married to you."

He pulled slightly away in order to peer into her face. "Do you have regrets?"

"Of course not." She let her fingers drift around to his back and with a few tugs, had the ties of his waistcoat undone. "I didn't think I would have the opportunity again to have a third husband."

"Then it's fortunate I accidentally came to visit when I did."

The stormy depths of his eyes darkened as he cupped her cheek and brushed his lips against hers. "Imagine you marrying a different man, one who might not wish to live to make your last days enjoyable."

"Imagine." The truth was, she didn't want to. He was here, and there was no doubt he'd been meant to be so. Longing shuddered through her; she lifted up onto her toes and kissed him back. Gentle, tender, light, none of them tipped her into passion but they did light tiny fires in her blood. When she broke the kiss, she grinned. "If you don't wish to go forward tonight, I'll understand."

"One thing you'll learn about me is that I never back down from a challenge." In a twinkling, he removed his waistcoat and threw it in the direction of another chair. "However, so you don't think I'm going to be England's best lover immediately, I have never... uh..."

Poor, dear man. "You've already mentioned you were inexperienced. But have you truly never bedded a woman? Not even during your salad days?" It hadn't occurred to her that a man could still be considered an innocent at his age.

"No." A flush rushed up his neck. "It's pathetic, I know, so please don't tell your brothers. They would think less of me. To say nothing about teasing me incessantly. I put on a decent act around them tonight and made them think I knew more than I do."

That brought out another giggle. "Of course, I won't. There is nothing to be ashamed of, though." She took his hand and drew him away from the window. "Were you not interested in relations with women before?" They would have a different issue entirely if he were attracted to men, but she would still welcome him as her husband.

And his sacrifice to marry her would be even larger.

"It's nothing like that. I merely hadn't given it thought." He pushed up his spectacles but stumbled after her until they reached the foot of the bed. "I was all too focused on academics and then taking on the responsibilities of clerking for various heads of state, and after that came ambassadorial duties." His shrug was an elegant affair. "And of course, the never going past kissing as I mentioned."

How adorable he was! The task of teaching him how to pleasure a woman was heady stuff, and she reveled in it. Never had she held that position before. Sophia rested her free hand on his chest. "There is no cause for embarrassment, Ambassador. We all had to begin somewhere." Slowly, she trailed her hand downward. As her fingers glanced over his abdomen, his muscles clenched, and she grinned. Already, he was so responsive. Gingerly, she stroked the building bulge at the front of his trousers. "Have you ever pleasured yourself?" Anticipation buzzed at the base of her spine, for she couldn't wait to touch him, learn every nuance of his body, discover what would send him over the edge into bliss.

"Oh, God." The whisper was choked with emotion. Then a moan shuddered from him when she continued her gentle exploration. "I have, of course."

"Good. At least there is something to work with." As she brushed her fingers up and down, tracing along his growing length, she met his gaze. "You can tell me what you like, and I shall do the same for you." How big would he be? Her first husband wasn't well-hung, but her second? He'd been *quite* satisfying.

He took her hand, removed it from his person. "I feel like a boy still at school."

"Mmm." She untied the sash at her waist. "I don't mind being your teacher."

Splotches of color blazed on his face, appearing mottled in the dim light from the one candle burning on a nearby table. "It's hot in here, don't you think?"

"Oh, indeed." She was enjoying this entirely too much. "Perhaps you should shed some clothes." With a shrug, her dressing gown slipped from her shoulders. Clad in a matching nightdress of the same silk, Sophia tugged his shirttails from his trousers. "I can help with that."

"Allow me one moment." Her husband raked his gaze up and down her person. "I can't wait to see you—all of you—but right now, you are simply astonishing."

"I'm glad you think so. That's quite a compliment for a woman my age, but I must warn you. In recent years, my need—my craving perhaps we should say—to lie with a man and be pleasured by a man have increased exponentially. The older I grow, the more pronounced the urges come, so if I frighten you just now, I apologize." Truly, it had been long years since she'd felt wanted, desired, by a man. It was good for her ego that he appreciated her.

"I will let you know, but this is all new for me."

When he stepped away, she frowned. "Where are you going?"

"Away enough so I can remove my clothes." That certain gleam in his eyes sent a shiver down her spine despite the heat in the air. "Then, you shall have my undivided attention."

"Oh." There was something to be said for marrying a relatively younger man, for his form was impressive. As she crawled onto the bed, her throat went dry once his trousers came off. "You are nothing to sneeze at either."

And he was fully aroused. The thick length of him curved slightly outward, and his belly was neither chiseled nor had gone to fat. A thin sprinkling of dark hair decorated his chest, and when he grinned, she gave into another shiver. He had a bit of a golden tan; the contrast of pale skin and golden where his cravat usually lay, as well as at his wrists, amused her. The man needed to be outside more. Truly, he was so adorable and ordinary that her heart squeezed. There was much fun to be had with him.

She welcomed him into her arms and met him with a kiss. After pulling slightly away, Sophia carefully removed his spectacles, set them upon a bedside table. "You won't be needing these, I think." Her hands trembled, for the instant his body lay pressed against hers, the need for him, to feel his member deep inside her throbbed into her consciousness.

"Did you know that without them, I am unable to see past the end of my nose?"

"I suspect that won't be an issue right now." Then she resumed her intention to memorize the shape and feel and taste of his mouth. To his credit, he kissed her back with equal enthusiasm and a definite skill that had her breathless with longing. For the time being, she avoided his rampant length. That she would save for later, to enjoy almost as a dessert.

But right now, she wanted so much more.

Gently pushing him off her, she encouraged him onto his back then she kneeled beside him and proceeded to explore every inch of him with her lips, tongue, and teeth. The scent of him—citrus and sage—flooded her senses. She was nearly drunk on him, especially when he caressed and touched her when she came close again. His every reaction, each tiny moan and exhalation he uttered, the way his eyes dilated spurred her onward until she feared she would burn to death from the fires in her blood.

"Touch me, Oliver. Show me that you want me, that you haven't married me only out of pity." For her own peace of mind, she needed to know that.

"Of course, I haven't." With a chuckle that tickled her insides, he maneuvered Sophia onto her back. "I will admit, I don't know what good I've done in my life to have deserved you, but I'm so glad you are mine."

He nuzzled the crook of her shoulder, spent copious amounts of time pressing feather-weighted kisses to the base of her throat and gliding his lips along the bodice of her night dress. Then, apparently, having a barrier of fabric between them grew too frustrating, for he took the hem in his hands, tugged the garment up, and when Sophia wriggled into a sitting position, she assisted him in removing it from her body.

"I knew you would be beautiful," he whispered before claiming her lips in a searing kiss that had her head clouding with desire. Gently, tenderly, he laid her back down. Seconds later, he made love to her breasts, working them over with his hands and fingers, teasing the buds into aching peaks with his lips and mouth. "So soft, so fascinating."

The steam of his breath increased the need circling through her insides. Her back arched of its own accord, which put a nipple more securely into his care. "Oh, it's been such a long time…"

"We shall go down that path together." But then he paused in his ministrations. He released one of those aching buds and rested a hand on the other breast. "Are you certain this activity won't send your heart into too much of a shock?"

"I cannot say with any certainly whether it will or won't, but that doesn't mean we shouldn't try." Would hitting release tax her body? She didn't know, for it had been a while since she'd last pleasured herself with her fingers. There had simply been too much to worry about. "At least I'll expire while flying."

"That is the hope—yet let us hope you do not." He again dragged his lips along the side of her neck.

"Touch me, Oliver." Would he never get on with it? Taking his hand, she guided him between her thighs. "You are an intelligent man. I'm quite certain you know how to do this."

He snorted. "I'm glad one of us is sure." The second he glided his fingers along her sensitive flesh, she shivered. "Perhaps I'm getting close?"

Oh, he was ridiculously adorable and naïve. "Like this." With a shaking hand and a racing heart, Sophia showed him how to caress her, how to open her up and find that all-important tiny pearl at her center. In some breathlessness, she said, "Apply various degrees of friction as the bud swells. You'll soon find a rhythm."

Of course, the ambassador proved a quick study in that as he had in everything else. "The female form is mysterious and amazing."

He laid to her side while continually rubbing the pads of his fingers over that nubbin. First with authoritative caresses then with the lightest of touches. Always, he kept her guessing, and as her body strained with coiled bands of pressure, she writhed from his torment. With a pleased chuckle, he took possession of her lips while granting her no mercy from his ministrations. Over and over, he plundered her mouth, and then he surprised her when he penetrated her with first one finger and then two.

Never, not even once, did he cease to boss that little pearl. That determination was the catalyst for the bands inside to break. Sophia tumbled over the edge into bliss before she was ready. The wave of pleasure crashed into her, and it stole her breath. Immediately, every muscle in her body went taut. She pressed her hand over his and clutched at his arm with the other while a cry of surprise left her throat. Contractions fluttered through her core, carried her away into the dark void that she both welcomed and feared, where her heart raced entirely too fast and heat blanketed her body, and through it all, Oliver watched her with heavy-lidded eyes and a grin of pure male satisfaction.

"The fact that you were able to hit release merely from my touch is breathtaking." He kissed her, again and again, and Sophia wrapped her arms around him to hold him close.

Perhaps she'd been entirely too primed, had thought about joining with him entirely too much, but knowing she'd found bliss so quickly was a positive sign. "Some men pleasure women with their mouths. So that's something to think about."

He lifted his head. "Do you enjoy that?"

Gooseflesh popped over her skin, for he had *that* look in his eye. "My first husband used to do that, and it was quite lovely."

Oliver kissed a path down her neck. He teased a nipple before continuing between her breasts, along her torso, and over her abdomen. "And your second?"

"It wasn't something he liked overly much." *More's the pity.*

"Well, then, let's see what side of that coin I fall on, hmm?" Down, down, down he went until he kneeled at her bent legs. With a grin that accelerated her heartbeat, he buried his head between her thighs and touched his tongue to the spot he'd only just tormented.

"Ol-i-ver!" It was too late to recall the startled cry, and truly, as soon as he warmed to his task, he was in complete control.

Sophia clutched the bedding in her fists, and when he slipped his hands beneath her buttocks to lift her more comfortably to his mouth, she lost all semblance of control. His lips and tongue were seemingly everywhere she wanted him to be. Probing and nibbling gave way to licking, sucking, and even penetrating her body with his tongue until once more she danced on the edge of bliss.

"I can see why this would prove highly stimulating." When he chuckled against her flesh, she bit her bottom lip, for the sensations were exquisite. "But let's finish the job, hmm?"

Where she had at first thought his fingers on that nubbin were wonderful, she hadn't counted on him being so accomplished with his lips or tongue, for he suckled that bud until she cried out for the torture to end then he soothed it with his tongue before beginning the process over again. All too soon, she toppled over the edge, fell hard and fast into that realm of brilliant light and then darkness where nothing except pleasure waited.

And she tumbled down, down, down, at first as light as a feather and then quicker, faster as the contractions caught her up as if she were as heavy as an iron ball.

In the end, Oliver caught her, came back over her body with his arms wrapped around her and his lips pressed to the crook of her shoulder. He murmured endearments and words of calm, some of which implored her to come back to him and out of the darkness, for it simply wouldn't do to expire on their wedding night.

Why the devil were there tears on her cheeks? She had no idea she'd been crying during that flight, but the release of emotion had left her deliciously relaxed and ready to return the favor to him. When she opened her eyes, immediately her gaze crashed into his. "That was incredible." As she kissed him, tasted herself on his lips, the longing inside grew into something more entirely. Would that she could have a lifetime with this man instead of the weeks or months the doctor had warned her about.

But then, that *was* her lifetime. There was no wry amusement in the thought.

"I rather think that it's you who made the difference."

For a few moments, she let him hold her, then she reached between their bodies and gently took his hard, hot length in her hand. "Turnabout is fair play, is it not?"

A moan shuddered from his throat. "I cannot guarantee it won't end in disaster."

"Not disaster. Only learning, and we have all night to indulge." Slowly at first, Sophia stroked her curled fingers up and down his shaft. "I think for this first time out, I'll simply bring you to release like this. That way, when we *do* couple, there's a better chance we'll come together." Knowing no other woman had been with him thusly was quite heady indeed. This man was all hers, would forever know her touch, would remember how she'd pleasured him first.

No one else could say that. Finally, she understood why men enjoyed that so much.

As she worked, she planted tiny kisses and nibbles to the underside of his jaw. He was an easy conquest, for everything she did to him made him moan from enjoyment. Up and down, up and down she pumped, and with each pass, his length stiffened further. His hips moved in time to her ministrations, and she could imagine what it would feel like having that hardness inside her. When she left off long enough to massage his stones, a cry of warning left his lips, and she smiled.

It wouldn't be long now.

"Sophia, perhaps you should leave off." Frantic warning echoed in his tones. He fisted the bedding in one hand, plucked at her wrist with the other.

"Oh, I think not. We're arriving at the fun part." With a laugh, she renewed her efforts, and once more took his member in hand. "You have quite an impressive tool here, Mr. Mattingly."

"Sophia, please…"

"Please, what?" Her strokes came faster and faster with varying degrees of pressure.

"Please, I… Oh, God." His hips bucked, which put him more firmly into her hold.

"I adore it when men beg." She kissed his chin. "Hold tight. I expect you'll go over soon." Quicker and quicker, she stroked him. With each pump, she slightly twisted her hand to give him additional stimulation. His length pulsed, heated and ready, and for a moment she closed her eyes as she imagined how that appendage would feel inside her. When need throbbed through her core, that's when Oliver broke.

"Ah, argh!" His body went taut, and as he threw back his head, an expression of complete bliss lined his face in the dim light.

In her hand, his member jerked as he thrust over and over. Seconds later, the warmth of his ejaculation spattered against her belly and thighs. And he'd been magnificent in that moment, looking as if he'd seen the very face of God.

Spent, he sagged into the pillows and pulled her close. "I apologize. That wasn't well done of me. I should have had enough control to stave that off in order to join with you."

"Hush, Ambassador." Sophia rested her head on his shoulder and slipped her hand around his waist. "All of that will come in time, and as I said, we have all night to do that together." This form of intimacy was perfectly acceptable, and it had certainly brought them closer.

"But there's now a mess—"

"I'll attend to it in a minute." For a long time afterward, they lay together as the shadows made by the moonlight danced through the room. "Falling asleep in my husband's arms is one of my most favorite things about being married."

"It's an honor I'll cherish." Emotion clung to his whispered tones, and it brought tears to her eyes.

"Thank you for what you did today. It gives me a modicum

of peace."

"I'm sorry you even need to worry about this." He pressed his lips to her temple. "But you are not alone any longer."

She snuggled closer to him. "At times, it is much to struggle with."

"For as long as you need me, I'll be beside you, holding off the darkness."

A tiny piece of her heart flew into his keeping. Yes, this had been the right decision. She only hoped it didn't leave him destroyed once her time was up.

CHAPTER ELEVEN

July 12, 1819

O LIVER CAME AWAKE to the sensation of someone watching him.

When he cracked open first one eye and then the other and Sophia's face swam blurrily into view, he grinned and cast about the bedside table for his spectacles. "Good morning." This was the best morning of his life, awakening next to a beautiful woman, who held a sheet to her person that barely hid her breasts.

Breasts he'd pleasured more than once during the night.

"Good morning." Her voice was still throaty from sleep, and the sound went directly to his length. "I trust your first night as a married man was satisfactory?"

"Oh, yes." Once he'd donned the eyewear, he turned onto his side, and an involuntary groan escaped his throat. Hell's bells. His body ached, but in a good way. "I cannot imagine a better morning." A low rumble of thunder rolled through the area, which explained the gloomy interior of the room. "In fact, the typical rain of England can fall all it wants, I refuse to succumb to a grouchy mood."

"I'm glad to hear that." His wife leaned over and lightly brushed her lips to his. "Last night was quite... eye-opening. I heartily enjoyed myself."

"So did I." He'd thrived under her tutelage, and some of the things she'd taught him, he'd never been privy to before. When he slipped a hand along her shoulder and down her arm, she shivered. "Tonight won't come quick enough for me."

Her grin turned positively wicked. "Just as long as you don't come the same once it finally does." Then she winked and wriggled from the bed, giggling as she went out of reach of his fingers. Then she yawned. "You have quite worn me out."

Concern immediately gripped his chest. "Should you rest today?"

"I will not." Though there were fine lines of exhaustion framing her eyes and mouth, she shook her head. "There is much I wish to do." Sadness clouded her eyes. "Once I am dead, there will be time enough for rest." Her voice faltered, but she offered him a smile. "Right now, I am famished. Will you join me for breakfast?"

"Are you certain you don't wish to take a tray here in bed?" The very idea of dining in bed beside his naked wife had his member hardening with renewed arousal. "We could request a pot of honey. I'm sure there are a few different uses for such a thing that are unconventional." Licking off the sweet, stickiness from her skin sounded like a more than acceptable way to start the morning.

Sophia's eyes darkened, but then she shook her head. "While it's quite tempting, if I don't wish Hannah a good morning, she'll began a search for me." As she padded over the floor to the adjoining dressing room, she shot him a grin over her shoulder. "And doesn't absence make the heart grow fonder?"

"I don't know about that, but yours held up fairly well after those sessions last night." They had coupled twice during the wee small hours following their first foray into carnal pleasures. Though she'd been properly and quite thoroughly stimulated enough to need a couple hours rest between bouts, there hadn't been pain or more tightness in her chest than usual, according to her.

"Yes, it did." Her giggle was muffled, which meant she must be rifling through her wardrobe.

"But one wonders if our next session will be too intense for your heart to withstand," he said in a quieter voice, for the reason for their union was never far from his thoughts.

They both knew it was only a matter of time.

When she returned to the bedchamber, she wore a fine linen shift and held stays in her hand. "That is the risk. However, if you are truly worried, we can leave off with our marital endeavors."

"Uh…" It was a difficult choice, for he didn't wish her to die sooner merely due to excitement in bed, yet he was entirely too selfish and didn't want to give up their couplings. Finally, he sighed. "For your health and well-being, I will make the sacrifice."

Sophia rolled her eyes. "Oh, stop." As she approached the bed, her brow creased with worry. "We already know my lifespan is nearly at an end, and you were the one who urged me to live that life without hiding behind fear. That is what I plan to do." She leaned over him and once more kissed his lips. "Don't make me feel guilty about that any more than I already do."

The subject matter caused his chest to squeeze with anxiety. "We could always go on a short honeymoon trip. Perhaps up to London? Or elsewhere that you've enjoyed."

"Oh, Oliver." She perched on the edge of the bed. "As much as I would adore that, since my time is limited, I would rather remain here so I can spend the days with my family. It's the right thing to do."

He nodded. "Agreed. I apologize I mentioned it."

"You have every right." She fussed with the laces on the stays. "If things were different…"

"If they were, you and I would have never met." Oliver caught one of her hands and brought it to his lips while holding her gaze with his. "I wouldn't trade that for anything."

"Me either." Tears welled in her eyes, but she blinked them away. "If we linger here too much longer, Hannah is going to burst in." She slipped from the bed. "Come and assist me with these stays. I'd rather not summon my maid just yet."

"Neither do I, for that means I'll have the opportunity to do a bit of exploration before breakfast." Never had he removed himself so quickly from a bed before regardless of his naked state. As he reached for her, she giggled and dashed into the dressing room.

If he were fortunate, he could keep her laughing until the end, yet that would usher in crushing grief for him.

BREAKFAST WAS A boisterous affair, where he took more than a few comments and ribbing from Sophia's male relatives. He merely grinned and introduced several different topics that had nothing to do with anything relating to wedding nights or beds.

It must have been the correct course of action, for his wife smiled at him in the way that had awareness prickling over him, while Hannah kept up a stream of conversation more or less related to the subjects at hand. Only once did a kitten jump onto the table, but when the other one vaulted onto the sideboard and leapt into one of the chafing dishes, breakfast was declared at an end, for no one wished for cat hair in their scrambled eggs or to partake of kippers licked by felines.

"If the weather clears this afternoon, perhaps we should attempt to play nine pins or even battledore and shuttlecock," the earl suggested as he stood up from the table while a footman removed the kitten from the eggs. "Hannah!" The earl gawked while bits of golden egg clung to the kitten's fur and whiskers. "Attend to your animal this instant."

"Apologies for him, Uncle Arthur. He's only a baby yet." Hannah hurried out of the room after the footman.

Ettesmere shook his head before including the remainder of the family in his gaze. "Julianna will come over and bring her father."

"You know battledore and shuttlecock is one of my favorites," Sophia said with a smile before she hid it behind a sip of tea.

"Then that's what we shall do." The earl glanced at his brother. "Gilbert, will you be joining us? We can form teams. Surely you can be a good sport, even with the limp?"

The other man pushed away his plate of half-eaten food. "Do I have a choice?"

Sophia pulled a face at him. "No, you do not. Be grouchy and morose on your own time, but I would love it above all things if you'll play this game with me."

Once again, the reality of the situation came home for Oliver. His heart constricted as she interacted with her siblings. Everyone in this room would mourn her loss quite deeply, and now his life was intwined with theirs. That thought had the power to humble him. They were his family. He had a family and was no longer alone. Why had that not occurred to him before? Perhaps he'd been so focused on Sophia, on telling her *she* wasn't alone that he'd completely overlooked the same was true for him. Forever after, he was connected with the Winterbournes. There was a certain warm comfort in that.

All too soon, he grinned at their teasing and bickering.

At some point, the earl frowned. "Why are you staring at us like that?"

Both Sophia and Gilbert glanced at him with interest in their faces.

Oliver shrugged. "I have a family—*you* are my family." A chuckle escaped him as he shrugged with a bit of scrambled egg sitting on his fork halfway to his mouth. "I'm not alone in this life any longer, thanks to my marrying Sophia." The awe and humbleness that came along with the knowledge didn't fail to astound him.

"As it should be." She left her chair, came around the table, and bussed his cheek. "We all need each other, Oliver. Never forget that." The subtle scent of roses wafted about him. "We both made a good decision yesterday."

"So it seems." Deeper he fell into love with her, and he refused to stop the slide even knowing the outcome. For the moment, there was no greater feeling than the contentment found therein.

BY THE TIME mid-afternoon rolled around, the rain had cleared and ushered in blue skies with partial clouds the sun flirted with, so everyone poured out onto the back lawn for a rousing game of battledore and shuttlecock.

Oliver had no idea how to play such a thing, but he was game to try, especially since Sophia's eyes sparkled when small rackets—battledores—were handed around. As he experimentally swished his racket through the air, Hannah joined them.

"Will you be on my team, Mr. Mattingly?"

"Of course." He glanced at his wife and then back to Hannah. "If you'd like, you may refer to me as Oliver. We are family now."

"I would like that very much." The girl nodded. She pointed to the fat beagle. "Did you know Regent snuck into the morning room an hour ago and stole all the sandwiches from my grandmother's tea tray when she wasn't looking?"

"Oh?" Despite his wish to remain a role model for her, a snicker escaped. "He is a naughty dog indeed. Will Lady Ettesmere join us this afternoon?"

"I don't think so. She is working on her costume for the upcoming masquerade."

Sophia poked his shoulder with her racket. "We need to peruse the attics and find you something to wear. With everything else going on, it slipped my mind."

"You *have* been preoccupied of late," he responded in a low voice, and when he met her gaze, heat twined up his spine. "I don't see that ending any time soon." His grin felt positively wicked, but he didn't care.

"Neither do I." The answering smile she gave him brimmed with the same deviltry.

Hannah snorted. She bounced her attention between them. "Adults are odd at times."

"Agreed." Oliver offered the girl his arm. "Shall I escort you over to the ground where the game will go on?"

"Yes, thank you." She slipped her gloved fingers into the crook of his elbow. "The object of the game is to keep the shuttlecock in the air. The person who lets it fall to the ground is out. A winner is declared when there is only one person left."

"I see. Sounds straightforward enough." He glanced over his shoulder at Sophia, who surreptitiously wiped at the moisture from beneath one of her eyes. "To that end, I might prove a challenge for you."

"We shall see, Mr. Mat… er, Oliver." Her grin was blinding. "I'm quite good."

Two teams were formed. Sophia ended up on the one opposite him, with the earl and Julianna. His team consisted of Hannah, Gilbert, and Emily. Ettesmere's son declined to participate. Instead, he opted to sit next to Julianna's elderly father, for a handful of chairs brought out to the lawn for the occasion.

When the earl produced two shuttlecocks, he asked, "Is everyone ready?" He then handed one to Oliver. "On the count of three, toss the shuttlecock up, and then we'll continue on until we have a survivor from each team."

Oliver looked about the gathering. It was exceedingly odd to have people to spend time with, and his chest swelled with gratitude.

"Three, two… one!"

The two white feathered shuttlecocks were in play, and everyone took turns hitting the objects and making them stay aloft.

Minutes went by in pleasant exercise before Gilbert missed a hit due to stumbling from his limp. Oliver followed a couple of hits later, as did Sophia, and then Arthur let one of the shuttlecocks drop. That meant Julianna and Hannah were the team winners and went up against each other. The grin on Hannah's face and her infectious laughter that echoed through the area buoyed his spirits.

Calls of encouragement went up for both players. At his side, Sophia hopped up and down much like her daughter did when in high spirits.

"You can do it, Hannah!" Twin spots of color decorated her cheeks. Had the exercise overtaxed her? Should he suggest she lie down?

Julianna squealed as she darted to hit the shuttlecock before it touched the ground. Apparently, the fat beagle took that as a sign of distress from his mistress, for he barked and ran toward her. Before either of them could do anything about his intrusion, Regent jumped, snatched the shuttlecock from the air, and then ran off with it clutched in his jaws.

"I guess that means the match was a tie?" Oliver chuckled at the look of outrage on Hannah's face. "There can always be a new game."

"Oh, that dog!" She threw down her racket and proceeded to give chase to the beagle.

Laughter circled through the company.

Sophia laid a hand on his arm. "She is such a spitfire." A giggle escaped her. "You will have a challenge ahead of you." Her amusement faltered. "I will miss participating in life as well as seeing how the two of you are getting on."

"None of that sort of talk right now." Oliver took the racket from her hand. He dropped them both on the lawn while the other players discussed the possibility of another game. "This time is for enjoyment and happiness, remember."

"It's difficult." The words sounded as if forced through a tight throat. "Soon, there will be... nothing."

"Come with me."

"Where are we going?"

"To stroll the property, unless you are over tired from your exertions already." Worry knotted the muscles in his belly. He needed to take better care of her.

"I'm fine, but perhaps we can stay in the vicinity? I'd rather not miss the family antics." The longing in her eyes tugged at his heart.

"I understand." Shoving aside his disappointment at a chance of being alone with her, Oliver led her to one of the chairs, and once she'd settled, he sat beside her. "Were you much like Hannah at her age?"

"Sometimes." Sophia took his hand and held it. "Having two brothers didn't help, I suppose. When we were in London, I had no choice but to act the proper young lady. Mama saw to that, and Papa expected it. I was nothing more than a pretty doll." She shrugged. "But here in the country, while we were at Ettesmere Park, there were no rules to follow. That glorious freedom, I remember it fondly. There was such a feeling of being deliciously drunk on it."

"I can just imagine." He brushed the pad of his gloved thumb over the back of her hand. "When the boys went out on adventures, it was only fair that you followed."

"Of course." When she shivered, that tremble transferred to him. "Such things we played at! We went swimming in the ponds, fished in the creeks, climbed trees, rode bareback, spent days doing nothing except lying in the meadows and watching the clouds." The tendons in her throat worked with a hard swallow. "None of us had any idea at that point what life would hold for us, or how death and grief would mar our existences."

"And neither should it. Childhood should be exempt from all that." He continued with his gentle strokes. "It's why I want to ensure the rest of Hannah's childhood is as carefree as it can be. Already, I feel her soul is older than her years, and I don't want her to lose the magic she's capable of by being lost to mourning and responsibilities that shouldn't be hers just yet."

"I'm so glad you are here." A tear escaped to her cheek. She glided her thumb along the side of his hand, leaving heated awareness behind. "Hannah will have an amazing life with you."

He didn't want her to cry or think of her abbreviated future, but it was inevitable she would. Mostly, Oliver wished he could take her in his arms and hold her regardless of the company. "That is my hope. I will, of course, remain in London most of the year, but I do wish for her to travel with me. There is no better education than seeing the world firsthand and recognizing one's privilege."

"I want her to make a difference, to use her position to help instead of spoil." Over and her, she caressed that tiny spot on his hand. Truly, he would go mad touching her but not able to show his affection.

"Agreed." As those gathered on the lawn got up another bout, he sighed. "Hannah's generation will see great changes in England, I believe, as well as around the world. Imagine what advances and inventions will be made in twenty years."

"It will be glorious. I hope you'll live every day to the fullest. In remembrance of me."

From two chairs down, a choking sort of sound issued from the young lordling. "For Jove's sake, Ambassador, kiss the woman, or at the very least, hold her in your arms. You are only just married, and due to circumstances, stuck here." Exasperation rang in his tones. "Hang the conventions and proprieties. See needs you right now, and women shouldn't have to bear the weight of the world alone."

When he peered into Sophia's face, saw that blatant emotion in her eyes, his reserve crumbled. "Perhaps you have the right of it, Charles." With a gentle tug on her hand, he encouraged his wife to sit upon his lap with her legs hanging over the side of his, modestly covered by her skirting. "In a moment, I'm going to suggest calling for tea right here on the lawn. The day is too lovely to waste by passing it inside."

"Perhaps later we could form a walking party and explore the maze?" She rested one hand on his chest while the other she furrowed in the hair at his nape.

"Your wish is my command." With a nod of thanks to the younger man, Oliver slipped his arms about Sophia and held her close. Not even the look of shock from the earl could mar the perfection of the moment. "If it makes you happy, that's what we'll do."

And wasn't that the reason he'd married her to begin with?

CHAPTER TWELVE

July 16, 1819

T HE MORE SOPHIA attempted to sleep, the more elusive that
state grew. While the soft sound of rain rapped against the
windows, she simply couldn't escape into dreamland, so she lay
in her bed beside her husband of a handful of days. While the
sound of his even breathing brought her a modicum of calm, her
swirling thoughts encouraged panic and fear. Since she'd married
him, she no longer slept with a candle burning at the bedside, but
now the deep, pressing absence of light bothered her more than it
should.

Beyond the rain, no other sounds reached her ears. There was
simply… nothing.

Is this what it will be like once I die? Will I even know?

Her chest tightened, and her heartbeat came a bit faster. It
was so unfair that she would leave this life prematurely when
there were truly horrible people out there who would enjoy their
existence well into old age. At the last second, she tried to stifle a
whimper, but it escaped anyway.

"Sophia?" Oliver's voice was rough with sleep, but he rolled
over to face her. "Are you well? Is your heart paining you?"

As always, the concern he showed toward her had the ability
to steal her breath. That this man would change the entire course

of his life for her, to make her last days easier and pleasant, had her gasping at the enormity of the sacrifice.

"As far as I know, all is well in that quarter." In fact, for most of the time she'd been at Ettesmere Park as well as being distracted by Oliver, the pain around that organ had faded. She didn't know if that was a symptom of the disease that plagued her. Did that mean it would attack without warning? "I am merely thinking of the future, the one I won't have, and what it will be like once I'm dead." Her voice broke on the last word, but there was no recalling the emotion.

"I've never claimed to be an expert in that, but I would imagine there will be great calm. Whether there is a heaven or not, I cannot attest to either. Yet all the suffering a person has known while alive will be over, and if it brings you comfort to think that you will again see loved ones who have gone before, there is no harm in that belief."

What if what they'd been taught throughout their lives by going to church services whenever they go had been wrong? She had seen passages in the Bible for herself, but with so many ways to interpret that text, it often left her feeling more confused than ever.

I wish I could know with some accuracy what will happen, but then, no one I've known as come back from the grave to bear witness.

"Some people say that when they face death, a certain peace steals over them, but I suppose I am not one of them, for that is not what I'm feeling just now."

"I won't pretend to understand what you are going through, but I can be here for you and listen if you wish to talk until you can come to terms with it."

She nodded even though it was too dark in the room for him to see the gesture. "I am growing panicked, quite frankly. As if I should spend every moment with my family, watch them sleep, sit with them while they eat or do mundane activities, but that is beyond silly. And would probably only bother them."

"That is a natural response." Bedclothes rustled as he situated himself closer. Seconds later, he wrapped his arms around her and pulled her backside flush to his front. There was no sexual innuendo in the overture, only security and a deep sense of belonging. With him, like this, she was safe, as if he could defend her against all the ills of life that threatened her. It was something she adored about being married. "However, I think your family would more appreciate your presence when they are awake or perhaps not brushing their teeth." A trace of humor clung to his words. "You can engage them in walks about the property. That would afford you the time you crave with them."

She couldn't help the shiver that went down her spine. "It is difficult, for I don't know exactly when I shall cease to be." Perhaps if she had a fixed date, finding calm in the face of death might go better.

Marginally.

"I wouldn't wish to know. It would take some of the spontaneity from life and only put worry at the forefront of my mind." When he nuzzled his lips into the curve of her neck, she sighed. "That would ruin the moments I had left."

Perhaps he had the right of it.

For long moments, she remained quiet. "My grandparents died when I was a few years younger than Hannah is now. I don't remember them much, and death certainly felt different back then than it does now."

"Possibly because we didn't know the depth or cost that death extracts." He glided his fingers back and forth over her belly, leaving heated tingles in his wake. "Once we become aware of that, it is something we fear or cannot fathom."

"There is some truth there. At least my death won't be the first Hannah will experience." That comforted her only slightly. "The poor girl has seen so many family members expire in her short life, I fear it's forcing her into adulthood all too soon."

"Perhaps it's giving her a healthy respect for the living. She won't grow into a spoiled young lady."

Sophia snorted. "With you at the helm, I'm certain she will

not."

"I cannot help how I look at life." His chuckle reverberated in her ear. "However, I *do* fear that since I'm an American, she might accumulate a skewed view of the English *ton*, of which she is a part, whether she wishes it or not."

"That's not a bad thing." Sophia frowned into the darkness. "There are times when I fear the *beau monde* isn't good for anyone's wellbeing. There is too much pressure to make one into an image that doesn't necessarily reflect the personal values they have." She took one of his hands, brought it to her lips, and pressed a kiss to the back of it. There was something so right about sharing this time thusly with him.

As if she'd been waiting for exactly him to walk into her life.

"If a child is reared to have enough confidence in themselves, none of those views will be able to harm them." He wriggled into a more comfortable position. "You have done that with Hannah already. She will turn London on its ear in short order."

"If we are fortunate, yes." Already, Oliver had silently been guiding her daughter. She'd been learning responsibility through caring for her kittens, and the fact the girl respected him enough to continue that spoke to the admiration they each had for the other. "I'm glad you formed a relationship with her from the outset."

"She was the first person I came across after my carriage broke down. I admired her poise and her ability to converse on topics beyond her age. After that, I was all too curious about her life and the people she spoke about." He pressed a kiss into her hair. "Thanks to Hannah, she led me to you in a way."

"Perhaps it was indeed fate all along." Even now, she couldn't wrap her head fully around the fact they'd wed, and she was lying in bed with this man. Her heart trembled, but it wasn't from any sort of defect. How she had come to rely on him so much in such a short period of time, she didn't know, but she was glad it had happened.

For a long time, they remained in a companionable silence

while the rain fell. Never had she felt so comfortable in the dark as she did now. When her eyelids began to droop, Sophia shook herself and turned in his arms. She rested her head on his chest while letting one hand drift up and down his back. He'd worn an adorable long night shirt in which to sleep, and each time he donned it, she never failed to smile. It made him so approachable and dear. There was something so intimate and satisfying about being in a man's arms, pressed into his hard body, and listening to his heartbeat to remind her that she wasn't dead yet and that she needed to remain grateful for all she had.

"Oliver?"

"Mmm?"

So he hadn't fallen asleep. It was lovely that he kept vigil with her. "What was the most favorite thing you remember about your father?"

"Oh, that is a difficult question."

She twined a leg over his. "Was he someone you aspired to be like?"

"Yes and no." His hand at her hip set off tiny flutters through her lower belly. "My father was a politician through and through. As such, he wasn't home as much as I would have liked." Over and over, he drew abstract patterns on her hip, her upper thigh, and each fleeting touch had shivers moving up and down her spine. "That's largely why I eventually became an ambassador—through my father's contacts."

"You didn't wish to follow in his footsteps?"

"The need to almost have two faces when one is a politician was off-putting to me." As had been his want since they'd wed, Oliver slipped the fingers of one hand through her unbound tresses. That gentle, rhythmic motion worked to further relax her. "I dislike the assumption they cannot act the same man in both side of their lives. Also, the underhanded dealings to bring supporters over to each side in a political race or issue goes against everything I personally believe in."

"Which is what?"

"Brokering peace between two countries or people. What I enjoy most is finding common ground between parties and showing each one that what they bring to a meeting is just as valuable as anything else." A chuckle escaped him. "The moment when two sides of an issue realize they need each other, can be enhanced by each other, well, there is nothing like it."

"I can see that about you, for that is largely what you did for me." He was truly a gem of a man, and she unexpectedly lost a piece of her heart to him. "Is that why you wished to eventually become an ambassador? To show your father there were other ways to effect change?"

"Perhaps. I haven't given much thought to the deeper reasoning." He smiled against the side of her neck. "However, the requirement for travel also assisted my intentions to move up the ranks and eventually gain this position."

"It does sound lovely." Though she'd been married twice, she'd never had cause to leave England. She'd gone as far at Bath once, but nowhere else. "I envy you that freedom, that knowledge you must gleam while you are out exploring and seeing new, different things." Now, there was no time left to explore, for she didn't wish to be away from home when the worst happened.

At least Hannah would have a taste of that life.

"I enjoy it immensely." Oliver slipped a hand down her back, and at the curve of her bottom, he squeezed a cheek. "If you'd like, I can entertain you with stories of my travels. Or, if you'd rather, I brought several journals with me that have detailed trips. It's a hobby of mine to infuse the spirit and attitude of a place with the people who populate it. Eventually, I'd like to try and have those journals published. Perhaps someday my words will provide insight and entertainment to others."

"What a wonderful idea." And it would give her a better understanding of him as person. Since they'd married, of course, they'd talked of everything and nothing, but there was still so much to glean. "I would like to read them while spending time with my family."

"I'll make them available to you in the morning." The happiness in his voice tugged a smile from her. "Should you have questions, perhaps I can deepen my descriptions that will help you to see these places in your mind."

"I have never met anyone quite like you, Oliver." At least having him with her did a decent job at distracting her from the worries.

"It's always a good idea to have original people around you to make you think." He brushed his lips fleeting over hers. "I'm beginning to enjoy these middle-of-the-night talks."

"As am I." Sophia snuggled closer to his warmth. "There is something so deliciously intimate and safe talking while surrounded by darkness, and I appreciate that your presence has dispelled some of the fear for me."

"Have you always been afraid of the dark?"

"Yes and no. It largely depends on what is happening in my life." She burrowed a hand beneath his night shirt in order to touch his skin. The fact that his muscles tensed, and he sucked in swift breath made it all the more amusing. "When times are wonderful, it's easier to think of the night as a friend, easier to let the shadows wrap around you as a comforting blanket."

"But when times are difficult, the night appears as an enemy of sorts, something one constantly needs to do battle with, a specter that brings you the worst of your fears and forces you to examine them," he added in a soft voice.

"Yes, exactly." She stilled her palm on his chest. "How is it you understand my exact thoughts on this?"

Oliver shrugged. "I have had those same thoughts over the course of my life." He spent the next several seconds decorating the underside of her jaw with feather-weighted kisses. The rasp of his overnight stubble sent tingles of need pinwheeling through her belly. "For now, you are not alone. How can I help fight those demons for you?"

Oh, he was so sweet it was almost too good to be true. Yet

there was something about him that was as sincere and innocent as a child's laughter. "When I was a young girl, my father used to check under my bed—as well as those of my brothers—for witches and ghosts that we feared might have hidden away while we were away from our rooms."

"He sounds like a special sort of man. No wonder you adored him."

"I did. Papa was larger than life. Ettesmere Park was his favorite place in all of England. He said a man was never meant to breathe in the pollution or fight through the prejudices found within society, which was why we were always here." For long moment, memories bounced through her mind. "Now, with Papa gone, I feel as if those monsters he used to defend against are creeping closer, ready to snatch me away from everything I love and hold dear." Tears prickled the backs of her eyelids, and she hid her face in Oliver's shirt. "When will I grow too weary of holding them back?"

For that was when they would win, the moment that she ceased to draw breath.

"Be strong for as long as you can. And when you are done, I shall take up the burden." The warmth of his breath skated over her cheek. "We shall take it moment by moment after that."

The open placket of his night shirt was all too tempting. She kissed the hollow of his throat. "I appreciate that, but can you do me one favor? It will sound all too childish, but…"

Oliver snorted. "Do you wish for me to look under the bed?"

"Yes." Would he think her unhinged?

"It would be an honor to take up that torch of your father's." With a rustle of bedclothes, Oliver removed himself from the bed. The sound of him fumbling at the nightstand for his spectacles let her know he was deadly serious about fulfilling the request. "Let's see what we've got down here, shall we?"

Unable to help herself, Sophia peered over the side of the bed while Oliver kneeled beside it. "Are they there?"

"Not that I can see, but to make fully certain, I'll crawl under it." Then the dear man was as good as his word. He shimmied beneath the four-poster frame, bumping his head once. "It would seem the only thing here is one shoe and a hair ribbon." When he slipped back, he rose onto his knees and regarded her with a grin that even the darkness couldn't hide. "There are no witches or ghoulies under the bed, my lady."

"Thank you."

But apparently, he wasn't done with making his rounds. After scrambling to his feet, Oliver checked that the door to the adjoining dressing room was firmly closed. Then, he opened a few drawers in various pieces of furniture and peered inside. He checked behind the draperies at the windows before returning to her in the bed.

"I am happy to report that the room is secure. You may fall asleep knowing that nothing will harm you." He removed his spectacles and then once more took her into his arms, but this time, he encouraged her onto her back. "Especially not while I'm on watch."

Sophia looped her arms about his shoulders and encouraged his body over hers. "What would I do without you?" But his humor and his dedication had managed to set her mind at ease slightly.

"For one, you would be lying here in the dark, allowing your fears and your frets to run away with you." He dropped his voice as he slid his hands beneath her shift. "But just to make certain I've properly vanquished those concerns for the night, I'm going to completely distract you with kisses, among other things."

The second his talented fingers found her breasts, teased her nipples into aching peaks, she was lost and ever so grateful for him. "You won't hear a protest from me." Besides, the gentle way he made her hit release always helped her to sleep deeply until the morning. They never indulged in frantic copulation out of respect to the state of her heart, but what they shared was enough.

It was certainly more than she'd had a month ago, and with him, she was no longer alone with the nights were long and crowded with monsters.

CHAPTER THIRTEEN

July 18, 1819

As time went by, Oliver couldn't help but think he was walking around with a cloud of gratitude clinging to his shoulders.

He'd married a wonderful woman, had a clever but energetic daughter, enjoyed a large, extended family, and quite honestly, he'd never felt as grounded or needed more in his life. There was no doubt in his mind that he was meant to be at Ettesmere Park for this time, for this season, and though his wife wouldn't have a long life, she had enriched his existence even in the short time that he'd known her.

Now, he was due in the attics for the purpose of choosing a costume for the dowager's masquerade ball that would go off in a handful of days. Sophia had promised to meet him there to help in the process since he had absolutely no idea of what he wished for a disguise. But when he reached the open door at the top of a set of narrow, wooden stairs, the sound of voices from within made him pause.

"Are you certain no one will know who I am if I wear this gown?" The speaker was Hannah, but as Oliver peered into the long attic, he couldn't readily see her.

"Absolutely." Sophia was there as well. "The skirts are rather more voluminous than the styles we wear today, but with the laced bodice and that white wig, you shall be transformed."

From his vantage point, the girl's long-suffering sigh held doubt. "The wig is ghastly and heavy. Did women truly wear such things in grandmother's youth?"

"They did. So did gentlemen."

"Ugh." Fabric rustled. Perhaps the gown in question was being folded. "What will you wear?"

"I haven't decided yet. There is so much to choose from."

"You should be a princess."

A pleased chuckle came from Sophia. "Why?"

"You have that sort of look, and I've always thought you secretly might be." Hannah's tone filled with sadness. "It might be the last time you can pretend you are one."

"That is very true. Perhaps if I discover the right gown, I will indeed pretend to be a princess."

Oliver knew exactly what Sophia's expression would look like. Her eyes would have filled with tears, and slight panic would mix with sorrow on her face. He'd seen the same countless times since he'd married her, but usually he was always there to cajole her into a better mood or encourage her to smile. Right now, he didn't wish to interrupt this tender moment, so he remained at the door, unashamedly listening.

"You and I need masks, Mama." More rustling ensued, followed by a thump as if something heavy had been inadvertently dropped.

"There are two masks made of lace and beads in my bedchamber. One for me and one for you. Your grandmother had them imported from Venice for this event."

"That sounds exciting!" Once more, Hannah's emotions had swung to the other end of the spectrum. Footsteps echoed. Perhaps they were moving toward the door. "May I ask you a personal question, Mama?"

"Of course, dear."

"Have you fallen in love with Oliver yet?"

Such an innocent question, but his ears strained to hear the answer.

"I am quite fond of him, yes." A guarded note had crept into Sophia's voice, but why? After everything, did she still not trust him? "But I must say he is a lovely man, and I'm glad I married him."

Oliver smiled. At least there was that.

"Is he a good kisser?" The bright note of curiosity in Hannah's voice never failed to lift his spirits.

"He is wonderful in that quarter. In fact, kissing Oliver is one of my favorite things." There was no mistaking the affection in Sophia's voice. "Sometimes, when I'm feeling sad, he'll come over and he'll kiss my forehead. I adore that, for instantly it makes me smile, and I don't feel so alone or hopeless."

At the door, his grin widened. His adjusted how his spectacles sat, but this was good.

Hannah snorted. "It sounds like love to me, Mama."

For long moments, the only sounds he heard where trunks being opened and closed, as well as the rustle of fabric.

Finally, his wife spoke again. "If I let myself fall for him, it will hurt all too much when I leave this world."

"Did you ever stop to consider that it's going to hurt regardless? We will all miss you." Hannah asked in her blunt, matter-of-fact way of speaking. "Oliver is tip over tail for you. Though he is not as goofy as Uncle Arthur is for Julianna, it is adorable all the same. His eyes light when you walk into a room." She chuckled. "And you smile when he comes near. Did you know that? It's how I imagine couples in fairy stories act toward each other. What else can it be other than love?"

The child was way too wise for her years, and his chest tightened, for she'd been correct on all counts. They'd been put upon this path together. Once Sophia died, it would hurt. Grief would come, but oh, they had made extraordinary memories.

"Perhaps you have the right of it, and my silly heart is trying so hard not to be broken."

Hannah scoffed. "Isn't your diseased heart why you married him in the first place?"

"Yes, but—"

"Then ought you to try and use that heart to its full advantage while you can?"

So easily could he imagine Hannah's expression. Yes, perhaps she would change the world more, sooner rather than later.

"If I promise to do that, will you drop this subject?" A tiny note of fond frustration rang in Sophia's voice.

"For the moment, but I want you to be fully happy until the end. The way you were with Papa." Fabric rustled, and the sound was closer than it had been before. "I remember how you were with him, even though I was little." When Oliver dared to peek inside the room, they were perhaps five feet away. Hannah laid her free hand on Sophia's arm. "You didn't care who was watching but would kiss him and hold his hand, and sometimes it seemed that you and he were the only ones in the world." Her smile didn't reflect in her eyes. "I liked that, and don't you think Oliver deserves that after what he's done?"

"Ah, dearest, you sound like an old village woman." Sophia hugged her daughter. "These things should be beyond your ken. You should be running over the lawn and finding adventures instead of counseling your mother at the end of her life."

"Well, Mama, if you weren't quite so dim as to what was happening around you, then I wouldn't need to be."

Oliver chose that point to announce his presence, for if he didn't, he'd dissolve into uncontrollable laughter from the girl's effrontery. He feigned surprise upon spying the two of them, and hoped they believed it. "Ah, here you both are. I'd been searching for you. How are my favorite ladies today?" He gave them both a wide grin as he pushed his spectacles higher onto the bridge of his nose. Sophia was especially fetching in turquoise dyed muslin.

Hannah gasped while a slight blush stained Sophia's cheeks. Then the girl sprang into action. Despite the armful of gowns, she rushed over to him, took his hand, and then kissed it. "I have to go, Oliver. Grandmother has seamstresses in to alter whichever gown I choose for the masquerade."

"Then I suppose we shall talk at tea later." When she fled the attic and the sound of her pounding footsteps faded, he glanced at his wife. "Is all well?" Not for worlds would he let on that he'd been eavesdropping.

"Yes. Of course." She raked her gaze up and down his person. A certain heat reflected in her gorgeous eyes that lit tiny fires in his blood. "Did you enjoy your walk?"

"I did. Now I'm understanding why titled men have such sprawling estates in the country. Taking strolls over the acreage affords a man plenty of time to think and gives good exercise besides."

"Oh?" Concern creased her brow. "Do you have regrets, then?"

"Never. In fact, I have never second guessed any decision I've made. While there may have been doubts ahead of one or two of them, once I committed to it, those vanished." He shrugged. "It's simply how it's always been for me."

"I envy you that calm." Sophia took his hand and led him through a warren of aisles in a series of rooms that comprised the attics. "Have you given thought to what you might wish to be at the masquerade?"

"I'm afraid I'm not the best person to ask because I've never wished to be someone else." Would she think him too dull?

She blew out a breath. "It is playacting, Oliver, not a commitment for the next twenty years." Then his wife pulled him forward into a section of the attic that looked relatively uncluttered and featured a small square window that had been propped open with a stick. "When I pawed through the trunks back here for Hannah's costume, I came across some impressive capes, cloaks, and boots that fold over at the knee."

"Interesting. Perhaps I can masquerade as Robin Hood." Anyone who sought to steal from the rich and give to the poor held a certain fascination for him.

"I was thinking more along the lines of a highwayman," she said as she cracked open a trunk and rummaged through the contents.

Apparently, thievery was a theme in all of these costumes. "Only if a cloak becomes me."

She shot him a glance that brimmed with mischief. "Cloaks are good for everyone."

In short order, Sophia tossed him a black cloak that would fall to his hips, a satin cravat in a red color, as well as a pair of the fold-over boots.

"Perhaps we can borrow one of Gilbert's lawn shirts. He's around your size, and I know he owns one with loose-fitting sleeves." Then she hooted with excitement and from yet another trunk she pulled out a cavalier-style hat, complete with rather bedraggled feathers. "We'll replace the feathers with prettier ostrich ones, but this is perfect!"

Oliver rested his items on the top of another trunk. "Perhaps I can attempt to steal your heart during the masquerade." He hadn't meant to refer to her heart or the state of affections, but it slipped out anyway.

"What makes you think you haven't done that already?" She kept her gaze on the contents of the trunk.

Because you haven't said it.

Sure, they indulged in intercourse regularly, but that didn't mean she loved him. Hell, it didn't even mean his infatuation had progressed past that. It certainly bore further thought.

"I merely assumed I hadn't managed that feat due to you wishing to keep yourself safe, in the event I might prove less than what I've promised." Feeling a theatrical flair, Oliver shrugged out of his jacket and then removed his waistcoat. The items dropped to the top of the trunk. Then he took up the cape and fastened it about his neck. "Regardless, do I have enough of a debonaire attitude to pass as a highwayman?"

When her head came up, she studied him. Finally, she nodded. "You'll do, but perhaps you need just a bit of help." After standing, Sophia crossed to his location, took up the red cravat, and wound it about his waist. "Ah, yes. The color is terrific here. Draws the eye to your hips and other interesting… parts of your anatomy." She met his gaze with blatant need building in her depths that stirred his length. "Pair all of it with the loose-fitting shirt, and you'll be certain to attract the notice of the ladies at the ball."

"The only regard I wish for is yours." And soon, for their time was, as always, limited. His chest tightened with the thought, but the longer he peered at her, the more he *knew*. He loved this woman with all of his being, and her returning those feelings wouldn't change his stance. "As long as I have that, I'm a happy man."

Her chin trembled. So much emotion shadowed her eyes, he couldn't discern just one. "Come with me." Once she'd led him to the far wall near the window, she turned about and faced him. "Will you please hold me?"

"Of course." He pushed his spectacles up the bridge of his nose. "Are you certain you are feeling well?" But he didn't delay, for any opportunity to hold her in his arms was time well spent. He cradled her against his chest and pressed a kiss to her forehead, just as she adored.

"You have been a place of shelter and security for me since we wed." She slipped her arms around his shoulders, and when she furrowed her fingers into the short hair at his nape, a shiver of want went down his spine. "And while I appreciate that, I need… I want…" A breath of frustration escaped her. "This is so difficult to speak aloud when I cannot make sense of it in my mind."

"I know." Oliver framed her head with his hands, and when she stared up at him with eyes wide and full of both wonder and confusion, he treated her to a string of tender kisses.

"Oh, you are so good for me. You will probably never know what this last week or so has meant," she whispered seconds before she lifted onto her toes and applied herself to kissing him back.

Then he lost himself to the wonder that was his wife. He moved over her mouth, tasting, memorizing every contour and detail of two petal-soft pieces of flesh. When he eased the tip of his tongue along their seam, she opened for him, invited him in. Her moan as the kiss deepened and their tongues tangled sent the blood rushing through his shaft. The warmth of her called to him like a siren's song, and he edged a hand along her spine. At the sweet curve of her arse, he squeezed a cheek, brought her closer still to his body enough that he ground his insistent erection into her hip.

"I want you, Sophia." Now and always, but since he wasn't given the always, the now would have to suffice. He dragged his lips beneath her jaw, traced the column of her throat—such soft skin—and when he kissed a path around her bodice lined with dainty lace, she arched her back, giving him a clear invitation.

"There is nothing stopping you from acting on that impulse."

"Such a vixen." Oliver glided a hand up her back. Quickly, only fumbling twice, he popped the few buttons of her dress from their holes, and when the garment sagged about her breasts, he tugged the bodice down, taking the fabric of her petticoat with it. "Never will I tire of unwrapping you." Why the deuce had he not done it over the course of his life? It was a mystery, but he still maintained that waiting for the right woman—here—had been more than worth it.

"Being undressed by a man is rather a favorite of mine," she said, and her voice was decidedly breathless.

"Mmm." She was perfection. He took her full breasts in his hands, gently squeezed while she shivered, and then with a chuckle, he worried the nipples into tightened peaks with the pads of his thumbs. "I will always remember you like this, with fire in your eyes, a flush on your skin, and that maddening smile on your lips."

"For an American, you are certainly a rogue." She lifted a hand, and with her fingers at his nape guided his mouth to one of those pebbled buds. "You make me forget everything the second you touch me, as if you are magic."

"Perhaps it's because I love you so damned much." Oliver didn't care if she didn't return his affections or that he'd made such a declaration. He'd said it, and it made him proud. When he shifted attention to the neglected nipple, and a shuddering moan escaped her.

"You are truly the sweetest man." Sophia pulled on his cravat as tears gathered in her eyes. "But Oliver?"

"Yes?"

"Join with me as if we have all the time in the world." One of her hands curled into his shirt. "Love me like I won't expire in the next few months. I want you without inhibition; I need you with abandon."

"Don't I always?"

"Yes, and each time, I fall deeper and deeper for you. It frightens me because…"

"Because you don't want me to mourn; you don't want to leave knowing you will leave pain behind."

"Yes."

"That is life, sweeting. It's how we know we're alive. Even if I had never touched you, never joined with you, never kissed you, just merely knowing you would make me sad once you expire." He brushed his lips over hers. "Because you're wonderful."

A tiny cry left her throat then she crushed her lips to his, and so much feeling lay behind the kiss that something strong shivered down his spine. His soul rejoiced from it as it reached out for hers. Sophia didn't stop kissing him. In fact, she clung to him, apparently sought to devour him, and the raw power of that embrace knocked him for a loop.

With a growl mixed with a laugh of amusement, he walked her backward. Eventually the wall halted further movement.

She stared up at him, nipped the underside of his jaw, her fingers abstractedly plucking at this clothing. "In this moment, I want to live. God, I want that so much."

"So do I." Renewed from the attraction that snapped between

them, emboldened by the love light in her eyes, he drew up handfuls of her skirting, wadded it at her waist. "You're certain? If things grow too heated or frantic, you could—"

"—I don't care. At least I'll be with you." Her fingers curled at his nape while she drew her free hand down to manipulate the buttons of his frontfalls. "Send me flying, Oliver. Love me. Love me with the whole of your being so that I can fill you with all that I am." When his hardened length fell heavily into her palm, she moaned. "I adore the size of you."

"Now I know where Hannah has come by her penchant for plain speaking." It made his spirit soar. Oliver put a hand beneath one of her thighs and encouraged her leg upward. She curved it about his hip, anchoring her heel into his backside. It was easily the most erotic thing he'd experienced, and the fact that she was doing it added wonder to the coupling. Her body was completely open to him, an offering of sorts, while the tip of his member glanced along her sensitive flesh.

"It's quite the only way to live. Now." Sophia kissed him, and the feeling imparted in that one kiss nearly saw him undone.

"Mmm." When he flexed his hips and buried himself as deep as he could go, she moaned in pure appreciation, and the sound blended with his. "This is my favorite part." Burying himself in her honeyed heat, going as deep as he could, irrevocably joining them together, yes, he had essentially waited to live for these moments. "Ah, Sophia, how I love you." Then he captured her lips once more while resting his free hand on the wall near her head.

Then there was no more need for words. They communed by touch and the brush of lips. Sighs and sounds of enjoyment and pleasure punctuated the silence of the room. The hot, stale air of the attics disappeared as he worked his length into her body, withdrew, and joined them again merely for the joy of it. Pure need reflected on her face, but that light in her eyes as she held his gaze sent tingles through his belly. Her fingers dug into his shoulder while she wriggled her other hand between their bodies to fondle and squeeze his stones. Intense sensation slammed into him, but he gritted his teeth against those feelings, for he wanted his joining to last as long as it could. Over and over, he speared into her. She met him thrust for thrust, pulled him closer with pressure of her heel to the small of his back and the gentle squeeze on his rear.

"Oliver." The name floated on a breathless whisper. Her eyes shuddered closed, and her head lolled onto a shoulder. "More."

"Gladly." He changed his rhythm as he snaked a hand to her waist, his fingers gripping her, holding her close. With every stroke, her breasts bounced, those pink nipples hard and inviting, but he was nearly gone. "This holiday has been life-changing," he murmured while peppering her jawline with feather weighted kisses.

"You have certainly changed mine, and I…" She panted, and the muscles of her core fluttered with tiny contractions. "I… I, oh…" A shiver wracked her shoulders. "I am coming to love you, Oliver, but it terrifies me."

"Then I must try harder to set your mind at ease." Yet, he silently rejoiced, for she'd finally said the words he desperately wished to hear. He continued to work her body as if he were a maestro and she a pianoforte. Harder and harder he pushed so that they slammed against the wall. Deeper and deeper, he stroked, and shivers of pure need streaked through him. Faster and faster his hips moved. Sophia clung to his shoulders, meeting him thrust for thrust, kissing his lips, his cheek, his chin.

When he met her gaze, the emotions there confirmed what she'd already said, and it was the most beautiful thing in the world. In that moment, pieces of his soul flew into her keeping while she gifted him with pieces of hers. It was the most rewarding, romantic moment of his life.

"Give me more, Oliver. I need you harder. Bigger."

"But your heart…"

"Then give me what you will."

As he did as she'd requested, he slipped his fingers between their bodies, found that slick, swollen button at her center, and applied friction to it until she writhed against him. Though he was nearly spent, he gritted his teeth, refusing to hit release unless she came with him.

Heat tingled through his stones; he wouldn't last. "Sophia, please tell me you're close."

She didn't answer with words. Instead, she threw back her head, dug her fingernails into his shoulder while tightening her leg about his waist. A muffled scream escaped her as she apparently fell over the edge into bliss. "Oliver!"

Damn, but she was beautiful while in the throes of passion. Her enjoyment ushered in his own release, and with each of her contractions, he was sucked downward into that spiral where there was no sound. White light sprinkled with rainbows wrapped around him. Pleasure slammed into him, washed through his body in a cleansing tide. He thrust once more time, spearing her to the wall as his member pulsed.

"I trust that was to your liking," he whispered against her mouth. Good heavens, the heat of her lips, the sweetness of her pulled him back like the unrelenting tide. He could spend hours merely learning how to kiss her properly.

"It was wonderful." With a satisfied sigh, she eased her leg from around his waist, and when her knees wobbled, she giggled.

The sound went straight to his heart. "It's always a good sign when a woman is unsteady on her feet after being thoroughly loved."

"Cheeky." But she didn't offer a protest.

"Perhaps you should rest. No doubt your heart is racing, and that isn't a good thing in your condition." As she tugged her bodice back into place, he guided her to a nearby trunk and encouraged her to sit. "How do you feel?"

She pressed a hand to her throat then her chest. "Wonderfully exhausted and spent." The drowsiness in her expression provoked a grin from him. Then her gaze travelled down his body to linger on his flagging length. "Do you think we might have time to do that again before we're expected for tea?"

"Now who's the cheeky one?" Oliver tucked his member back into his trousers and did up the buttons of his frontfalls. "Give me a half hour to refract then I'll answer you, but we should be careful and not overly tax you."

"I'll worry about my health, Mr. Mattingly, and I say I'm not quite done with you." Yet she looked fatigued and exhausted and all too pale.

"Message received." Truly, this was the best day of his life, and now that they'd shared soulful moments, he felt lighter than before.

How could he let her go when God decided to take her?

CHAPTER FOURTEEN

July 20, 1819
Masquerade ball

SOPHIA'S HANDS SHOOK as she donned a glittering tiara. If she were to become a princess tonight for the ball, she might as well play it to the hilt. A glance into the cheval glass that stood in one corner of her dressing room showed the diamonds and rubies winking like mad in the candlelight and put her in mind of the stone of her engagement ring.

It had been two days since she'd coupled in the attic with Oliver, but that night she hadn't slept well, and yesterday, she'd kept to her rooms, for her chest had been tight and she'd had trouble keeping her breath. Her husband had been beside himself with worry, thinking her decline had been his fault, but she'd waved him off and told him to play lawn games with the rest of the family while they had fair weather.

Mostly, she suspected her health woes stemmed from the fact that the walls around her heart had tumbled down more quickly than she'd anticipated and now she was more than halfway in love with him. Oh, it was a development she'd hadn't wanted, for knowing her life could end at any time brought her early grief. She hadn't wished for her marriage to deepen as it had, but there was something about Oliver that had made a leisurely slide impossible.

He would mourn hard, and so would she—for him before she even expired. She would mourn for a life together she'd never had the chance to cultivate. It simply wasn't fair. Why shouldn't she live to old age with him?

Thus, the reason she'd taken to her bed where she nursed a breaking heart.

Sophia had spent a large portion of today in her rooms, taking her meals on trays, but Hannah had visited and so had Oliver, but the worry and concern in their eyes had sent her deeper into that downward spiral. Because of her health, they already felt the effects of her looming absence.

I cannot bear it any longer.

"Oh, my dear, you are lovely tonight."

"Thank you." She turned about at the sound of her mother's voice. "Hannah wished for me to go as a princess, so here I am." The yards and yards of pale lavender silk felt like clouds around her. Clear glass beads and silver spangles decorated the overskirt and lined the low bodice. "I suppose my childhood self should thrill at this night."

"You always did like those fairy stories." Her mother, dressed as the goddess Hera, perched upon a chair nearby. "I came up tonight before the festivities begin because I'm worried about you." A frown marred her mother's face. "Are you nearing the end, then, since you've kept to your rooms recently? You are in pain, even though you don't speak of it."

"I can never be certain, of course, but of late, my chest has been tight and my heart hurts." Speaking about it was almost as exhausting as going through it. Sophia dropped onto the bench of her vanity table. "Since my wedding, I haven't been as careful as I should have been, and I've certainly let various activities carry me away."

But she wouldn't trade those times for the world.

When her mother tucked an escaped tendril of hair back into her Greek-inspired updo, the thin gold bracelets on her wrist tinkled together. "You worry that you should be living the life you have left, yet wondering if you should try to extend that life by sitting around doing little more than being a decoration."

"Yes." Even now, her chest was tight. It hurt to breathe. Why was it so hot? "As of yet, there haven't been large shocks or scares, so I don't know how well my heart will hold up if I encounter one, but perhaps I'm paying now for what I've been doing." *Had* the coupling with Oliver in the attics set off a chain of events that would eventually lead to her early demise?

"I'm sorry this is even a concern for you." Compassion and sadness shadowed her mother's eyes. "I am also sorry that you have inherited your father's weak heart."

Sophia nodded. "Did Papa have an inkling he would go when he did?"

"I don't believe that he did." Her eyes took on a faraway look. No doubt her mother was remembering those last moments. "We had thrown the anniversary ball, of course, for we both did so love to entertain." A rueful smile curved her lips. "We had danced many sets that night, and he'd tucked into his dinner with gusto. After the ball, we retired and went to sleep, the same as we had always done. But he never woke up." A shrug lifted her thin shoulders. "From how he appeared in the morning, I would like to hope he passed peacefully in his sleep. But know this, my girl, your father lived his life to the hilt. He didn't hide behind that fear, even when he probably should have, knowing that *his* father expired early of the same."

"It's a delicate balance." She'd never known that about her father. Yes, he had been a larger-than-life figure to her, but perhaps if she'd been privy to his struggles and the overcoming of them, it might have helped her in her own. "The boys don't seem worried that they might fall victim to the same state."

"Of course not. They are men and wouldn't show an insecurity if they can help it." Her mother chuckled. "Though I'm more at ease knowing Arthur will marry again soon and have someone to look after him. He'll be more apt to listen to Julianna than he would me."

"He loves her to distraction." Sophia fussed with how one of her elbow-length gloves lay on her arm. "I'm glad to see that, and his children adore her."

"It's refreshing, especially after he has struggled so long in coming to terms with everything. Gilbert, though, vexes me."

"I am worried about him, but it is not my problem to solve."

"No, it is not. I suspect both he and Madelene have gotten off-track, but if they still love each other, they can fix their union." She shook her head and focused her bright gaze once more on Sophia. "But your own marriage is nothing to sneeze at. That man of yours shows himself in a good light with each passing day."

"Agreed." Her cheeks heated as her thoughts removed to how they'd spent the afternoon in the attics, at how free she'd been during those sessions, at how easy it was to forget her health concerns when in Oliver's company. "He is an extraordinary man, and I'm only just beginning to realize how much."

"Do you love him?" Her mother tilted her head slightly to one side as she rested a speculative gaze on Sophia. "When you married, you didn't. I could tell, but you shared a connection with him, and you certainly didn't waste time taking him to your bed."

The heat in her cheeks intensified. "I won't apologize for enjoying intercourse. It is something I will miss once I'm gone."

"I'm not asking you to, but I *am* asking about the state of your heart, outside of its ills."

Sophia nodded. "If I asked myself that question five days ago, the answer would have been no." She pressed her lips together as she pondered. "But now?" They had connected deeply on a soul level in the attic, and it had been both wonderful and frightening. "Yes, I believe I am in love with my husband. What he's done for me, sacrificed for both me and Hannah..." A sigh escaped her. "It's incredible."

And she hadn't had nearly enough time with him.

"I'm happy to hear that. Mr. Mattingly *is* an incredible person." Her mother smiled. "When I'd told area gentry and a few members of the *ton* that the ambassador had married my daughter, so many of them had said you were fortunate indeed, for there was no man quite like Oliver. That he's honorable and forthright and willing to help anyone he comes across."

"All traits a woman searches for in a husband." Tears sprang to her eyes. "I don't want to leave him, Mama. I don't want to leave any of you."

"I know." Her mother sprang off the chair, closed the distance, and held Sophia's head to her while she stroked a hand up and down her back. "But he's right. You mustn't spend the remainder of your time thinking on the moment when you truly will leave. There is much living yet to do, and you can still be a bright spot in all our lives until then. Enjoy being his wife."

Sophia rapidly blinked away the tears lest they fall and spot the gown. "I intend to dance at least one set tonight if I can."

"And so you should." Her mother smiled down at her. "It's a pity the rain has returned. The terrace would have been a nice distraction."

"There are other places where couples can disappear to for a few minutes." It was one of the reasons Sophia loved balls and society events. The other being the need to don pretty gowns and wear sparkling jewels. "Since my toilette is finished and I'm wearing what has to be one of the most gorgeous gowns I've ever seen, perhaps we should go down and greet guests."

Her mother nodded. "We should."

As Sophia rose to her feet, she sighed. "This can easily be the last ball I'll attend, Mama, and I intend to enjoy it until the end." Though her voice wavered on the last word, she lifted her chin and gave her mother a bright smile.

A knock on the door interrupted their conversation, but before she could answer it, the panel swung open, and Oliver came into the room, and dressed as he was like a highwayman, she couldn't help but admire him.

"Good heavens, Sophia." He stared at her with awe in his

expression. "I thought you beautiful before, but just now, you are incredible."

"Oh!" Her cheeks heated. "How nice of you to say, and you are quite something too."

"I'll leave the two of you alone," her mother said on her way to the doorway with a smile. "Don't linger, else I'll send Arthur up here after you."

Oliver didn't waste any time. He tugged her into his arms and dropped a gentle kiss to her lips. The wide brim of his cavalier hat bumped against her forehead. Then he held her a bit away in order to rake his gaze up and down her form, and his eyes darkened behind his black domino mask. It was quite comical, for he wore his spectacles over the mask, which completely gave away his identity. "The persona of a princess was a good choice. You are suited to royalty."

A laugh escaped her. "I don't know about that." She plucked a bit of lint from the shoulder of his dark cape. "However, you are every bit a highwayman. In fact, this style of clothing is wonderful on you." The black silk waistcoat provided a pleasant contrast to his white lawn shirt with the loose, flowing sleeves. He'd even worn the red sash at his waist. "I especially like the boots." Somehow, with them—and good heavens, where had he procured the rapier slung low about his hips?—it seemed as if he'd stepped out of a story book merely to dance a waltz with her before he disappeared into the mists of time at midnight.

"Perhaps I'll spirit you away to a dark corner and try to steal a kiss from you before the night is over." He waggled his eyebrows. "Or something else if we're afforded good enough privacy."

"You are incorrigible, Ambassador." But she adored that about him.

"Or is it that I merely like my wife so incredibly much that I simply need to be everywhere she is?" He swept her into the first few steps of a waltz before escorting toward the door. "Truly, though, I'm glad for this chance to show the area notables that I've won you and that I'm proud to have you on my arm."

Her heart trembled while tingles sailed down her spine. "What am I going to do with you?" She grabbed her lace-edged masquerade mask on the way from her room.

"I believe I've already given you a few ideas," he whispered and then he nuzzled her neck as they made their way along the corridor. "If you still don't know, reserve a dance for me, and I'll be the happiest of men."

"Of course." She clung to his hand. The evening would prove bittersweet, for no matter how much fun there would be had, eventually, the hands of time would advance her closer to the day where she would need to leave him.

As soon as they gained the lower floor, Hannah bounded over to them. The skirts of her pink and sage gown billowed out behind her, but the most shocking thing about her were double wings like a moth attached to her shoulders and made with wire and tulle.

"Do you like my costume, Mama?" The girl twirled so they could both have the full effect of the gown. "I'm a fairy tonight instead of what I would have been."

"It's a lovely change." Sophia touched a finger to one of the wings. "Where did these come from?"

"Uncle Gilbert and Oliver constructed them." She shot a grin at him. He returned the gesture as if he were a child himself. "Aren't they wonderful?"

"They are, and I'm quite impressed." Sophia waved at Arthur, who came out of the ballroom. "Let's go see how many people are already here. Then we shall peruse the refreshments room to see what sort of edibles we'll look forward to." When Oliver chuckled beside her, she nudged him with her elbow. "None of that, else it will be all I think about tonight."

"As if that is a bad thing," he whispered while they strolled toward the ballroom. The sound of laughter and conversation grew louder the closer they came. "Can I help it that I'm completely enamored?"

He was certainly good for her ego as well as her heart. Everything was so easy with him, as if he enhanced life around him.

"Come, you silly man. Let me introduce you to a few of my friends." If she were to die early, at least she would enjoy every second she had remaining, just as her father had done.

And she would hope those she left behind would choose to remember her fondly instead of drowning in grief.

CHAPTER FIFTEEN

OLIVER GLANCED ABOUT the ballroom of Ettesmere Park with a grin from his position near the open terrace doors. Even though a steady rain fell, the relatively cool air the precipitation brought with it did much to combat the heat in the room. This was his first masquerade, and so far, it had been amazing. With the identity of most people hidden, he had the grandest time attempting to puzzle them out.

To say nothing to how beautiful his wife was.

Currently, Sophia danced a country reel with Hannah as her partner. Both of them laughed their way through the steps, and as he watched, his chest swelled with pride. They were his immediate family, his very own, and nothing could make him happier.

"The two of them are quite the pair."

He glanced up as the earl came over dressed as the Roman, Mark Antony, complete with a red cloak and a breast plate. Where he'd procured such things remained a mystery, as did the question of why he wasn't wearing his mask.

"Indeed, they are, Your Lordship." It was a bit of an annoyance trying to see past the slits of his domino mask and through his spectacle lenses, but it was manageable. Once more, Oliver rested his attention on Sophia and Hannah. Since it was a special occasion and due to Sophia's condition, Hannah had been allowed to attend the ball, at least for a short time. How could a man not smile when seeing them together? That bond between mother and child had never been stronger, even though all too soon it would break, and he'd be handed the broken pieces. "Are you enjoying the ball? You mother certainly has a knack for planning these sorts of things."

Colorful tissue paper flowers festooned the ceiling corners. The same decorated the windows and swags of them were draped over the terrace doors. Candlelight twinkled from the brilliant chandelier centered over the middle of the dance floor, while numerous potted ferns and other plants were grouped in strategic places around the perimeter that gave a sense of privacy to wallflowers and others who weren't in the mood for socializing.

"Oh, quite, on both counts." He shot Oliver a look that brimmed with ruefulness. "Though, if I'm being honest, I cannot wait until the ball comes to an end. It's not natural for a man's arms and legs to be on display." As the earl gestured to indicate his form, mottled red color crept up his neck. "Additionally, the lack of structure a tunic provides in various other portions of the anatomy is vastly unsettling."

Despite the utter seriousness of the conversation, Oliver couldn't help his chuckle. "While I can sympathize, I do admire your bravery for donning such an outfit. Was it your idea?"

The earl snorted. "Hardly." With his gaze, he searched the crowded ballroom. "Ah, there she is. The culprit."

Oliver nodded when he recognized the earl's intended, Julianna. She had dressed in a fair imitation of Cleopatra, though her gown was far less revealing that the original no doubt had been. "It's odd, isn't it, that when the ladies speak, we have no choice but to fall victim to their suggestions?" He pushed his spectacles back up the bridge of his nose. With the mask, the glasses simply wouldn't stay in place.

"That is exactly how it feels." The other man met Oliver's gaze and shrugged. "I had been perfectly comfortable and capable of making my own decisions, but then along came Julianna and everything changed. My thoughts, my wishes, were no longer my own, and suddenly I'm listening to her counsel on everything."

"They change us, make us into better versions of ourselves," he said in a soft voice as he found Sophia. The country reel ended, and though she pressed a hand to her chest, her expression didn't suggest she was overly fatigued or in distress. "Honestly, the right woman makes us believe in ourselves and what we can accomplish." When Sophia glanced up and their gazes connected through her sparkling mask, she waved. That smile would forever be seared across his consciousness for all the heat and welcome it contained.

"That is a good way of looking at it." Then the earl rested the whole of his attention on Oliver. "You have been good for my sister, by the by. The change in her has been remarkable."

"I don't know what you mean. Hasn't she been the same woman she has always been?" He frowned when a couple of gentlemen approached her on the sidelines while Hannah scampered off to presumably find entertainment or trouble.

"Don't play coy, Ambassador." Amusement rumbled in Ettesmere's laughter. "Before you came along, Sophia moped about the house, keeping inside, hardly daring to do anything that might bright on an attack of her heart." The skin at the corners of his eyes crinkled with a grin. "Now, it's as if she's found renewal. She dances, joins us for lawn games, takes long walks with us, quietly gives out advice even if we don't want it. Essentially, you've given her back her former self."

Oliver shook his head. "I don't know about that. The only thing I've done is told her that she should live the days remaining to her without fear. It's all anyone should do when faced with the knowledge that she is."

"So modest." The earl clapped a hand to Oliver's shoulder. The jostling sent his spectacles down the bridge of his nose. "While I was opposed to the suddenness of your marriage, I can see now it was exactly what my sister needed." All the gaiety faded from the earl's expression, replaced with worry. "Sophia is a woman who thrives best when she has a husband by her side. More than anyone I've ever known, my sister is the epitome of romance and hope. She champions love, and I'm glad you stepped in that gap for her."

Heat crept up the back of Oliver's neck at the praise. "I only did what my own heart told me. It's not a lie when I say from the first moment I saw her, I knew she was the one for me." People might scoff at the possibility of love at first sight, but he was living proof it happened, and what was more, it could put down deep roots. When he glanced again in Sophia's direction, sharp shards of jealousy speared through his chest, for she continued to chat with those two men. For the first time since they'd wed, he entertained the possibility that she might not be happy with him.

Did she regret marrying an American who didn't possess a fortune or hold a title?

"I can respect that. You know immediately what you want and why, and you don't accept anything less." The earl nodded. "It inspires me." He peered more closely into Oliver's face. "You've gone beyond being enamored with her, though."

"Perhaps." Oliver flicked his focus back to Ettesmere. "In the short time that Sophia has become my wife, I've fallen irrevocably into love with her. It's always been my intent to distract her from her fate and give her the best life that I can." He forced a hard swallow into his throat. "However, I won't lie. When death takes her, I'll be devastated, but I'm so entirely grateful that I'll be able to parent Hannah. At least in that way, I'll still have a piece of Sophia to take into the future."

God, it sounded pathetic, and it only made his chest hurt to speak about his wife's impending death. How did a man recover from knowing the greatest love of his life and then losing it?

"How well I know the conundrum, my friend." Sadness temporarily shadowed the earl's eyes. "For years I was lost to that grief. It wasn't until Julianna entered my life that I began to realize I could possibly find a love like that a second time."

"You mean well, of course, Your Lordship, but just now, I

cannot contemplate or even comprehend a life without Sophia in it, let alone entertain the thought of marrying again." The steady sound of the rain in the open terrace doors brought him back into the moment, and for the time being, his wife was still very alive and frankly the most beautiful creature he'd ever seen. "I'm not going to talk as if she's already gone. That's not fair to either of us."

"Fair enough, and I quite understand." The earl offered a small smile. "Thank you for what you've done for her. I wish I had words of wisdom to give you, for lesser men would have paled and not made the sacrifice at all knowing there wouldn't be a future. We all should live by your example, Ambassador."

"You flatter me." He put his spectacles back into place. Damned mask.

"I speak the truth." The earl's expression brightened, for Sophia had moved their way and was nearly upon them. "You are an honorary Winterbourne, and I don't say that lightly."

There was no time for a reply.

"Two of my favorite people," she said as she joined them, trailing the faint scent of roses. "What were you discussing with such intensity?"

He and the earl exchanged a glance. "How fortunate we are to have both you and Julianna in our lives," Oliver said smoothly as he took her hand and brought it to his lips. "And since the earl's nuptial ceremony is in five days, it was only natural we discussed marriage." Not that any of it was a lie per say, but she didn't need to know the exact subject matter.

"Oh, I'm so glad you're nearly wed, Arthur." Sophia touched his arm. "You and Julianna will make a splendid couple, and she'll do you proud as a countess."

"I appreciate that." Genuine affection lined his face. "It's quite surreal yet." He glanced across the room. "If you'll excuse me, though? I promised I'd sit with Julianna's father for a bit tonight before she takes him home."

Oliver nodded. The care and concern the whole family

showed toward each other as well as their extended relatives never failed to amaze. "Enjoy the remainder of your evening." He squeezed Sophia's fingers. "And now, it seems they are preparing for a waltz. If you will indulge me?"

"Of course." She glanced between them with narrowed eyes behind her sparkling mask. "Why do I have the distinct feeling you are not telling me everything?"

"Such gammon, Sister." The earl leaned in a bussed her cheek. "Enjoy yourself."

Once he left, Oliver led her to an open spot on the dance floor. "It's a pity the rain hasn't let up. I'll wager a moonlit walk in the gardens would have been just the thing to add to the success of the evening."

She rested the fingers of her free hand on his shoulder. "Didn't you promise to spirit me off somewhere else? That you said rain wouldn't deter you?" Her eyes sparkled with mischief.

"I did indeed, but first, I want this waltz with you. That is, if you are feeling well enough?" Always, her health came first.

"I am. Just slightly fatigued."

"Good." When the opening notes floated into the air, he set them off into the first steps. "Where is Hannah?"

"She went into the refreshment room. Who knows what trouble she'll find after that, for she'll probably avoid me to postpone my order for her to retire."

"Let her enjoy this moment of her childhood." When the steps of the dance took Sophia temporarily away from him, he watched her, and his heart brimmed with pride. As she returned to him, he grinned. "There is something delicious and naughty about dancing with a woman in disguise."

Her laughter set fire to his blood. "Why, Ambassador, are you flirting with me?"

"Perhaps I am." He dared to pull her closer. "Truth be known, though, I am tempted to spirit you into the first unused room we come to tonight and do unspeakable things to you." As he'd talked to the earl, it had been pressed upon him that his time with Sophia was limited indeed. And if he were to lose her, he wanted her to know exactly how loved and adored she was; he hadn't a lifetime for that.

"You have my attention." Her eyes darkened, but before either of them could say more, the steps took her away from him.

Oliver's length twitched to life as soon as she rejoined him. The warmth of her in his arms, the scent of her, the soft play of candlelight on her face, the sparkle of light on the beadwork of her gown worked to send him into a spiral of need that would only end with them both naked and satisfied.

He dared to put his lips to the shell of her ear and whispered, "I want you. Right now. In any way you'll receive me."

Twin spots of color blazed on Sophia's cheeks. From the exertion of the dance or from his words, he couldn't say. "How do you know that I won't take advantage first?"

"Oh? Then you think to ambush me?"

"Not exactly, for I'd want your full cooperation." Again, the steps took her from him, but her eyes never left his. When she returned, there was no mistaking the blatant need in those blue depths. "In fact, tonight since I'm feeling quite heated, I might take my time in working you over before we finally join."

Oliver cleared his throat. His fingers tightened on her hip. "Meaning what?"

"Just this." She dropped her voice so that he had to draw her closer still in order to hear. "I would order you stripped down for my inspection, but you should keep the domino mask on."

Perhaps he didn't despise the mask after all. "That is a good start." The images her words conjured had desire rushing through his member and tingling at the base of his spine.

"Agreed. After that, I'd kneel before you, being certain to lick every centimeter of your erection." Her words sailed out on a bare whisper, but there was no mistaking her meaning. "Then, I'd take you into my mouth, over and over and over again, encourage you to go so deep that when I swallow, the muscles in my throat would massage your tip."

Oh, God.

"Impressive," he managed to gasp out at the same moment that he missed a step. Then he was obliged to put his spectacles back into place.

Sophia chuckled. "Some say it's not ladylike, or the act more suited for harlots, but there are moments when it gives me immense pleasure to do that." For the last time, the dance took her away from him, but when she returned, he nearly begged her to continue the story. "And perhaps when you were almost on the edge of spending, I'd release you but make you watch as I pleasured my breasts with *my* fingers to further bring you to that precipice."

It was more than he could bear just now. His engorged length pressed painfully against the front of his rather tight breeches, and he was forever glad he'd worn black over tan. "What do you intend after that?"

"When you simply cannot endure any more teasing, I'll push you onto your back, straddle you, and then take your impressive equipage into my wet and very needy heat." How she managed to make her voice sound like a smoky purr, he would never know, but he wanted to throw her over his shoulder. "I would work you over faster and faster, bobbing up and down harder and harder, impress upon you that you are mine as I claim you until we are both sweaty and lost to passion."

A shudder lanced down his spine. "That sounds like just the thing to pass a rainy night." Now he wanted her beyond measure. It didn't matter the unmasking would occur in just over thirty minutes, he had to couple with his wife else he'd embarrass himself. Finally, the waltz came to an end, and he was forced to relinquish his grip on her but stood staring as if he were a green boy at university. "I can honestly say that was the most interesting waltz I've ever had."

"Good." Sophia smiled and her gaze dropped to his mouth. She made no move to leave the dance floor as couples flowed around them. "I am going abovestairs to our room, for I believe

I've become overly taxed and need to take to my bed for a while." A wink followed the obvious lie.

"I'm sorry to hear that. Do you wish for assistance up the stairs?" he asked, and if possible, his cockstand swelled further. "After all, I *am* a concerned husband."

"That might be best." She did a fair imitation of sagging and leaning into his side as he put an arm about her waist. "I might need some very *specific* attention."

Truly, he was the most fortunate man alive. Perhaps there was something to this living as there were no tomorrow. And above everything, he loved his wife.

CHAPTER SIXTEEN

July 22, 1819

SOPHIA'S SPIRITS RAISED exponentially, for the rain that had plagued the area for the past three days had finally cleared and left behind blue skies with warm sunshine. Both she and Hannah were beside themselves, for there was a picnic in the offing for the afternoon, and Oliver had spearheaded the outing as a surprise.

"There is something truly lovely about walking through the world after rain has come." She held hands with her daughter while the other rested securely in the crook of Oliver's right arm. This little family of hers was too precious for words, and she remained amazed that she'd been fortunate enough to secure both Hannah's future as well as her husband's. "The air smells fresh and new, and the grass sparkles where the raindrops cling to it."

"I see wetness, Mama," said the practical Hannah. One of the kittens—the white and orange one—trailed after her. He had refused to remain in the basket Hannah carried. While that one seemed to enjoy adventures outside, its companion kitten preferred to remain inside.

"Well, yes, there is that." She chuckled, as did Oliver. "You must use your imagination a little bit."

"Would you enjoy a bouquet of wildflowers today?"

"Always." Soon, the season for the blooms would be over… as would her existence. "There is never a day when I won't enjoy flowers."

Hannah nodded. "Then as soon as we choose a spot for our picnic, I'll pick some for you." She smiled. "So will Oliver."

"What?" The ambassador looked baffled. "I rather thought to enjoy the time at the side of the creek. It's more emboldened than the stream at the other side of the property. A smaller sister of a river, if you will, and I would imagine with all the rain we've had, it will have more power."

"No, silly." Hannah laughed as if that was the funniest joke she'd ever heard. "I named this kitten Oliver. Since he's a boy."

"I see." Oliver—Sophia's husband—glanced at her with an expression of confusion mixed with pleasure. Clearly, he did not. "Why would you name a kitten after me?"

"Because he's nice, and he makes me happy, and he's good to talk to. Just as you are." Her grin widened as she rested her attention on Sophia. "Do you want to know what I named the other kitten?"

"Dare I guess that it is called Sophia?"

"No." Hannah snickered. "I named him Gilbert, because he's grouchy like my uncle."

"Of course." Sophia shot a glance at Oliver, who shrugged but chuckled. "Your Uncle Gilbert is in a mood, of that there is no doubt." Again, she wondered if it had anything to do with the state of his marriage, for she'd more or less forgotten about everything over the last week or so while she'd committed to living her own life.

"Do you think he would like a bouquet, too?"

Sophia squeezed her daughter's fingers. "It couldn't hurt. Maybe they'll cajole him into better spirits once he sees all the colorful flowers."

"Good." Hannah released her hand. "I'm going to go right now and pick them. Then I'll run back to the manor and give one of the bouquets to Uncle Gilbert."

"What about our picnic lunch?" Oliver asked as he hefted the lidded basket. "I might eat all the food before you return."

"You won't." Hannah waved to him. "Truly, you will spend your time flirting with Mama, probably kissing her, and you'll forget to eat until I come back and scold you for it." Her sigh sounded all too grown up. "*Someone* will have to look after you once Mama isn't here, so you'd best come to terms with that."

Oliver cleared his throat. "Actually, I intend to employ a few tutors once we're in London to occupy your time while I'm involved in business." One of his eyebrows rose as he peered at her. "At least one of them will travel with us when the need arises. I refuse to neglect your education, no matter what you have planned."

"Fine." Hannah shrugged. "But keeping house for you might be fun, especially while in London. I've always wondered about how a household is run."

"Then you agree to the tutors? I'd like you to learn at least two foreign languages. Not only will it help when we travel, but it will serve you well into adulthood."

"I agree. Besides, the tutor who visits me now doesn't understand I'm more advanced than the lessons she gives me. A challenge is most welcome." Then she scampered away, the basket swinging on her arm while the kitten raced after her through the tall meadow grass.

"She is quite the dervish and will prove a handful for anyone I bring on as staff," Oliver said as he pushed his spectacles back into place on the bridge of his nose. "I have a feeling I won't be allowed to linger in mourning for long."

That knowledge both cheered her and sent knots of worry into her belly. "Hannah is becoming a bit managing, though. Perhaps it stems from not being properly stimulated with schoolwork." That might have been a mistake on her part, for Sophia had grown lax in her daughter's education ever since the news of her diseased heart came to light.

"She is merely concerned. Too much death is truly too much. It changes one's perspective." He remained silent for a few seconds. "However, she is too young to put herself on the shelf, so to speak, merely to look after her stepfather." A sigh escaped him. "I'd hoped I haven't given her the impression that I'm a doddering fool already."

Sophia snorted with laughter. "I'm sure she doesn't think that." She squeezed her fingers on his arm. "Though, it is sweet she wants to take care of you. It's incredible how well she's adopted you as a parent."

And I won't be there to see how their relationship progresses.

"Perhaps, but I meant what I said. She will have a well-rounded education. At least I can do that much for her."

"Yes." A ball of unshed tears lodged in her throat. Oliver would no doubt go on to do great things in his role as an ambassador. Hannah would grow into a wise and well-traveled young lady whose mind would be opened seeing the world. Truly, she would become a force to be reckoned with, and she would have to do that without her mother's support.

"It makes me sad all over again that the two of you will have adventures without me, but at the same time, I'm glad you'll have each other." She looked away, for she didn't want him to see her with tears.

Again.

"I cannot imagine how this time must be for you," he said in a low voice. "Certainly bittersweet but regretful."

"Yes." She released her hold on his arm. Moving away from him, she concentrated on the meadow grass and the slight dampness of her hem. The walking dress of ivory muslin stamped with raspberry-colored rosebuds was another favorite and made her look a bit more youthful than her one and forty years. "Don't forget me, Oliver."

That sounded like the worst thing in the world. Had she made enough of an impression on him that he would always hold her in his mind with fondness?

"As if that is even possible." Quickly, he caught her up, took possession of her hand, and promptly kissed the back. When he met her gaze, the intensity of his stole her breath. "Sweeting, you are imprinted on my soul, my heart, my brain. There is not chance on this Earth that I will ever forget you or what you've meant to me in the short time we've known each other."

Her chin trembled. "I appreciate that, but it only means you'll hurt longer and harder once I'm gone, and that was something I wished to avoid."

"It will mean I loved you to the best of my ability, and that I used my heart instead of letting it linger fallow." He tugged her into a loose embrace. The picnic basket jostled against her hip. "And it will be my pain, for I will miss you fiercely, but at least I was able to love you for as long as I could."

Before she could reply, he claimed her lips with a kiss so tender and romantic that it brought tears into her eyes. Gently, he made love to her mouth right there in the meadow where anyone passing in a carriage might see them, and it was one of the best moments she'd ever passed. All too soon, he pulled away merely to peer into her face.

"I guess Hannah was right." A self-conscious chuckle escaped him, but his eyes had darkened slightly behind his spectacle lenses. "I've already been distracted by kissing you and we haven't even reached our picnic destination."

Heat infused her cheeks. How had she fallen so hard so fast for this man who lit her soul and fired her imagination? To say nothing of how he'd smashed down the walls around her heart like a hero with a sword of old. "Then perhaps we shouldn't linger here, for the sooner we set out our blanket, the sooner we can return to kissing before Hannah returns."

"In this we are of one mind." Oliver slipped an arm about her waist and set them into motion once more.

Sophia relaxed into his side. He was strong and wonderful, and he smelled so good! "Do you believe that the heat and passion between us would have been this powerful if I wasn't due to die soon?"

"That might have had a little to do with it, but truly, as soon as I saw you, I knew you would be my wife." He squeezed his fingers at her waist. "Sometimes, two people are just attracted to each other regardless of the circumstances."

"Perhaps." Unbidden, her mind jumped back to the masquerade ball two nights prior. After blatantly teasing him with her words, they'd had removed upstairs for a quick, frantic bout of intercourse that set her heart to racing dangerously fast. Afterward, she'd taken the opportunity to rest, and in that it wasn't a lie, for when her mother had come up to check on her, she'd truly been exhausted and lying beneath the bedclothes.

The fact she'd corrupted her husband into doing such things had only made him appeal to her more. And love making was such a delicious way to pass the time. Hers was limited so why not throw caution to the wind?

She came back to the present with a sigh. There was no cause to worry over any of it, for she would leave this mortal coil soon enough. Would he eventually marry again? He was still young enough that he might wish for children later in his life. The thought sent a swift stab of jealousy through her chest. If things had been different, that could have been her, but in looking back over her life as she'd spent it, there were no regrets. She'd loved both of her previous husbands to distraction; it was no different with Oliver.

Fate was fickle and oftentimes unforgiving, and it was up to each of them to enjoy the time they were given.

Eventually, they arrived at the creek, and just as he'd predicted, it had swollen its banks from the recent rains. A fairly strong current moved the muddy waters, but it was a lovely area. Beneath a stand of oak trees, Oliver began the task of spreading out a worn quilt whose colors had faded in places and was stained in the others while she stood at the edge of the water and peered into those muddled depths. That rushing current called to her, whispered into her ear, beckoned to her to investigate, but for the time being, she ignored it.

When he called to her, Sophia gladly joined him on the quilt. The gorgeous day plus his company and the sound of the gurgling creek waters worked together to relax her.

"This is exactly what I needed today." She smiled as Oliver rested his back against the stout trunk of an oak tree. He'd been very much in the same repose that seemingly long-ago day when she'd told Hannah of her heart condition, the day he'd given the child the kittens. Then, as well as now, he had the power to settle her nerves and usher in a feeling of calm.

And oh, how she loved him!

"I'm always glad to be of service." He stretched out legs encased in tight-fitting trousers in a brown color. The slight scuff on the left toe of his boot and the brown tweed of his waistcoat—obviously a favorite—put her in mind of a gentleman of leisure, when he was anything but. "I brought one of those Gothic novels that are your favorite in the event you'd like for me to read a couple of chapters aloud."

"So romantic." She hitched up her skirts and crawled over to his location. "I still cannot fathom why some other woman didn't snap you up."

He rolled his eyes. "If she had, then you and I would never have met." One hand rested on the edge of the picnic basket. "Also, your superior cook has put a few of your favorites as well as Hannah's into our lunch. There is even a carafe of tea, though I rather doubt it has retained its warmth, but even cold tea is preferable to none. Isn't that the English way of thinking?"

"Oh, you adorable thing." Unable or unwilling to remain parted from him, Sophia climbed into his lap, straddling him with her skirts bunched between them.

Immediately, his arms went around her, and she relieved him of his top hat, tossing it to the side. "Or we could spend a few minutes doing other things that have nothing to do with luncheon."

"That is perfectly acceptable. Might as well since once Hannah returns, we'll have no choice but to act proper."

"Proper, I've found, is much overrated," he murmured and slipped a hand up her spine to tangle in her hair.

"Indeed." This time, she initiated the kiss, and all too soon the embrace grew heated. Over and over, she plundered his mouth, sought out his tongue with hers, for that thrust and parry of a French-style kiss was one of her favorite things to do with a man.

Oliver, as was his wont, refused to be a passive participant in any of their embraces. He broke the kiss merely to drag his lips down the side of her throat. When he followed the cut of her bodice, she trembled in his hold, and with a smug chuckle, he took one of her taut nipples into his mouth and worried it through the thin fabric of her dress. The other he rubbed and rolled until her back arched and she writhed from his erotic attentions.

"It's unseemly for a woman my age to enjoy carnal relations this much," she managed to gasp out as her head lolled onto one shoulder. The evidence of his desire rubbed against her center, and it only served to ramp her need.

"Nonsense." He delved a hand beneath her skirting and seconds later, those questing fingers were between her splayed thighs to play at her sensitive button. A chuckle left his throat when she uttered a moan mixed with a sigh and curled her fingers into his lapel. "Physical pleasures can—and should—be enjoyed at any age. And if I had the honor of growing old with you, I could guarantee we would have indulged long after our hair turned gray."

With a tiny cry, she claimed his mouth in a savage kiss while he continued to rub that nubbin for all he was worth. It took next to no time for her to fall over the edge into bliss with a soft-pitched cry; perhaps that spoke to his skill or the fact that she enjoyed these times all too much, or perhaps her body, changing as it grew older, was more inclined to hit release sooner.

It mattered not, and temporarily she went blind and deaf as waves of sensation rushed over her. Finally, Sophia sagged into his chest, and as his arms once more went around her as he held her close. The race of her heart, the sudden strike of heat that enveloped her body, the contractions that rocked her core all worked into ushering her into a state of exhaustion where she wanted nothing more than to lie down and rest.

No doubt the end was drawing near, but now, in this one moment, she didn't care, for she had Oliver and he had her.

Eventually, she stirred. "Shall I return the favor?" Teasing him beyond the edge was another of her favorite things.

"Not just yet." He pressed a kiss to her damp forehead. "We both know that Hannah will return shortly, and I'd rather not appear in such a scandalous position."

That tugged a smile from her. Already, he doted on the child. "Then tonight."

"Most definitely." His grin was dazzling as she eased from his lap and into a standing, though wobbly, stance.

"Good." A sense of lightheadedness plagued her, but with a shake of her head and a few practice steps, the feeling passed. Worry knotted in her belly. How many days—hours—did she have left to her? "Since I'm overheated, I'm going to stand at the creek's edge, perhaps splash some water on my chest and face. Then we'll do justice to Cook's picnic."

"Be mindful, love. It would only take one misstep for you to have a fall."

"I will." Good heavens, the heat on her skin made her want to rip off her clothes and jump into the waters merely to cool herself. Couple that with the unrelenting exhaustion that had steadily built over the last handful of months, and it became something of a concern. Where they the final symptoms of her diseased heart? Was that what her father had felt shortly before his demise? With those thoughts floating through her mind, Sophia moved to the creek's edge.

Hannah, please come back soon. I want to see you one last time before I go.

CHAPTER SEVENTEEN

AFTER A FEW moments of watching Sophia at the creek side, Oliver let his eyes drift closed as he willed his rampant cockstand to fade. His wife was voracious when it came to all things carnal; he'd never met anyone quite like her before, and though he was thoroughly glad to indulge her, he only hoped that added stimulation and excitement wouldn't hasten her premature demise.

It was only a matter of time before she experienced that one large shock that would cause her heart to seize.

She assumed he hadn't noticed that her symptoms had increased and now came at greater frequency, but he had. Of course, he had. Sophia was his life, his very reason for being at present, and he wouldn't give her up without a fight.

A sense of pride filled his chest, for he'd given her the best end of life he could have possibly provided, and what was more, he and the Winterbournes had become close as a family. That bond would serve him and Hannah well as they attempted to traverse the future without her.

A sharp cry of fear rent the air and brought his eyes open. A weird sucking sort of sound followed. "Sophia?" He scanned the immediate area as well as the creek side, and he watched in horrified fascination as his wife, who'd been kneeling at the side, tumbled into the seething water due to the crumbling earth upon which she'd perched. No doubt the strain of the rains and the swelling creek had deteriorated it.

And now she was floundering in the water.

"Sophia!" He was on his feet in seconds, and shoving a hand through his hair, Oliver rushed to where she'd last stood, but time seemed to have slowed down. The rush of the swollen creek, the sharp, earthy scent of both the water and the mud clogged his nose, the heat of the sun as it beat down upon his back, the sounds of her frantic struggles and splashes all worked to send panic through his chest and fear twisting down his spine.

"Oliver, help!" She threw out an arm, but the fast-moving current prevented her from coming close to the bank.

Brown pieces of the bank continued to crumble beneath his boots, so he followed the creek even as she attempted to gain her footing on the slippery bottom.

"Please, try to grab hold of anything you can find." There were some medium-sized boulders within the creek, but due to the muddy water, she might not be able to find them.

"I cannot." With a squeal, Sophia ducked beneath the water where it had pulled her under.

His heart lodged in his throat. "Sophia!" But then her head broke the surface. The current had tugged her a few feet from him.

"I'm trying!" Again, she went beneath the surface, and when she came back up, she coughed and sputtered. "The bottom is slippery. There is no purchase." She grabbed at exposed tree roots, branches that floated in the water, had nearly grasped a patch of grass at the bank's edge, but the current worked against her effort. The water carried her body as if she were a child's doll, and her drenched skirting probably weighed her down.

Oh, dear God.

Time accelerated once more. His pulse pounded in his temples while every muscle he possessed went taut. He couldn't lose her now. Not like this. If he didn't do something she would surely drown. "I'm coming after you." Oliver darted over the grass as he followed the creek's direction. Once more Sophia went beneath the surface. Never had he asked if she knew how to swim, and the fact that she might not terrified him. With his heart in his throat, he frantically scanned the water, hoping to see any glimpse of her glorious blonde hair or the ivory dress she wore.

Finally, she emerged, yet another few feet off from his location. "Sophia!"

"Oliver!" Her wail held so much terror in it that his heart threated to burst from all the fear it carried. "I'm so tired." She coughed and spat water. "My arms won't obey my command."

"Summon strength, love. I'm coming after you." As Oliver vaulted through a cluster of cattails, mud sucked at his boots, but he continued on with as much determination as he could muster. He kept his attention fixed to the rapidly churning creek water and where Sophia bobbed, temporarily waylaid by a large tree branch.

"I'm stuck." Her announcement came with so much fear that his own chest heaved. "My dress is snagged. It's pulling me; I cannot get free."

"Dear God, keep her safe until I can reach her." Never in his life had he been so frightened as he was now. His hands were cold, his mouth dry, and his stomach muscles quaked. "I'm coming in." When she screamed because the tree branch had caught in the current and was dragging her with it, he looked again at the water. Her head bobbed above the water line, so close to him that the terror was evident in her overly pale face. Her hair lay plastered to her head.

"Help!"

That terror-filled entreaty spurred him into action. "Hang on." Oliver scrambled down the muddy bank. Water sloshed over his boots. There was nothing for it but to dive into the angry, murky creek and hope for the best. With his heart pounding hard and his stomach in knots, he launched from the bank.

Immediately, cold water broke over his body, closing him into it, drenching his clothes and tearing at him with greedy fingers, but he pushed toward the surface. Truly, the swollen creek was a force to be reckoned with. Water droplets dotted his spectacle lenses, but thank goodness, he still had them.

"Oliver!"

"Sophia!" He wasn't the strongest of swimmers, but a man with a purpose and everything to lose was quite motivated. Stroke after stroke, he moved toward her location in a diagonal line. The tree branch had once more stalled, held up by a boulder, which would buy him time. "Try to keep your head above the water." As if that suggestion was so easy. Already, he'd had to spit out foul water. It stung his eyes, making it even more difficult to see and gain his bearings.

"I'm so tired." Her voice was weak, and that brought with it a new terror. Was this the large shock that would finally take her life? "It is too hard to fight."

"Do it for me. Try for Hannah." Another two strokes carried him to her and the branch, but it was a constant fight against the current that wished to sweep them both away.

She shook with exposure and fright by the time he joined her. "The skirting is hopelessly snagged. I cannot unravel it." Exhaustion had seeped into her voice.

"I will take care of it. You just keep holding onto that branch."

As best he could with the current jostling and yanking at him, Oliver clung to the gnarled wood with one hand while he explored her skirting with the other. Ducking beneath the muddy water line, he attempted to keep his eyes open for as long as he could before they burned too much. The branch was quite large and the bulk of it was beneath the water. Sure enough, the delicate muslin had been snagged and the yards of fabric wrapped about the debris. The water had done the rest, and Sophia was more or less a prisoner of her skirting.

Once he'd broken the surface once more, he jerked his head in the hopes of removing his sopping hair from his face. "I'm going to need to tear the dress. It's the only way to free you."

"Do it." She nodded, but he didn't trust how pale her skin had grown. Her lips held a faint bluish tinge. "I'm fading."

"Stay with me." Oliver grabbed a handful of her skirts where they remained snagged on the branch. It was only a matter of time that the current would quicken, and the branch would continue on its way. Using strength he didn't know he had, he wrenched at the fabric. Though it was wet, it eventually tore, and he kept on with his task until a large panel of the gown had come free. She would have to endure embarrassment when returning to the manor house, but at least she would be alive. "You're free."

With a cry, Sophia she clung to him, her arms securely about his shoulders. "Please don't let go." She shivered in his hold.

"Never." He glanced toward the creek bank. It would be a perilous crossing, but damned if he wouldn't try and extricate them both. Pressing a kiss to her wet temple, he forced down a hard swallow. "I'm going to try to swim back to the bank. Do you have enough strength to hold tight to me?"

"Yes." Her voice wasn't as strong as he would have liked, but he couldn't worry about that now.

"Good." His pulse still pounded as he gauged the distance between the tree branch and the bank. "It will seem as if we're moving too far down, but it's easier than fighting the current. Ready?" A few yards away, there was a stretch of grass bank that he could hopefully use to pull them both out of the water.

Sophia nodded.

Though his body already ached from exertion and the relatively cold temperature of the water, Oliver released his hold on the tree branch. Immediately, the current caught at his body, pressed Sophia more tightly into him, but he wrapped one arm around her waist and used the other to execute awkward half-strokes that would hopefully pull them both toward that grass.

He moved diagonally through the current. Sophia's whimpers in his ear both alarmed and comforted him. And still he concentrated on the task at hand. Water continuously splashed into his face, stung his eyes, speckled his lenses, but he ignored it all. His first priority was getting his wife to safety.

Soon enough, his shin bumped what would have been the natural creek bank had not the recent rains swollen the waterway. Ordinarily, the creek probably would have come to his thighs, but trying to find purchase on the slippery bottom with the waves smacking him at chest level made everything more difficult. "I'm going to give you a boost, but I need you to climb upward until you clear the current. Can you do that for me?"

An expression of shock etched her face, but she gave him a curt nod.

"Good. Here we go." Turning them about so that the raging current slammed against his back, Oliver put both hands at her waist, and with clenched teeth, he heaved her out of the water and then released her.

Sophia landed on the patch of water-logged grass. She scrambled upward, grabbing at the grass with both hands until her fingers were muddy. At some point during her impromptu swim, she'd lost a slipper. The backside of her dress was, of course, gone, but the linen shift kept her from being exposed, and she climbed.

"Mama!" Hannah arrived at that moment, and he breathed a sigh of relief. She dropped the flower bouquet that she carried. The scattered blooms provided an odd splash of color in the drama. "Oliver?"

"Help your mother. Get her to dry land." When the girl did exactly that, he took hold of the grass and began the task of pulled himself upward as well. The mud-slick bank proved a challenge, but finally he gained the more solid ground at the side of the gurgling water. He collapsed onto his back as his chest heaved and his heart raced. *Dear God*, he did not wish to do that again any time soon. "Is she well? Please tell me she's still breathing," he finally croaked out and turned his head to glance at Sophia, who lay on her side facing away from him.

"She hasn't moved." Panic threaded through Hannah's voice. "Her eyes are closed. What should I do?"

Well, damn. Oliver's mouth tasted of grime and dirt. Grit crunched against his clenched teeth. "I'll have a look at her." As every muscle in his body protested, he scrambled to his knees and then crawled the short distance to his wife. "Help me move her onto her back."

"Is Mama going to die?" Hannah's eyes were wide and full of worry as she rested on her knees. Obviously, strain was becoming too much for her.

"I don't know." Gently, Oliver eased Sophia onto her back. When she still didn't stir, he hauled her body into his lap with her head resting on his chest. "Sweeting, please let us know you are well." Fear put a waver into his voice, but he didn't care. This was no time to be strong. Hannah needed to see that emotions were a part of life and that it didn't make one weak to show them.

"Why isn't she saying anything?" A whine had set up in Hannah's voice mixed with fright. "Is she dead?"

"Give it some time."

Finally, Sophia opened her eyes, and he'd never been so glad to see those blue depths in all his life. She stared up at him. Realization clouded her face as well as shock. "I didn't die."

"No, love, you didn't." He grinned, and with a glance at Hannah, he brushed the wet hair from Sophia's face.

"But I should have. That was the largest shock I've experienced since I was given the news of my condition. The doctor told me to avoid anything of that nature." Awe lingered in her voice along with fear. Slowly, she brushed at the droplets of water that splashed upon her cheek from his dripping hair. "*Why* didn't I die?"

Then that same awareness plowed into his chest with the force of a blow. His wife was correct. She hadn't expired, and by all rights should have. If her heart was truly as weak and diseased as her doctor had indicated, she shouldn't have been able to survive the terror of being swept away in a rain-swollen creek and the fight for survival afterward.

"No, you didn't." But why? He stared at her and she stared

back. Horror crowded her eyes and her chin quivered. Hannah kneeled beside them and quietly cried. "Why *didn't* you die? The doctor was certain that a shock of that magnitude would have done you in." It wasn't a question, but he desperately needed to know the answer.

"I don't know." Her face was pale, her lips had a slight blue tinge. She shivered in his hold despite the July sunshine that bore down on her. "My chest hurts, but not as acutely as it has before, but my whole body aches, as well, so it could be due to that whole incident." Sophia reached out for Hannah and touched her hand. "I'm still here, dearest. In fact, with the exception of being tired from that dunk into the creek, I'm feeling quite… fine."

"Then you won't die?" Hannah bounced her watery gaze between Sophia and him. "Is she cured?"

"I don't know, Hannah." Her head dropped again to Oliver's shoulder. "We need to summon a physician."

"Of course. That's exactly what we should do." Was it possible her doctor in London had made a mistake in diagnosis? Medical knowledge wasn't that accurate no matter how much skill a physician claimed to have, and with women's health, even less so. His heartbeat accelerated the longer he thought about the possibility. Did that mean he would indeed have years with his wife, a future to look forward to with her? He would do everything within his power so that she received the best care, because he loved her to distraction. "Do you think you can stand? We'll walk back to the picnic site, and you can have a rest there before we return to the house."

I need answers and quickly.

Once he had them, he would ride for London. It didn't matter how long it took, but he would return to Town and summon the best physicians and surgeons he could find, have them come out to Ettesmere Park and examine his wife.

If there was a chance, however slim, that she could be healed of whatever illness she struggled with, then he would pay whatever it took to see that she received that care.

"I suppose I can." She offered a hand to her daughter. "Help me up. At the very least, I can wrap the quilt around me since my dress is ruined. And a cup of tea sounds marvelous right now."

Hannah tugged Sophia up into a standing position and then threw herself into her mother's arms. "I am glad you are here."

"So am I." Over Hannah's head, she looked at him. "I'm so sorry."

He frowned. "For what?"

"For falling into the creek. For needing a rescue."

"Well, didn't you say I'm your hero?" His chuckle fell flat when she didn't join in.

She didn't smile, which had been his intention. "I'm sorry that you married me in haste while we repented at leisure."

What the devil did that mean? Shouldn't she be ecstatic that there was a chance she would live to old age? That they could perhaps enjoy a long and happy marriage?

But she obviously struggled with her thoughts and wasn't inclined to share. He would question her once they were alone. Before he could lead the way back toward the picnic area, Hannah released her mother only to bounce into his path and then she threw herself into his arms.

"Thank you for rescuing my mother, Oliver." She clung to him as if he would vanish in the next second. "You are exactly what a papa should be."

His chest tightened, not from worry this time, but from the pure thrill of hearing those words. For a few seconds, Oliver held the girl close. "You are quite welcome. I would do anything for you and your mother."

And if that meant calling in favors from London's peers, then he would. He wouldn't stop in his quest until someone told him that Sophia would return to full health.

I simply cannot lose her.

CHAPTER EIGHTEEN

July 24, 1819

I T HAD BEEN two days since Sophia had gone through the harrowing fall into the rain-swollen creek. Two days since life had been as idyllic and perfect as it could be. Two days since she and Oliver had slept in the same bed.

And two days since her worries truly began.

She hadn't expired after that horrific afternoon, when, by all rights she should have, and neither had she died that night when she'd spent the remainder of the day in bed. After being forced to explain the accident to various family members, exhaustion had returned and forced her to rest, but she felt as far from death as a person could be.

That terrified her in a way far different from waiting to die.

Had the family doctor in London misdiagnosed her condition? Sophia shifted against the nest of pillows she leaned against. Every decision she'd made in the last six months had been because of that diagnosis. Had everything she'd known been a lie?

And worse yet, had she tricked Oliver into marrying her? Did he now feel well and truly trapped?

"Sophia?"

So lost in her thoughts, she hadn't heard the knock on the corridor door, nor had she been aware the panel had opened. Her husband stood on the threshold, and when she beckoned him in, he stepped forward a few steps. "What is it?"

"Do I have permission to send in a doctor? Yesterday, I summoned one from the neighboring village, but he wasn't available to make a call until now."

Oh, dear lord. Knots of worry pulled in her belly. If his results were different than what she'd already been given, she would have definitive answers... and her life would crumble in a different way than it had before. "Is the man here?"

"Yes. He's downstairs in the parlor." Concern clouded his stormy eyes. "Will you let him give you a cursory examination?" Oliver rubbed a hand along the side of his face. Suddenly, he appeared old, tired. "I've already told him of your history and what happened the other day."

"I suppose that's a good idea. We should know... *I* should know if my heart is truly weakened."

With a nod, he came further into the room. "Sophia, please let me in."

"You *are* in. At least the room." But she knew to what her referred, and she couldn't risk it. The walls around her heart were back in place, for if the new doctor had a different diagnosis than the previous one, she would have to set Oliver free.

"I don't appreciate being pushed away, especially during such a critical time." He paused at her bedside, but his customary grin was missing. "I am your husband."

"Only because we suspected I would die early!" She hadn't meant to let loose her fears quite yet, but it couldn't be helped. "Don't you understand, Oliver? We married under false pretenses. You only asked for my hand because you expected this marriage wouldn't last beyond six months, and you followed my wishes of Hannah having a parent." The urge to retch grew strong, but she staved it off with a few swallows.

"That doesn't discount our feelings for each other."

"Feelings based on an expected limited time." Her eyes welled with tears. "Even you cannot deny that." She clasped her hands in her lap atop the bedclothes. "We made no secret of why we wed in haste—we were in lust; there weren't any further expectations beyond that."

His expression fell. Despite the afternoon sunlight spilling into the room, agony and desolation twisted through his features. "You don't believe that, surely. We have shared our feelings…"

"I don't know." Her heart ached so fiercely it was as if she were mourning for a husband all over again except hers was still standing there at her side facing the widening rift between them, perhaps of her making, but their marriage hadn't been fair to him. She glanced at the windows, away from the shock, the disappointment, the angst on his face.

"If you'll only listen to me—"

"I rather think I'm done listening for a while." Her chin quivered, and she swallowed again, for there would be plenty of time to indulge in tears later. "Send in the doctor."

"Very well." Once he left the room, her composure cracked.

Until she had answers to her questions regarding her heart, her life was in a sort of suspended hold. Decisions couldn't be made until something definitive was said.

In short order, Oliver returned with an older gentleman with thinning blond-gray hair. He carried a worn black bag, which he set on the foot of the bed. "This is Doctor Braun. He's from a village the next county over, and if you wish for a reference, I can fetch one from your brother Gilbert." His voice was dull and devoid of the life he usually had. "Apparently, during your brother's time at Ettesmere Park, he has called upon the doctor a time or two."

That was surprising news. What did Gilbert need to see a physician regarding outside of his limp? "It's not necessary." All she wanted to do was either cry or have an honest talk with Oliver, but her feelings were too fragile, so she would keep her own counsel. "Please, just conduct the examination. I'm rather fatigued."

At least that wasn't a lie.

"Of course, Lady Sophia." The doctor removed an instrument he referred to as a stethoscope. "Please breathe normally." He came toward her, held the narrow end of the hollow wooden monaural tube to her chest above her right breast and placed the funneled side to his own ear. "I'll be able to listen to your lungs and heart with this." With a nod he repeated the routine with the left side of her chest. Then he did the same to her back. "Your pulse is quite rapid and thready at times, but your lungs are clear."

She glanced at Oliver, but his attention was riveted on the doctor, and his arms were crossed at his chest, which meant he was closed off or protecting himself from terrible news.

What diagnosis did he want to hear?

The doctor cleared his throat. "When you engage in regular activities throughout your day, does your heart feel strained?"

What did that mean? "For the past six months or so, I have made it a point to do nothing more strenuous than walking." She ignored the heat in her cheeks. "Of course, I have been intimate with my husband, but there again, we have been careful and haven't done even that with abandon or let passion carry us away."

Except that glorious day in the attic when they'd enjoyed each other with abandon.

And that was perhaps a regret now.

"Are you often out of breath?" the doctor asked without looking as if he'd heard her.

"Sometimes."

"The fatigue has become worse than when you were first diagnosed with the heart ailment?"

"It has. In the past several weeks, I've had to take naps or lie down during the day." Trying to keep up with Hannah was sometimes too much.

"When you are in the country, do you feel better overall than when you are in London?" The doctor stared at her as if she were a bug in a jar.

"In some ways being here has made me feel more relaxed, but I yearn for the excitement of Town, and I miss the faster pace I enjoyed there." Though she didn't look at Oliver, she felt his gaze on her. "However, I have less anxiety here than there."

Even less so once Oliver had come into her life, but would all that go away soon?

"Is there anything different about your lifestyle or daily living now than when you were first diagnosed?"

"Besides being married?" This time she did glance at her husband. He tried so hard not to show his reaction, that she had learned about him, for his jaw was set as if he clenched his teeth. His eyes were slightly narrowed behind the lenses of his spectacles. "Besides living every day behind fear of dying?" Except when she met Oliver. He'd taught her to stop wasting the time she'd had left and to start living. "I worry less."

Oliver nodded. "I can attest to this. She has relaxed by increments, and I haven't known her that long."

Again, it was due to her husband. How could she let him go, but how could she expect him to stay if her diagnosis wasn't what he was promised? With every shred of willpower she possessed, Sophia tamped the desire to cry.

"However, the fatigue is debilitating even if I've spent the day lounging about." She pressed her lips together. "My emotions often swing wildly back and forth between happiness and the depths of despair without warning. I can cry for no reason." Previously, she'd assumed it was because she'd been facing death. Now, she might as well confess everything she'd felt recently. "There is also the feeling as if I shall burn to a crisp at any given time. Applying cool, wet clothes or splashing water on my face or chest have no effect. Sometimes, my thoughts are murky, and I imagine the worst scenarios." Thus, being frightened of the dark.

"Interesting." Yet his expression suggested she was bound for Bedlam. "I have not encountered anyone having all of these symptoms together before."

"I'm afraid of that." Yet, how sad was it that she clung to the hope that the first diagnosis still stood, for that would mean she could keep Oliver in her life, shortened as it was. "There is also feeling faint at times."

"Before or after manipulating the stairs or walking?"

"It comes and goes."

For long moments, the doctor peered at her as he stroked his chin. Finally, he nodded, pulled a brown vial with a glass stopper from his bag and set it on the bedside table. "There *is* something unequivocally wrong with you, but it is *not* your heart."

"Even though my father died of a weak heart?" His diagnosis left her more confused than before.

"These things present differently between men and women, and quite frankly, we know almost nothing about women's health." He pointed to the bottle. "This is laudanum. Take a few drops when you find the pain—any pain—unbearable or the chest tightness unwieldy. Or perhaps even when those, er, ah… urges you told me about start to bedevil you." Dark color crept over his cravat. "Take it also when you feel the other symptoms are out of hand."

So, because this man wasn't familiar with a woman's body or how it worked, she was to spend her days under the influence of opium? How convenient for everyone. In that state, she wouldn't be a bother.

But that is no life either.

Basically, she was back where she started.

"Then what the devil ails her?" Oliver asked as he came closer to the doctor. One hand had curled into a fist. "Surely, it's *something*, else she wouldn't be feeling as she does. I've never known Sophia to lie or concoct stories for attention."

Her heart squeezed. Oh, he was such a noble sort, a true hero, and he truly didn't deserve any of this.

"I would have no idea, Mr. Mattingly, but from what she's said, I am confident in saying that she *is* ailing. However, I am just as confident that her heart is *not* diseased." He bounced his gaze between them. "She is not weak bodily. Her color is good."

Sophia despised being discussed between the two of them as if she didn't exist. "The event of distress a few days ago didn't harm her more than abrasions and contusions. She appears hale and hearty still." He bestowed an indulgent, smug smile on her. "In simple terms, she is growing older, and some women have a tendency to trend toward symptoms of hysteria or decline as they do."

"What?" Sophia sat up as straight as she could in the bed.

"Damn it all!" Oliver's exclamation came the same time as hers. "Do you mean to say my wife is merely agitated because she is aging?"

"Well, Mr. Mattingly, the lady is no longer a young woman. It's only natural." The doctor closed his bag with a snap. He took it in hand. "In cases like this—and if her condition grows worse, you might think upon moving her to an asylum or some other place where women of her... ailment can be given more specialized care."

Sophia snorted. "So I can be ignored, or worse. Poked and prodded, have medical experiments performed on me so men like you can *understand* women better?"

"Absolutely not." Oliver's words were adamant as he shook his head. "I don't accept any of this."

Did he refer to her health or the situation they were both currently in?

"I would advise discussing it with Lord Ettesmere, and if you decide on an asylum, there is one three counties over for women like Lady Sophia." The doctor glanced once more at her then back at Oliver. "Count yourself fortunate, Mr. Mattingly. Some women devolve into snarling, snapping, horrid-tempered beasts with ailments of the mind during this time of life. At least your wife remains congenial. Good day."

Left alone with her husband, Sophia merely stared at him. What else was there to say? Her heart was perfectly fine, but the rest of her was not? And whatever ailed her wouldn't necessarily kill her immediately? When he would have spoken, she held up a hand. "Please, don't say anything." It was becoming nearly impossible to hold back the tears that gathered in her throat.

"I must, for I refuse to give up on you or have you sent away." Emotion graveled his voice as he stumbled toward the bed. "There must be some way of ascertaining answers."

"The doctor didn't appear to have them."

"Then I'll find one who does."

"Just stop." She shook her head. Tears stung her eyes. "Obviously, I am not expected to expire any time soon, and because of that, you are leg-shackled to me upon a false pretense." An ache set up around her heart that had the power to steal her breath.

"Don't say it." He rested a hand on the mattress near her knee.

Oh, how much did she want to feel his comforting touch? Have his lips on hers? Hear him tell her that everything would come out right in the end? But she didn't want him to hate her as the years dragged on.

"I must, Oliver," she whispered as a tear fell to her cheek. "This isn't fair to you. None of it is." Her throat hurt from the effort of keeping her emotions in check. "You were assured freedom in less than six months. And since you won't have that with my death, I am setting you free with my words."

"No." He shook his head. Pain reflected in his eyes. "I refuse to hear it."

"You must, for as the years go by, you will grow to resent me, perhaps even hate me. You could have had such a different life." At the last second, she stifled a sob. "If you remain here, your life will be wasted, and you were meant for so much more than a husband to a woman who is apparently bordering on hysteria." *Dear God*, would she be thought of as a detriment to him? Would a wife such as her stunt his ability to move up in his position?

I cannot bear that.

"Sophia, listen to me. This is merely reaction talking, making you think worse than the situation truly is. I mean to—"

"Please go." The words were tearful, and the longer he lingered, the hotter her cheeks and chest grew, just like that time at the creek. The she uttered the speech she knew would make him leave. "I only married you because I knew I would die, because I wanted the thrill of bedding you, because you would be a wonderful father to Hannah."

With each point, pain and denial were etched into his face. "You don't mean that." But his skin had paled. "I've seen how you truly feel…" Denial shadowed his eyes.

"I do, and now with everything else we've heard, I find I no longer wish for your company." She would set him free, and perhaps someday he would find it in his heart to forgive her. "I will ask my brother to help me to apply for a divorce based on being misinformed as to the state of my health. He has the coin for it." The words felt thick and heavy, and with each one, it was as if she'd thrown daggers into his chest.

Could she even do that, though? The potential damage to her reputation was enough to give her pause, and she didn't give a fig for her family's reputation. Each member had already added enough scandal upon it, and the Winterbourne name seemed to still stand tall. However, divorcing Oliver might also have repercussions on Hannah's prospects because of the stigma. Yet, her dearest daughter was quite unconventional and headstrong. The gossip wouldn't be too terrible after a few years. Besides, Hannah wouldn't be one to rush herself onto the Marriage Mart.

Yes, her original thought still stood, as much as it would pain her to do so.

"I won't give up on us." Moisture gathered in his eyes, magnified behind his spectacle lenses, and a drop wet his cheek. "But for the moment, I shall leave, give us both the time necessary to digest the news and plan our next course."

"Oliver, you are not listening." Dear stubborn man!

"And neither are you, but we *will* talk again once I have a stronger argument to rout you." With a glance that would forever be seared onto her brain—at once both terrifying and wonderful—he turned on his heel and took his leave.

Only then did she allow herself to give into the sobs that battered her insides. The best thing to ever happen to her in years had just walked out of her life on her order, and she'd stupidly let him. He'd done nothing except support her and had sought to make her days full of happiness and joy, and she'd tossed all of it away out of fear.

Fear of everything.

Her chest tightened and hurt. She might not be quite so frightened of the dark since Oliver's advent, but now that he took his light away, would the night swallow her whole? Perhaps it would, for the fear of losing him couldn't be borne.

CHAPTER NINETEEN

July 24, 1819

OLIVER FELT LIKE a shell of his former self.

His life had suddenly gone topsy turvy and nothing was as it seemed any longer. Two days ago, his wife had more or less told him to go away, that she was giving him his freedom and would pursue the possibility of a divorce if such a thing would even be granted, and that what she'd felt for him had only been based on the circumstances of the that moment.

Had they truly married by mistake? Or worse yet. Had Sophia lied to him about her heart condition merely to justify taking him into her bed?

I simply cannot believe that of her.

It had broken his heart and crushed his spirit. Of course, it would. Such a thing would shatter any man, but there was a chance she'd only spoken those words out of fear or confusion. A person couldn't be told horrible news one day and then have all that challenged and changed on another mere weeks later without their mind playing tricks upon them.

But he vowed to still do everything within his power to make certain there was nothing wrong with her heart and to discover exactly what it was she suffered from.

After that, if she remained steadfast in her wish to send him away, so be it.

The musings didn't help the state of his heart. He doubted that if he ripped said organ from his chest it would stop the fierce ache, but he ignored it as best he could while methodically packing a change of clothing into his valise. The earlier plan of riding out of Ettesmere Park neck or nothing for London had changed slightly. Since he wasn't familiar with the area, setting out alone would prove foolish, so he'd ordered a carriage to be brought around. Taking a driver with him who knew the roads and the directions would be the more prudent plan. It would make for a longer trip, but there was no other choice.

Just as he buckled the leather straps that held the valise closed, Hannah pelted into his room.

She held a basket of wildflowers in one hand, and the colorful blooms temporarily cheered him, but it was the shock and slight betrayal in her round eyes that gave him pause. "Are you leaving?"

There was no sense in lying to the girl; she was too clever for that. Oliver's shoulders drooped. "Yes." While she stared, he donned his frock coat of brown lightweight wool. As he smoothed it over his tweed waistcoat, his resolve crumbled. "I am going to London," he said by way of avoiding an overly complicated explanation.

A trace of a frown took possession of Hannah's lips, and in that moment, she heavily resembled her mother. Then her eyes narrowed, and he was certain she meant to argue. "Mama told me she'd sent you away."

"She did." It was the truth, and this child deserved to know that from both parties.

"So, then, you are just going to do what she says? All of a sudden." She set the willow basket of flowers on a small round table nearby. "When the two of you have always bickered like people in love do?"

Exactly how much had this girl seen and observed in her short lifetime? Oliver grabbed his beaver felt top hat from the foot of the bed and set it upon his head. Then he pushed his spectacles back into place on the bridge of his nose. "I have no choice." Neither he nor Sophia could move forward until they knew exactly what her health complications entailed.

"You know, for an ambassador and an intelligent gentleman, you certainly have shown yourself for a bacon-brained idiot." The insult had been delivered in such a matter-of-fact way that Oliver didn't know if he should feel offended or laugh at the joke. Before he could respond, Hannah came toward him a few steps. "Will you stay married to my mother now that she might be well?" So much hope and longing rode on those words that his chest hurt all the more.

Oh, how to answer when he didn't know how to navigate such complicated waters? With a sigh, he nodded. "If she wants me as a husband, but circumstances between us have changed since we married. We are both trying to make sense of it all, and it's… confusing."

Yet, here he was, packed and readying to leave while Sophia had refused to see him for the past two days. This was the bedroom they'd shared since their nuptial ceremony, but she had removed to a different room directly following the doctor's examination.

The girl snorted. "Every day brings some sort of confusion."

"True."

She glanced from the valise resting at his booted feet to his face. "Where are you going?"

"As I said, London."

"Why?"

Ten minutes ago, the answer had been simple. Now, standing before this slip of a girl that knew more than her years indicated, he wasn't entirely certain. "I wish to gather the best physicians and surgeons, implore them to return to Ettesmere Park with me so they can examine your mother. Perhaps they will have insights into her health concerns." When the child didn't appear convinced, he let loose another sigh. "In essence, I want your mother to know there is no danger to her heart, if that is indeed the case." His own heart squeezed with pain so great that it stole his breath. "And if that is so, I hope that one of these men—or even the most highly rated midwife—can tell us why your mother is feeling the way she is."

All he wanted was for Sophia to be well or, at least, live out the remainder of her life without worry and hopefully without pain.

Everything else could be worked out after that.

"That is quite sweet of you." Relief shadowed her eyes. "But she has refused to see you," Hannah continued as if attempting to work out the problem on her own. "She has even told me not to talk about you with her."

The pain in his heart increased. "This is so, and until your mother comes to peace with all that has occurred, I rather believe our union will remain strained." Why wouldn't Sophia believe him when he told her that he loved her? No matter how their marriage had come about?

Then his thoughts swung the other way, as they had over the past two days. Perhaps Sophia truly didn't need a husband who spent his time split between England and America. In fact, if she had only married him on the assumption that she would be dead soon, then their union wouldn't work regardless of how he felt about her.

"How frustrating."

Did she refer to his situation or how this affected her life? Oliver shifted his weight from foot to foot. The longer he delayed, the more difficult the journey, for already it was past time for tea. Daylight for travel wouldn't last forever.

"Agreed." He rubbed a hand along the side of his face, upset the set of his spectacles, and then was obliged to reorient them. "It is quite a mess."

Hannah frowned. "I rather think it is not."

"How do you figure? Your mother is stubborn."

She snorted. "So are you, but she wouldn't have chosen you if you didn't possess some sort of backbone."

There was that. He shrugged. "Yet here we are."

"You must look at the problem with logic." The child jumped onto the bed and regarded him with hope in her eyes. "You either love Mama or you don't. Which is it?"

Direct as always. A grin tugged at the corners of his mouth. "I love her to distraction. Nothing has changed in that quarter, but she refuses to believe it as truth."

"Yes, well, Mama has had a bit of a tough go of things lately." Hannah shook her head as if that explained everything. "And on the reverse side, Mama either loves you or she doesn't." She looked at him with expectation. "Does she?"

"A few days ago, before the incident at the creek, I thought she did." Her actions, her words had indicated such. The way they got on together was a testament to that fact. Yet, was it possible it had all been an act because she'd believed she was dying and that she wouldn't need worry about a long-term marriage?

Oh, this is untenable!

"And now?"

He shrugged. "I don't know."

Hannah's frown had returned. "You must talk to her instead of assuming things, Oliver." Her tone of voice suggested he was an idiot to even think along such lines. "Even if Mama's life is spared now, life itself is still too short for silences and misunderstandings."

Dear God, the girl was wise beyond her years! "I…" What else could he say? The truth stared at him in the face. Not only did he love Sophia more than everything, but he was exceedingly fond of Hannah. If the marriage fell apart, he would lose that connection with her, and his chance to finally be a father would dissolve.

It was something he'd not considered when grappling with the woes between himself and Sophia. This time, the pain that gripped his chest prompted a gasp from him. He rubbed his fingers over his stinging heart. How did one fix such a coil?

"Additionally…"

"Yes?" he managed to gasp out around the fierce ache in his heart.

Tears pooled in Hannah's eyes. She fiddled with the end of her golden braid of hair that rested over one shoulder. "I'd grown rather used to having a father about again." Then she burst into sobs, and once more resembled her mother.

Well, damn.

The sight of a woman—no matter the age—in emotional distress never failed to reduce him to the strength of jelly. "Oh, Hannah. You poor thing." Swiftly, Oliver sat next to her on the edge of the bed and dared to put an arm around her shoulders. Moisture gathered in his own eyes with such force that he couldn't hold back his tears. "I'm so sorry that the ignorance of adults is throwing you into a quagmire of feelings."

"Why can you not stay here and fix it?" Hannah turned into him, buried her face in his cravat, and set out to apparently give life to every tear in creation as her arms went around his middle. "You fixed Mama's life before when you came to us."

Never in his life had he imagined that he could know that such exquisite love existed or that it would come in the form of affection between a father and a daughter. He hugged her and cried along with her, for in that shared grief and confusion and heartache, there was no shame. There was only understanding and the will to do something that would make things right again. At the very least, he owed the girl that much. It wasn't fair to her to come into her life, promise to be a replacement father, and then leave again without the guarantee that the relationship between him and Sophia would be repaired upon his return.

No longer was he the only person he needed to consider when making decisions, and for the last two days, he'd forgotten that.

For long moments, they vented pent up emotion with each other—a broken family who still clung to hope—and finally Hannah pulled away, wiping her eyes.

"Oliver, please don't go," she implored him with a splotched face and luminous eyes. "I need you here. Mama needs you."

Then the decision was made for him. Perhaps the children did indeed lead the adults in their lives. Nothing else mattered except for keeping his bond with his little family intact. He nodded, removed his handkerchief from a jacket pocket, and then handed it to her. "I suppose I shouldn't delay further in talking to your mother."

Hannah sprang off the bed and stared at him as she mopped at her cheeks. "Truly?"

"You have my word." Slowly, he rose to his feet. "Where is she?"

Some of Hannah's enthusiasm faded. "I honestly don't know. She's been scarce since luncheon. Hiding from all of us, I suppose."

"I shall locate her. Have no worries." Oliver forced a grin for her benefit. "Will you accompany me downstairs? I need to cancel the carriage I ordered."

"Yes!" She caught at his hand and practically tugged him from the room.

Then minutes later, Oliver returned to the entry hall after explaining to the driver that he wouldn't need the carriage or the man's services after all. Hannah trailed behind him, talking an unending stream of information regarding the kittens' growth and maturity, and telling him that the one called Gilbert had caught a mouse and left it in Hannah's bed, but the rodent had still been alive. Obviously, she assumed everything would come out right.

"How dare you!"

Fury rang in the earl's voice as he strode through the entry hall and didn't stop until he'd landed an unexpected punch to Oliver's right cheek. The force of the blow knocked him backward. He stumbled, crashed against the opposite wall with his spectacles hanging askew from one ear. But Ettesmere's temper hadn't abated. "You promised that you would take care of my sister, and now you are running away when there is a chance you could have a lifetime with her instead of a few weeks." His expression resembled a thundercloud, and his hand had curled once more into a fist.

"That's not well done of you, Ettesmere," Gilbert said in a droll tone as he joined everyone in the entry hall. The tip of his cane thudded on the marble floor. "But I understand the sentiment."

Oliver lifted a hand to ward off another attacked while the side of his face throbbed with pain. "Hold, Your Lordship. Let me explain."

"I should toss you out on your lying arse," Ettesmere threatened with all seriousness. "My sister asked for my help in securing a divorce. What the hell did you do?"

"Nothing!" Oliver shook his head. The situation kept moving from bad to worse. "Why do you assume it was me who cocked everything up?" That was quite aggravating.

"Uncle Arthur, stop!" Hannah sprang between the earl and him with her arms outstretched. "Oliver hasn't done anything wrong. In fact, he is going to talk to Mama and make things right again."

"Hannah is correct." He put his spectacles back onto the bridge of his nose. "Yes, I had intended to remove to London, but *not* because I'm running away." With a tug to the hem of his jacket, he explained further. "I wished to engage the services of as many surgeons and physicians and midwives as I could muster to explain your sister's health worries."

By increments, the earl's ire began to fade. "Then you are not abandoning her?"

His brother snorted and crossed his arms at his chest, his cane leaning against his hip. "Not that anyone would blame you. Women are often nothing but trouble, as you've had cause to witness. It was just a matter of time."

"While I understand you are bitter due to your own martial difficulties, that doesn't mean the rest of us are in the same way."

Quick anger cut through Oliver's chest, but he tamped down the urge to lash out further. "I love your sister more than everything, but Sophia is laboring beneath a misconception given to her from a physician. She's also trying to make sense of what life might be for her now. I can't blame her for the confusion."

To say nothing of moving through murky emotions.

"Or she's got some maggot in her brain, and everything is twisted," Gilbert replied with a roll of his eyes. "This is why no one in their right mind should ever ask for a woman's hand."

"Enough!" Oliver's patience snapped. "I won't have you disparaging women and my wife especially. Whatever is between us is a private matter. While I attend to my own affairs, perhaps you should do the same with yours."

Slowly, Hannah lowered her arms. She glared at her uncles but then rested her gaze on the earl. "Do you promise not to hit Oliver again?"

A red flush rose above Ettesmere's cravat. "I promise." He extended a hand to Oliver. "My apologies for planting you a facer. I'm afraid you'll have a rather ugly bruise tonight."

Gilbert scoffed. "And you will have no doubt invoked Sophia's wrath. Providing she wishes to keep the ambassador on." But a flush of red had risen above his collar.

"I understood the reasoning behind it," he said to the earl as he shook the man's hand. "Hopefully, I can convince your sister to forgive you."

"Thank you." Embarrassment remained in the earl's expression. "You make your living talking to people, Ambassador, and hopefully you can sway my sister over to your way of thinking. She is still a bit lost, I'd imagine."

"Let us hope the task ahead will be as easy as you say."

The earl nodded. "Don't be late for my nuptial ceremony on the morrow. That I won't forgive you," he said with a smile.

"Of course, I won't." Though he feared it might take until eleven o'clock tomorrow morning to convince Sophia they had always been meant to be wed. "Now, do either of you know where your sister is currently located?"

Both of the brothers shook their heads. The earl frowned. "Honestly, I have been preoccupied with wedding details and haven't looked for her since breakfast."

Gilbert shook his head. "I arose late this morning and must have missed her."

"I shall find her." Oliver raised a hand to his throbbing cheek. "Perhaps once she sees me partially battered, she'll be more apt to listen to what I have to say." Though, he didn't want her pity.

The earl snickered. "Again, I apologize for the punch. I'm rather overprotective of my family."

"Truly, I understand, and I feel the same way regarding mine." He glanced at Hannah, who beamed. "Now, if you will all excuse me, I need to make inroads into securing my future."

Hannah put a hand on his arm. "May I come with you? It's my future too."

He glanced at the earl, who frowned. "I rather think this is something I should accomplish on my own." For his wife might need convincing. "But please believe me when I tell you I'll do everything in my power to convince your mother she needs me."

"Mr. Mattingly is correct, Hannah." The earl drew her away from Oliver and rested a hand on her shoulder. "I believe your grandmother wishes for you to have a bath and to take to your bed early so you'll prove rested for the festivities tomorrow."

"Please?" She looked up at the earl with round eyes. "I cannot lose another father, Uncle Arthur."

Oh, God.

The earl put his free hand over his heart. "In this I won't budge." He glanced at Oliver and the worry in his eyes matched his own. "Good luck. I assume if all goes well, we will see the both of you at the ceremony."

Oliver nodded. "From your lips to God's ears."

Hannah frowned. "You *will* convince Mama she should stay married, won't you Oliver?"

"I shall do my best." Then, with a wave to her, he quit the

area in favor of returning to the room he'd shared with Sophia until she'd moved out two days ago. There was no trace of her there. Not immediately concerned, he moved on to various rooms around the manor house. She proved elusive. He even visited the attics, but his wife wasn't there either.

Worry pulled knots in his belly, but as he passed a window that looked out onto the back lawn and the maze, he *knew* where she would be—the heart of the maze. Oliver grinned. It was fitting since that was where she apparently went when she wished for security and for thinking.

He vowed to himself as he made his way outside the manor, he wouldn't leave that maze until he'd secured her promise to remain with him for the duration.

When he reached the heart, the respite from heat and the sun was welcome, but that wasn't the reason he forgot how to breathe, for Sophia sat upon the picnic quilt with her back to the roses in the center. She wore the wonderful pink gown that she had for their wedding ceremony, and with her hair piled atop her head and the enamel rose pin deep in the tresses, she remained every bit the dream of his heart as she was that day. At least twenty clipped roses of varying colors littered the quilt around her—no doubt to represent hope.

His heart skipped a beat, and he finally drew in a shaky breath. "My God, Sophia, you are a vision." And he'd missed her so damned much.

"I knew you would come here and find me." When she smiled, he groaned, for in the shadows and with that come hither twinkle in her eyes, all he could think about was kissing her.

But that wouldn't solve anything.

"How so?" Where had the woman gone who had tears in her eyes and determination in her expression when she'd told him to go two days ago?

She shifted and rearranged her skirting over her folded legs. "You are the hero I needed when we first met, and you are my husband now—still that hero. And I still have need of you." A tiny waver echoed in her voice, and it tugged at his chest. "You don't quit something until it's done to your satisfaction."

"No, I don't. This is true." Oliver came forward until the toes of his boots aligned with the edge of the quilt. "I must say that this change in attitude has left me reeling." But perhaps it would make his work easier. "We need to talk." He couldn't live in this nether world where he didn't know where he fit.

"I know." She nodded. "Everything has been so…"

"Strange?" he provided.

"Yes." Sophia held out a hand to him. "But then, normal is so boring."

"Indeed." The second he took her hand, need shivered along his spine.

I'm not giving up on us.

CHAPTER TWENTY

SOPHIA'S NERVES CRAWLED and knots of worry pulled in her belly as she tugged Oliver onto the quilt beside her. Never in her life had she been so anxious regarding one of her husbands, but this time was different.

She had changed.

Life had changed.

Expectations had changed.

Now they needed to manage them—together—and if ever there was a time when she should pursue Mr. Mattingly, it was now.

I have to fix this

"I apologize for how I've handled things these past couple of days," she said by way of introducing the subject. She smoothed one hand over the raspberry pink silk gown and hoped that him seeing her in the frock she'd worn for their wedding would help to win her argument. "The news was certainly frightening in a different way than I'd become accustomed to." It was never easy admitting when one was wrong, but for this man, for their union, she would. Twenty times over if need be. "But when Hannah said you intended to leave, that you'd packed a bag... Even if it was my fault that you were doing so..."

"You reacted with fear." Understanding reflected in those stormy eyes of his. "It's what you felt when the village physician said there was nothing wrong with your heart. Everything you'd previously known came tumbling down."

"Yes." She nodded. For whatever reason, Oliver had always known her thoughts and why she did the things she did. "I couldn't help but imagine the worst-case scenario."

"Because that's what you've always done."

"It's as if my mind compels me to think that way just now, and sometimes, it frightens me. I don't know myself as I did perhaps ten years ago." Sophia looked at him, as he rested his weight on an elbow like they were attending a picnic instead of discussing the most important topics. Oh, he was such a handsome man, and so dear with those wire-rimmed spectacles, that the real possibility of losing him brought tears to her eyes. "Perhaps that was why I consented to marry you. I'm *different*, somehow, at this time in my life, and I don't know why. I don't understand myself any longer."

"We all are different as we age." For long moments, he regarded her, but his emotions were too difficult and hooded to read. "When you told me two days ago what you felt for me didn't matter any longer, when you removed yourself from our literal marriage bed, that you ordered me away from you, I was hurt; my heart broke, Sophia."

"I'm so sorry." Her chest tightened so much that it stole her breath. She pressed a hand to her heart. "I didn't want you to think I'd trapped you into this union on false pretenses."

One of his eyebrows rose. "Then you would have done so under true ones?"

"What?" His words made no sense. "No. That's not what I meant." She shook her head. "The attraction that sprang between us from the outset was all too real. It still is." A shuddering sigh escaped her. "And when I said that I loved you not long ago, that wasn't a lie."

"Then what, exactly, are you struggling with, sweeting?" A faint grin tugged at the corners of his mouth. "I'm afraid I don't see the problem."

Of course, he wouldn't. "There might not be anything wrong with my heart, but there is definitely something not quite normal with my health." After pressing her lips together in an effort to stem their trembling, she shook her head. "I don't wish to consign you to a life where you might need to look after me if my faculties leave me, and I certainly don't want you to decide that I'm fit for Bedlam or an asylum that the doctor spoke about." A sob rose into her throat, but she tamped it. "My grandmother, from all accounts, was insane. Perhaps that is my fate, but I couldn't bear to have these things weigh upon your shoulders."

"That is the responsibility of a husband, Sophia. No matter what."

"But—"

"Hush." He gave her a small, tight smile. "First of all, once you and I repair what is between us now, there will *never* come a time when you and I are parted again. I would never consign you to such a place." His voice was full of firm determination, and his expression stole her breath with its fierce protection. "You are my wife. For better or for worse. For now and always. For sickness and in health. That's what I promised you, and I never go back on my word."

"I…"

He heaved out a breath and frustration went through his expression. "Nothing will work, we won't move forward, unless you trust me and trust yourself that you've made the right decision. That we belong together."

"If I hadn't trusted you, I wouldn't have married you."

"Then, again, love, I fail to see the problem." His eyes twinkled with amusement. "Nothing has changed between us except your expiration date."

Such a cheeky devil. *I love him so much.* She'd been a silly widgeon to ever think either of them could merely walk away.

"I don't know… There is surely something off with my health. I don't want to be a burden."

"You aren't."

"That being said, I want to return to London. I'll submit to as many tests or as many examinations as you order if that might allow us to determine what it is that I'm suffering from." If that was even possible. Men who studied medicine knew next to nothing. It was entirely possible they would never find answers.

"We will do whatever you want—and that was my only intent by wishing to leave just now—but please know this." Oliver moved into a sitting position. He held her gaze with his. Never had she seen him as somber as he was now. "I have *never* stopped loving you. Not with knowing your heart was diseased, not through knowing it wasn't, and I won't as we go through whatever else you currently grapple with."

"But you have your whole future ahead of you. An ailing wife you married for the guarantee of a short union will only hinder you." That idea refused to leave her.

"Not this again." In some agitation, he removed his brown jacket and then tossed it to the side of the quilt. Clad in his shirtsleeves and waistcoat, he was the perfect picture of the country gentleman, and her mouth watered. "Whether you expire next week, next month, next year, or twenty years from now is irrelevant. Don't you see that?" He rested a forearm on his bent knee. "You are mine in every way that matters, Sophia. I won't give you up and neither will my devotion to you waver. Whatever fate holds for us, we will meet it together, for I only want you. Need only you."

Her heart trembled. "Oh, Oliver." Tears welled in her eyes.

"When you more or less told me you would seek a divorce—which is apparently prohibitively expensive and elusive in England—my heart was battered. I won't lie; it took me by surprise." The amusement faded from his expression as apprehension stole it. "It made me think you didn't value me as a man, a husband, a person. That you had only married me to avoid the scandal that would have followed once I bedded you… or rather it was the other way around that first time."

Heat filled her cheeks from more than one count. "I didn't

mean to hurt you," she admitted in a whispered voice. "I was only looking out for you, and I thought that by setting you free, you wouldn't eventually come to hate me... for living." This time, a sob tore from her throat, and she couldn't stem the falling tears.

"Never."

"My heart has already been through so much, you see."

He nodded. "It was only natural for you to build walls." For long moments he remained silent. "So, where do we go from here?" There was an air of vulnerability about him that tugged at her chest and made her fall ever deeper into love with him. "If you need me to court you all over again, I will do that. If you wish for time away as you gather your thoughts, I will give you that. But whatever it is you need, please know that I refuse to give up on us as a couple, and I will scale those damned walls time and time again until you believe in my earnestness."

"I can see that about you."

"And I refuse to leave Hannah. She doesn't deserve that, and quite frankly, the child needs to see how adults work out their problems."

"Agreed." Flutters of need moved through her lower belly. He was certainly a hero, and he was hers, straight out those storybooks she used to read to her daughter.

"However, I must tell you that I adore my position as ambassador. If our living both here in England and at times in America is something you simply cannot square with, *then* we will have a bit of friction in our union." His expression was guarded. "I believe traveling will be good for Hannah, but if you refuse to leave English soil, I suppose we'll be destined to be apart for half the year." That tiny little catch in his voice sealed her decision. "And that I couldn't bear. I suspect that is one of the issues that has set Gilbert's union lopsided."

She gawked at him. "Possibly." Then she shoved that thought from her mind. "It will be a fine life indeed, for all of us."

"And?" His body was taut as if he would run.

How had she found such good fortune as to land him? *Stop being a ninny, Sophia. Fight for him!* After scrubbing the tears from her cheeks the best she could, Sophia shifted on the quilt. She kneeled before him and took one of his hands in hers. "Oliver Mattingly, I'm desperately in love with you but was too foolish and fearful to know that state has sprung from my heart instead of the situation surrounding it." Her hand shook in his. "Putting all of that aside, will you stay married to me? Perhaps for the next twenty years or so if we are blessed?"

It was as if the clouds had parted, and the sun shined brightly when her husband grinned, and he was easily the most handsome man she'd ever seen. He scrambled to his knees and held her head between his warm palms. "I do, I will, and I give you my promise to make those years the most wonderful you've ever passed." Love light gleamed from deep down in his eyes. "I love you, Sophia. That has never changed." He retrieved one of the cut roses and tucked the bloom behind one of her ears. "If we remember to carry hope, there is nothing we won't overcome."

"Oh, Oliver." There was no opportunity to reply with more words, for he brought his mouth crashing down on hers in an intense kiss that would forever be seared upon her brain. Perhaps words weren't needed, not when she could show her appreciation with other creative ways. When she moved to have better access to him, he toppled onto his back, and she sprawled over his body with yards of skirting around them.

"Not a bad position if you ask me," he murmured before he wrapped his arms around her and set out to apparently kiss her senseless.

And there was nothing she wished to do than return the sentiment.

Each meeting of lips, every touch and caress, each glide of tongues sent her closer to that sought-after edge before any clothing had been removed. The scent of sage and citrus teased her nose and drove her further onward in the quest to claim him as hers.

With no reservations this time and no fear looming over them.

Need and desire twisted down her spine. She couldn't have enough of those feelings or of him. What had begun as a plan to spend her last days in happiness and provide a parent for her daughter had grown into a romance of a lifetime with heady days of wonder—years of them—suddenly stretching before her.

I have a future with this man.

Sophia straddled his waist. The waning sunlight sparkled on the thousands of tiny clear beads on her gown as if the fairy folk were rejoicing right along with her. After tugging her skirting free of her legs, she slowly drew the bodice of the gown downward, and while he watched with passion-drugged eyes, she continued onward until her breasts were bared. "Love me."

His chuckle reverberated within her chest as he took those globes in his hands. "I don't believe I have ever stopped." Then, as she leaned over him, he sucked one of the erect nipples into his mouth, and she sighed.

Exquisite sensation washed over her the longer he played with her breasts or teased her sensitive buds. For a distraction, she nuzzled the crook of his neck, nibbled a line of desperate kisses beneath his jawline. The rasp of his evening stubble enhanced the desire already ricocheting through her body, and she shivered, which only brought his member to a more straining state.

"I need you." Wanted to feel him moving inside her, wished to have his thick length in her palm, taste him on her tongue. In short, she wanted him in every way a woman could have a man. And to enjoy that with abandon this time.

Her husband's eyes twinkled with affection. "There is nothing stopping you from taking what you will." He removed his spectacles and tossed them in the direction of his abandoned jacket. "I will give it to you time and again."

One of the things she adored about him was his willingness not to dominate the coupling every time they came together. Some men wished to remain in control at all times, but with

Oliver, if she felt more amorous and initiated intercourse, he always led her guide it. And there were times when she wished to feel cherished and protected during love making, and that was when he took the lead.

That give and take, that exchange and balance of power was key to finding contentment within a relationship.

"Good." As if she had all the leisure time in the world and they weren't in a semi-public area, she slid down his body, wrenching his shirt tails from his trousers as she went. As soon as skin was somewhat bared, she pressed her lips to that hot skin and laughed when his muscles clenched and went taut.

It took next to no time to manipulate the buttons of his front-falls, and when his engorged length sprang free, she sighed. "You are truly a gorgeous man."

He snorted. "You would say that about anyone with rampant equipage and you in that certain mood." Teasing threaded through the words as he caught a hand into her hair and guided her toward that straining member.

"No. Truly." Sophia took the hard, hot shaft in her palm. It twitched from her touch. "It is due to your selfless sacrifices and the fact you've traded parts of your soul for mine." She glanced at him, met his darkened gaze. "You are mine, and I cannot have enough of you." Then she lowered her head and took him into her mouth.

"Damn. I am glad you have found adequate satisfaction with me." A moan sailed onto the tail of the oath. He bucked his hips, clutched the quilt in one hand while she continued to move on his manhood. A strangled cry escaped him. The fingers in her hair tightened and he thrust into her mouth. "You must leave off else I'll come down your throat."

As if that is such a horrid idea.

With a humming sort of chuckle, she eased off him and instead, kissed a path up his body until she reached his lips. The scrape of his clothing against her sensitive nipples only heightened the need she had of him. "What else do you wish for me to do since you're shying away from that sort of pleasure?" But tonight, oh tonight, she would tease and torture him to her heart's desire.

"Enjoy while I give you tit for tat." His muscles went taut, and seconds later, he wrapped his arms around her, flipping them both over so that she was on her back. When he delved a hand through her skirting and between her thighs, she shook with anticipation. "Let's see how much you can endure before you fly."

"Do your best." *Or your worst, depending.* The moment he spread her open and found that tiny nubbin, Sophia shuddered. She adored when her husbands fully embraced everything the marriage bed could entail. Some had done it more than others, but truly, she had been satisfied with each one. Oliver, however, had shown himself as the greatest risk-taker of them all, and never would she have enough of that.

He claimed her lips and at the same time worked over that swelling button with various levels of friction until she squirmed from that attention. No longer did she care that her heartbeat raced or that her breathing was labored; it wasn't a danger. In fact, she craved those reactions, for it meant she could finally enjoy everything that was happening to her without fear. She shoved her hands beneath his shirt, and the rasp of that sprinkling of hair on his chest against her palms only increased the sensations pinging wildly through her. Naked or half-dressed, it didn't matter. Every time she was intimate with him was her favorite.

For long moments, they communed with kisses and touches. Then the unrelenting pressure that stacked inside her broke. Heated waves of pleasure caught Sophia up in their vortex, and she gave herself over to them. A keening cry of surprise and enjoyment ripped from her throat, and for the first time since marrying him, she didn't care if it was heard. Now was the time to fully embrace having intercourse with her husband, and she did so with aplomb.

"You are transcendently beautiful when you claim release,"

he whispered. Oliver shifted position; the wide head of his shaft glanced along her damp flesh and set off another series of flutters. She curled a hand on his chest, her fingers catching a few hairs that made him gasp, and before the contractions deep in her core ceased, he thrust into her body with such authority that she cried out again.

His moan blended with hers, and as he held the bulk of his weight on his forearms, he peered into her eyes. "Ready to embark into our new life together?"

"Oh, yes." She slipped her free hand to his nape, furrowed her fingers into his hair, and pulled him closer. "Show me why I was clever enough to marry you in the first place."

"Gladly." Slowly, oh so slowly, he moved with tender strokes that rocked her body and brought tears to her eyes.

Sophia clung to him, met each thrust, and all too soon they found the familiar rhythm. The scent of roses filled the air, for their exertions had crushed many of the blooms she'd cut to plead her case. Their gazes remained locked, and it was the most extraordinary thing to watch the emotions play through his stormy depths and know that affection, that pride, that love was all for her. "Give me all of you. There is no need to hold back now."

The dear man did as instructed. As she canted her hips and wrapped her legs about his waist, he pushed into her with more frantic purpose, going ever deeper, claiming her body harder and quicker until they both panted with need and clung to each other. He dug his fingers into her hip and continued on his quest to apparently join their souls. The second he shoved his other hand between their straining bodies and worried that already sensitive nubbin, Sophia's hold on sanity slipped.

"I… I'm… Ah, Oliver!" The vortex once more sucked her under, hurling into a swirling white world of colored pinpricks where there was nothing except intense pleasure and warmth and *him*.

Over and over and *over* he continued to work her body, and it responded with fall after fall until she shook from it and exhaustion blanketed her. Eventually, he found his own release, and with a hoarse shout of her name, he collapsed into her. His member pulsed and jerked, still embedded deep in her core, but he wrapped his arms around her, pressed his lips to the side of her neck, and simply held her as her heartbeat thudded wildly and sweat plastered the back of her gown to her skin.

For long moments they remained locked in the embrace with limbs and clothing twisted, and when Sophia came back to herself, she opened her eyes to find Oliver watching her. "That was… amazing." This man who'd come so suddenly into her life all because of a broken coach axle had managed to break through the defenses she'd thrown up, and even though she was still a bit vulnerable, she knew they would weather all obstacles.

Together.

"*You* are amazing, sweeting." He brushed his lips against hers. "I cannot wait for you to come to London as my wife, to show you my office in America, and if you'll agree to it, visit France for a honeymoon."

"That all sounds wonderful." But truly, she didn't care where she went, for wherever Oliver was felt like home.

July 25, 1819

ARTHUR'S NUPTIAL CEREMONY was due to begin in ten minutes. Sophia stood outside the drawing room doors, smoothing the fabric of her silk gown of robin's egg blue over her stomach while waiting for Oliver to join her, which he did in short order. He was magnificent in dark evening clothes, and he escorted Hannah on his arm, for the girl doted on him.

"You never cease to surprise me with another beautiful gown," he said by way of greeting as he leaned into her and kissed her with slow leisure as if they were alone.

From beside her, Hannah made a gagging noise. Soon after, the girl shoved at her shoulder until they broke the embrace. "Really, Mama. Have *some* decorum. There is plenty of time for all of *that*." The admonishment in her voice made Sophia laugh. Oliver's chuckle added joy to the moment. "The sooner Uncle Arthur weds, the sooner we can eat. I'm starving."

"You can fill your belly in short order." With a wink at Sophia, Oliver offered his arm to Hannah. "Come. Let us go in and find a seat."

"At the wedding breakfast, you can tell me about France, since we're going there soon…"

The sound of their voices drifted away as the two moved into the drawing room where Arthur's nuptial ceremony would soon begin. She and Oliver had decided to take Hannah to France on their wedding trip, for it would initiate the girl into travel. Since they were truly a little family now and had all been through so much, this trip would further serve to bond them together. Beyond that, this trip would mark the official beginning of her new life.

Together.

A soft grin tugged at the corners of her mouth as she peeked inside the room where the rest of her family had gathered. Oh, they made a fine picture indeed, and she would have them all with her for a long time indeed.

What more could she ask for from fate?

"Lady Sophia?" The butler approached her with an expression of confusion.

"Yes? What is it, Landers? You seem perplexed."

"I am, my lady." He wrung his hands. "There is a new arrival that might prove a fly in the ointment."

"Oh? Who is here?" They weren't expecting anyone else.

Landers cleared his throat and patted a flyaway strand of gray hair back into place. "It's Lady Yeardly. She has arrived and is asking that her husband attend her as soon as possible."

For a few seconds, Sophia stared in astonishment at the butler. "Gilbert's wife is *here?*" When he nodded, her eyebrows rose. At least they would finally have answers to why her youngest brother was so out of sorts regarding his marriage. "Uh, there might be... strong words involved with her return, so leave Madelene in the parlor with tea. Gilbert can attend to her after the ceremony. I don't wish for his private business to sour Arthur's wedding."

"Of course, my lady." The butler glanced into the room. "You will tell the dowager as well as Lord Yeardly?"

"I will, after things conclude here." Once Landers left, she sighed.

It remained to be seen how that tableau would play out, but if Gilbert and his wife were as willful as the rest of the Winterbournes, it would certainly be a tale to remember.

Perhaps that was the glorious mess a family should be.

And there was nothing wrong with that.

The End

About the Author

Sandra Sookoo is a *USA Today* bestselling author who firmly believes every person deserves acceptance and a happy ending. Most days you can find her creating scandal and mischief in the Regency-era, serendipity and happenstance in Victorian America or snarky, sweet humor in the contemporary world. Most recently she's moved into infusing her books with mystery and intrigue. Reading is a lot like eating fine chocolates—you can't just have one. Good thing books don't have calories!

When she's not wearing out computer keyboards, Sandra spends time with her real-life Prince Charming in central Indiana where she's been known to goof off and make moments count because the key to life is laughter. A Disney fan since the age of ten, when her soul gets bogged down and her imagination flags, a trip to Walt Disney World is in order. Nothing fuels her dreams more than the land of eternal happy endings, hope and love stories.

Stay in Touch

Sign up for Sandra's bi-monthly newsletter and you'll be given exclusive excerpts, cover reveals before the general public as well as opportunities to enter contests you won't find anywhere else.

Just send an email to sandrasookoo@yahoo.com with SUBSCRIBE in the subject line.

Or follow/friend her on social media:
Facebook: facebook.com/sandra.sookoo
Facebook Author Page: facebook.com/sandrasookooauthor
Pinterest: pinterest.com/sandrasookoo
Instagram: instagram.com/sandrasookoo
BookBub Page: bookbub.com/authors/sandra-sookoo